SWIFT HORSES RACING

VICTORIA KAZARIAN

FOG HOLLOW BOOKS

Do you remember still the falling stars
That like swift horses through the heavens raced
And suddenly leaped across
The hurdles of our wishes–do you recall?
And we did make so many!
For there were countless numbers of stars:
Each time we looked above we were astounded
By the swiftness of their daring play,
While in our hearts we felt safe and secure
Watching these brilliant bodies disintegrate,
Knowing somehow we had survived their fall.

Rainer Maria Rilke

For Stanley Vierk, my father,
who first explained flight to me
and later shared my fear of it.

1

—————

Detective Mario Flores scrolled through his phone as he waited for his drink.

He checked emails, then every social media site on his phone. Faces of girls he'd known, posing in sunglasses, doing duck face pouts and laughing.

His finger swiped up, down, left, right. They rifled past him hypnotically, like images in a kid's flip book.

His legs dangled off the stool, the toes of his shoes knocking up against the wooden bar. The smell at Someplace Bar & Grill wasn't pleasant—popcorn drenched in artificial butter, canned nacho cheese, sour spilled beer—but it was familiar.

He'd taken a seat at the bar because that's where you sit when you come by yourself. For the first time he wasn't waiting for someone. He was waiting for the bourbon. He'd be drinking it by himself.

For the last month he'd come here to meet Ruiz. Jimmy Ruiz, of Monte Verde PD up on the peninsula. Ruiz sat across from him, his padded baseball glove of a hand wrapped around his beer as they talked about the Schuler homicide. Threw out theories and talked about suspects. Over time, they cautiously ventured into talking about their lives apart from the force. Ruiz's big frame hunched down over the table, lips turned up at one corner. His voice cut through with a low, rumbling laugh; he couldn't help but crack up at his own jokes.

Tara, daughter of the owner, handed him his bourbon. She had the same warm smile for everyone. It was possible she'd heard the news; police gossip spread like a virus here. But in her eyes, he saw acceptance. He needed it. He drank it up.

Then Flores remembered, took out his wallet and lay some bills on the counter. Before he took a sip, Ruiz would always lay out a big tip for the waitress so he wouldn't forget. A guy who does what's right, in little things and big things. It was built into him like a compass or GPS. Reyna had told Flores once: *He's the kind of guy who always returns the shopping cart at Safeway.*

Flores's first sips of bourbon went down smooth, the warmth spreading through his body and melting down every jagged edge. He took in a deep breath and felt the burn make its way down to his fingers, his gut. He couldn't make a habit of this. It felt too good.

In his peripheral vision, he saw a large man at a table at the back of the room. The guy faced the front of the bar like Ruiz did: the cop on alert, watching the door. In the mix of voices in the bar, he heard low grunts of laughter. Flores turned his head quickly and scanned the back of the room.

He saw a young guy, thickly built, at a table of guys with fresh haircuts, all of them looking exposed and naive. New academy grads. The group of newbies looked back at him, startled as if he'd shone a flashlight into their car.

Jesus, he was maybe seven years older than they were.

The bourbon had reached Flores's brain and was stirring up a mix of thoughts. He was sixteen years old again on an August night, face down against the warm asphalt of a Target parking lot, his cheek scratched and bleeding. An officer patted him down. He'd stolen a car with his friends. None of them needed it. It was for the excitement, in an Orange County suburb where you had to cut or punch yourself every once in a while to remind yourself you were alive. Desperately seeking an edge in a town where all falls were cushioned and the thrills were as manufactured as the coasters in nearby Disneyland. His friends, all of them, were from well-off families. After a night in juvie, they'd been bailed out by their parents. He remembered the faces—his older sister Dawn, his mother and father, and later, girls at school he'd dated. Disbelief, disgust, shame.

He'd come before the judge, an older Black woman, who looked down over her glasses at him and told him he had more privilege than 98 percent of the kids his age, and he was too smart to be pulling shit like this.

Let this be that one time, Mr. Flores. That one time.

She sentenced him to community service in the Police Explorers. In the youth program for two years, several officers mentored him, spent more time with him than his dad ever had. He made friends with the kind of kids he'd never bothered talking to at school. And he'd stayed friends with them.

After college and a few months in Europe, he'd applied for the academy. Not in Orange County, which he felt a strong desire to leave. Not in the rural community of Davis, where he'd gone to college. In San Jose, a place where nobody knew him and they were hiring to rebuild their force.

He took one more sip and swirled the glass around,

watching the reflection of the bar lights shimmer in the amber liquid. Maybe it was time to move on again. Seattle. Maybe Austin or Atlanta. It almost didn't matter where. Every person who had been a bright spot in his life here a month ago was gone.

In his mental flip book, they fluttered past him again. A pretty face splashed with light from the police cruiser on the expressway that night. That glare from Mandy Dirkson, angry at him for shirking his duty to the force.

Then Ruiz's heavy-lidded eyes leveled at him for the last time, pain on his face—at least as much as his pride would let him show.

Flores, how could you have done this?

It was a look no amount of bourbon could wash away.

Detective James Ruiz was tired, cold and entirely done with New Year's.

The beer he'd nursed all night and the conversation he'd had at the party in South San Jose hadn't been worth the drive. It was his least favorite holiday. The men he'd talked to, husbands and boyfriends of Reyna's coworkers at the dental office, engaged in the kind of chest beating that happened when drinking alcohol. Ruiz kept up the sports talk for as long as possible because he actually enjoyed it. Then he waited for the flurry of desperation partying to end. At 1:30 a.m., he approached Reyna in the kitchen. She nodded that she was ready and downed the last of her cosmopolitan.

As he pulled his Ford F-150 onto the side street that led to the expressway, he wished for some kind of sci fi wormhole to speed them to their home in Santa Clara. Eight-year-old Jacky was at his *lola's* tonight. The one bright spot in this evening was, he and Reyna would have the next twelve hours or so to themselves.

He pulled onto Almaden heading north. A mist hung

over the road, turning streetlights ahead into blurry red and green circles on the damp pavement. A car passed on the other side of the median, no headlights. He shivered. A drunk or someone too tired to drive. An accident waiting to happen.

Apart from that, the lanes were empty. In the corner of his eye, he saw Reyna shivering, pulling her thin jacket up around her neck.

"My Niners jacket's in the jump seat, hon. I don't need it."

She twisted around and pulled the jacket out of the back. She leaned forward in the seat and slid the gold and red jacket on, putting a delicate arm into each sleeve. She wrapped the sides of the huge jacket across her chest and settled back in the seat. He liked the look of her in it.

They had just passed Branham Avenue, when Ruiz saw an SUV pulled over to the narrow shoulder, idling.

"Bad night for car trouble."

"You're not going to stop, Jimmy. Tell me you're not going to stop. I just want to get home and go to bed."

He shook his head. "Me, too." He wanted to be in bed with her, too, though the odds of anything happening between them there were low.

Suddenly he heard the roar of an engine coming up behind them. The SUV had pulled onto the expressway and was revving behind them. It swerved into the left lane and zoomed ahead.

A white sedan had just turned onto the expressway from a side street. The SUV ran the light and pulled up until it was on the left side of the white car.

Two shots echoed in the cold air. Ruiz felt adrenaline hit, a sudden surge of hyperawareness that woke every cell in his tired body.

The white car that had entered the intersection continued, lurching toward the row of trees on the shoulder, no loss in speed, with the abandon of an out-of-control vehicle. Ruiz felt the boom as the car hit the trunk of a large eucalyptus, with a screech of bending metal.

Ruiz watched as the SUV sped off, a good twenty yards ahead. He squinted and caught the glimmer of a California plate, reflected in the streetlights. He called out to Reyna, keeping his eyes on the road ahead.

"You get the plate number?

"Nine something, I think—"

"Call 911. Now."

The SUV was 200 yards ahead of them, taillights dimly glowing like red eyes in the mist ahead. His senses buzzed. He pulled over fifteen feet behind the white car, the Ford's tires bumping up over the low curb.

He opened the door and ran to the car, a white Camry, now twisted around the trunk of a eucalyptus. A branch cracked and fell just as he approached, landing next to him. Scythe-like leaves, their menthol smell released, fluttered down.

The driver's side window had shattered into jagged diamonds, lit by the yellow streetlight above. Through a hole in the shards, he saw a flood of red, a bright white shock of hair. Santa Claus colors. He pulled at the bent door, which resisted, then opened with a low scraping noise. The thin and frail body had twisted up and sideways from the impact.

An elderly man. The bullet had entered the side of his head and, it looked from the quantity of blood, the other shot had hit his chest.

A siren wailed in the distance, coming closer. Ruiz felt for a pulse in the thin wrist. To his surprise, he felt a beat.

The shots had been at fairly close range—and targeted. The old man should be dead. He should have died instantly.

Under the wail of the approaching sirens, Ruiz heard a sound. A gurgle, a rasping sound, as if the man was trying, against all odds, to form words.

He suddenly remembered a hospital room. His mother. Three years ago, life leaving her as her body gave up its fight with ovarian cancer. Her lips had moved as if to say something, then her spirit left her mid-thought. Nothing.

He bent closer toward the man. Then he heard it.

It made no sense. It sounded like the old man whispered the word *saloon*.

Then quiet. No rise in the man's chest.

A deep stillness filled the car.

3

The cold air hit Flores in the face as he opened the back door of the 1950s-era apartment lobby and headed to the covered parking area in the rear of the complex.

The crisp air cut into his lungs and energized him, reminded him that he liked his job, even when it called him out at 2 a.m. He hadn't been surprised at a call on New Year's; he was especially lucky it was less than two miles from his home. He had no desire to run into any drunk drivers making their way home at this hour.

He wound around the narrow off ramp from Lincoln Avenue to Almaden, which funneled his Prius around a curve, like a Hot Wheels track he'd had as a kid. Almaden was the offramp from the quaint area of Willow Glen to the rest of San Jose, a wasteland of strip malls, auto parts stores and drive-through fast food. Stucco bungalows and large oaks lined the quiet, narrow streets of Willow Glen. Lincoln Avenue formed an old-timey downtown, with shops and decent restaurants. In Willow Glen, people walked. Couples leaned into each other as they strolled along Lincoln Avenue. Families walked together, hand in hand.

Completely unlike his Orange County neighborhood.

He'd chosen it for that reason.

AS HE HEADED SOUTH, Almaden Expressway opened like the maw of a whale in the mist, lit by the glow of yellow streetlights. Not far down the road, he saw the flashing lights on the opposite side of the median.

Flores made a U-turn and drove onto the shoulder when he spotted the cause of the call: a white Camry bent against the base of a large eucalyptus tree. The impact had forced the driver's side up at an angle. The firemen had lights in place and EMTs had a stretcher set up.

The slow, methodical pace of the firemen made the bottom of Flores's stomach drop.

This was a recovery. There was no rush.

Just beyond the Camry, he saw the patrol car, and two officers who looked familiar. They were talking to a Latino with the build of a linebacker, dressed in his best for a night out.

Flores approached and called out to the patrol officers.

"Detective Mario Flores, Homicide."

The air felt cold and stiff like a starched canvas backdrop.

He walked toward the Camry, and one of the officers followed him. Flores looked into the shattered window and saw the blood-covered body of an old man, a bullet wound in the side of his head, his body jutting sideways at an unnatural angle.

"The witness here called it in right before 2 a.m. There's a bulletin out for the SUV the witnesses saw. Flores, this is

Detective James Ruiz, of Monte Verde PD. He and his wife were coming home from a party."

A detective. The desolate feeling he'd had seeing the old man lifted. This guy would give a decent account of what he'd seen. Flores could trust what he'd hear. Flores reached out to shake hands and felt his own hand get lost in the man's large one. Flores felt the man's hand was trembling. From the looks of it, it wasn't from the cold.

"Good to meet you, Ruiz. Let's step over here and you can tell me what you saw."

They stood by the concrete block fence, marked with splotches covering up graffiti. The outline of the F word hissed from behind the gray paint. Ruiz paced in a tight triangle in front of the fence, flexing his hands.

Ruiz was angry.

"Hey, man. You okay?"

Ruiz looked at him, actually down at him, since the Detective was a good six inches taller than he was. Ruiz frowned and looked to his right, down the shoulder at the Camry.

"You and your wife coming back from a party?"

Ruiz nodded, probably knowing he'd be asked about what he'd drank. "South San Jose. Neither of us drank much. I had a beer, Reyna had a cosmo."

Flores wondered if this guy was for real. He raised an eyebrow. "That's pretty tame for New Year's."

"These parties aren't my favorite way to spend an evening. I worked patrol on New Year's for five years. I learned to hate it."

"When did you first see the SUV?"

"We passed it on the shoulder. Then it pulled onto the road and sped up behind us."

Ruiz rubbed his flushed face. He enunciated carefully as

if determined to get the words on the record. Clouds of breath came out into the cold and dispersed as he talked.

"As soon as the Camry turned onto the expressway, the SUV changed lanes and sped up. It swerved into the left lane so it was almost even with the Camry on the driver's side. Whoever was in the passenger seat fired two shots. Then the SUV revved up and headed north on the expressway."

Flores wondered if Ruiz was thinking the same thing. The neighborhoods on either side of the expressway were a combination of seniors, the original owners, along with young families who'd bought from owners who'd retired and moved away. This looked like a gang hit.

This was not a neighborhood where that kind of thing happened.

"They targeted the Camry. Pulled out and headed straight for it." Ruiz's voice grew progressively louder, his anger surfacing again. A scruffy cat making its way across the top of the concrete fence took one look at Ruiz and scuttled away. "The SUV was waiting. If it was random, he could have gone after us."

"You get a plate number?"

Ruiz slowly shook his head, his face reflecting his disappointment. "It happened fast. California plate. As it passed, my wife saw it started with 9—then the shots happened. It headed into the mist. She saw everything, too. It was pretty far ahead of us. She says she got a picture on her phone."

"Make? Color?"

"Ford Explorer. Early 2000s. Black."

"Show me where the SUV was on the shoulder."

Ruiz pointed at the spot on the shoulder, a hundred feet beyond his truck. They both walked in that direction, passing Ruiz's truck. The face in the passenger seat of the F-150 looked up suddenly. A smooth, oval face. Pretty.

"We called it in. I pulled over and ran up the road to get to the driver in the Camry. I opened the door to get to him. It was hanging." Ruiz's voice was hoarse.

Flores stopped and looked both ways at the expressway, picturing the events Ruiz described. He looked at the twisted white car.

"Must have been dead before he hit the tree."

"He wasn't." Ruiz croaked the words out, startling Flores. "He said something before he died."

"What?"

"It was hard to hear but it sounded to me like he said, "Saloon.""

Flores studied Ruiz's eyes for *nystagmus*, involuntary eye movements caused by intoxication. Could he have been drinking more than he'd admitted to? Only a partial on the plate. And *saloon* as the guy's last words. His eyes looked just fine.

The two detectives stood on the shoulder staring down at fresh tire tracks. Flores saw the skid marks in the lane. The nearest streetlight was a good hundred yards down and wasn't helping much. He took out his phone and turned on his flashlight. Then he took a few photos.

Ruiz looked down the expressway at the big houses, now going for a million plus, visible over the fence on the side streets.

"It's New Year's, but it's still a weird thing to happen here."

"No kidding, James."

"Call me Jimmy."

"I'd like to get your wife's account now, Jimmy."

They walked back toward the truck, then Ruiz gave a

curt nod. "Her name's Reyna." He said it in a way that made Flores look up at him. Like he'd shown the trace of something he shouldn't. Softness. He watched as Ruiz turned and continued down the shoulder back toward the Camry and the patrol officers.

Flores tapped on the passenger side window of the truck. The woman opened the door. She was wearing a huge gold and red Niners jacket, which had to be Ruiz's and a red scarf wrapped around her hands. She was shivering. It was 34 degrees out, which was as cold as California was going to get this time of year. And she'd just witnessed a murder.

"Mrs. Ruiz. I'm Detective Flores of San Jose PD. I need to ask you a few questions about what you and your husband saw."

Reyna Ruiz wrapped the jacket around herself and turned to step down from the high truck, putting out a shapely little leg in black stockings and high heels. She was a fine-boned woman, cut like a gem, a contrast to the bear-like Ruiz.

"Mrs. Ruiz. Stay inside." He held his hand up. "It's cold out here. Can you tell me what you saw?"

Reyna Ruiz closed her eyes. "We were coming back from my friend Corrine's party off of Coleman in South San Jose. We were both tired. It was strange to see the SUV was on the side of the road. At first Jimmy thought they were having car trouble. Then the SUV pulls out and speeds past us."

She pulled her hands out of the red scarf to gesture as she talked. She had an easy, physical way about her; she involved her hands, her eyes and her body in the telling of her story. She filled the physical space around her in a way that was out of proportion to her small body.

"I could tell it was heading for the white car. There was a sound—*pop pop*. Like fireworks, only then we saw the car swerve toward the trees. Oh, my God, it was horrible. That crunch." Flores noticed her hands were shaking under the scarf.

"Jimmy wouldn't say." She searched his face. He wasn't sure if she was looking for news of the old man or checking him out. "The driver couldn't have lived through that. It wouldn't be possible, right?"

She looked so hopeful, he was sorry to disappoint her. "He didn't."

Tears welled up in her eyes. She leaned back in the seat and blotted her eyes with a tissue.

Flores gave her a minute, while he took a look at her face unobserved. Hispanic or Asian? Maybe Filipina.

"Were you able to see the license plate number?"

"By the time we figured out what had happened, it was far ahead of us. I took a picture on my phone. It's not very clear though."

She pulled out her phone and swiped through screens with manicured fingers till she came to the picture.

Flores took the phone and zoomed in on the photo. All he could see was the back of a dark vehicle. The plate was a tiny, reflective rectangle, even enlarged. It didn't look helpful, but there was a possibility the tech team could do something with it.

"Can you send this to me, please?" He gave her his phone number.

In a minute, he felt his phone buzz that it had been received.

"Thank you, Mrs. Ruiz. Now you guys stay safe on your way home tonight."

She looked up and smiled faintly. After he turned away, she was still imprinted on his retina, a flash of light from the emergency vehicles highlighting her face.

4

Duke Sorenson stayed up just past midnight watching old movies on the set in the bedroom. He turned the volume up until it drowned out the sound of the neighbors' illegal fireworks. The nice thing about living alone in a house was that you could turn the volume up as loud as you damn well pleased without anyone complaining.

He was watching *The Thin Man* with Myrna Loy and William Powell. William Powell was a kick, always a drink in his hand, ready with a smart comeback to his wife or to anyone around him. Duke loved the banter between Nick and Nora Charles. In the days before they had children, Joanne had that feistiness. It had been one of the things he'd been attracted to. It had disappeared with the dementia.

When Joanne had stopped recognizing him, it felt like the ultimate snub. At first he thought she'd done it on purpose, payback for his ditching her with the kids while he worked late all those years. When she turned a blank face to him, it looked like the silent treatment she'd given him for a good part of their marriage. Maybe he deserved it.

While he'd stayed till midnight working on government contracts, she'd managed the house, the kids, the finances. He knew she'd felt stranded by herself and longed for adult company. He'd heard her say she was lonely, but at the time he didn't get it. *You talk to your friends on the phone, you have them over for coffee every week. You're always at parent meetings at school. Don't tell me you're lonely.*

He wanted to say it but never did: *Do you know what it's like to be the only one left in the building at night, saying goodnight to the janitor?*

He pulled his dinner out of the microwave and set the tray on a plate on the table. He poured a glass of milk and set it at the top of the tray, then lined up a fork and spoon— spoon on the right, fork on the left with a folded napkin under it, as Joanne had instructed the kids how to set the table. When you have little left in your life, rituals are important.

He felt bad thinking it, but retirement had been as big a blow as Joanne's illness. He'd worked in aeronautics for forty-five years. He'd gotten up every morning excited to go to work. He had a purpose. The longer he stayed, the more he was able to get done. The more he got done, the more he was given. He was the one to receive special clearance. The trusted one. He was gliding on the wings of a great machine. When he saw the final form of the planes he'd worked on— on the news, on the cover of a trade magazine or in the skies —he felt he was part god. He created this sleek thing that inspired awe. That raced through the skies, breaking the bonds of earth.

Of all people, Karl understood. They met at the donut shop with a small group of retirees on Friday mornings, all but one were in aerospace or aeronautics. There had been seven members of the donut gang at one point, but after illness and moves out of the valley to more affordable areas in the Central Valley or Arizona, they were down to four. It reminded him of a group of native American elders sitting around a fire, telling stories—pictures that drifted up in the smoke of a great fire as they talked. They hung in the air between them, vivid and pure—all traces of sadness, of lost dreams, of estranged children and angry wives burned off.

Now he sliced his microwaved Salisbury steak into tiny pieces, scooping up rice from its compartment and mixing it into the gravy. He'd talk to Karl tomorrow. If his children weren't visiting on the weekend, maybe they could go down to the museum at Moffett Federal Airfield and look at the planes.

He tried to put something on the calendar every day. To have a reason to get out of bed.

IN THE MORNING, he sat at his small, new dining table, drinking his coffee and eating a plate of scrambled eggs, which doctors now said were okay to eat, in moderation. He was watching a World War II documentary on the little TV he'd gotten after Joanne's death. He needed noise. It was too quiet this morning.

As if they'd read his state of mind, his daughters called, one after the other, to wish him happy New Year. Their condescending chatter made him feel more alone. He was an item on their to-do lists.

After the calls, Duke scrolled to Karl's contact on his phone. There was something refreshing in talking about *things*. Talking about who had cancer and whose spouse had passed wore on him after a while and his mind moved on to other thoughts.

How will I fix that leak in the sink?

Is that plane overhead an Airbus 320?

Duke called Karl. He let it ring nine times, then replaced the handset. He was probably at Rose's for the holiday. Karl was fifteen years older than he was and had told him his children Rose and Christoph were pressuring him to move in with one of them. Duke laughed at the thought. Karl was a stubborn cuss and would fight them off as long as he could. He saw no signs of the cognitive decline in Karl that he'd seen in Joanne. He worried about what would happen when he did. He could not handle another person slowly backing out of his life.

As the day wore on, Duke kept himself busy, sweeping out the garage and cleaning Yeager's cat box. Then he sat down at the computer his son Rick had built for him last spring. He used it for email and checking stocks. His daughter had set him up on Facebook, which he'd thought was a big waste of time. Why not just talk to people?

Duke opened up the program and scrolled through the news feed. Theo, one of his grandkids, had been in Times Square when the ball dropped. He'd posted lots of badly lit, blurry photos of young people in the dark. Then Duke watched a short video of his daughter Kathleen banging a pot on her front porch wishing the neighbors happy new year.

He kept scrolling through the news feed.

Then he saw it.

When he grasped what he was reading, it sucked the air out of his lungs. He felt like something immeasurably heavy had landed on his chest. His sight flickered, like lights right before a blackout.

It was a news blurb from a local TV station someone had reposted with an orange angry emoji: **OMG. Who would do this?**

He saw the photo. He recognized Karl's white Camry, bent around a tree on Almaden Expressway, driver window pocked with bullet holes.

92-Year-Old Aeronautics Pioneer Is First Murder of the New Year

5

By the time Flores got home, it was 7 a.m.

Crime Scene Investigation had gone over the site, taking molds of the tracks on the shoulder and photographing the marks in the right lane, the damaged car, the old man in position in the car.

The medical examiner from the coroner's office had come to have a look at the body. He remarked that the wounds were "surprisingly precise." Then the old man was taken away.

In the interminable time it took for the flatbed tow truck to chain up the car, he'd verified the name: Karl Schuler. He'd lived a half a mile away, in the maze of streets that wound around in curlicues and cul de sacs and then emptied onto the expressway. He'd owned the house for forty-eight years. After googling him, Flores found out that he'd been a celebrity in the field of aeronautics. Before his retirement he'd worked in Silicon Valley since the late 1940s.

Since the DMV's 1980s-era database wouldn't be fast or helpful with the partial plate number, he had Mandy

Dirkson from his team run the partial – with make, model and color through Carfax. That gave him the VINs for the DMV search.

CSI had found shell casings at the scene and was now processing them, but it would be a day or two before he got the results.

Later this morning, he'd interview Schuler's daughter in South San Jose. Right now his limbs felt wiry and stretched out. His brain buzzed tiredly, to the point where it would begin misfiring soon. He needed sleep.

He'd hoped Oksana was still in bed, but she sat upright at the kitchen table, eating a piece of toast, ear buds in, her abnormal psychology textbook in front of her. She leafed through pages then typed on her laptop. It wasn't till he opened the fridge that she took the ear buds out and looked up at him with bored, impassive eyes.

"Happy New Year," she said with a trace of a Russian accent and gave him the side eye. The scent of her lotion reached him from the other end of the kitchen. Summer flowers in the winter. "What the hell took you so long?"

Feeling happy he'd been missed, Flores poured a glass of water and shook some vitamins into his hand. He felt dehydrated. "An old guy, shot on the expressway. His car slammed into a tree. Bad crime scene, even for New Year's." He gulped down the vitamins.

He wanted badly to head back to the bedroom with her, but she was already dressed in jeans and a sweater, her long blonde hair damp from the shower. Oksana kept to a schedule. Grad school was top priority, and she'd sacrifice him for her studies in a minute. Which made her a good match for him, as he often did the same to her, ditching plans at the last minute for a case.

When she took her ear buds out and looked up at him,

he bent down and gently pressed his lips to hers. She'd looked so resolute, her finger in her textbook, that he wasn't expecting anything.

But there it was. A little give in her lips.

Soon his tongue was in her mouth, and her arm was around his neck. He lifted the hem of her sweater, sliding his hands up beneath it.

"You're awake enough for this?"

"This is a make-up session for last night. Or a make out session." He held her hand and pulled her up out of the chair and led her down the hall to the bedroom. "Both."

He saw she'd made his bed neatly, propping the throw pillows in a tidy row against the pillow shams. He surveyed the bed with satisfaction.

"Neatness in a woman." He spoke in the voice of a Bond villain as he raised his eyebrows and lifted her sweater over her head. "I find it quite...*arousing*."

She picked up one of the pillows and threw it at him in response, hitting him square on the nose. She stepped up on the bed, slipped off her jeans and stood above him. He pulled her down onto the bed laughing, and she lay on top of him, her long legs stretched out even with his. He felt the pressure of her body on his, her skin bonded to his by a light sweat, and he wanted to rush into her, but he waited. It would be better if he waited.

Her still damp hair swept across his face, tickling his lips and making him laugh.

His phone rang in the kitchen. He'd be an idiot to take it. He ignored it and surrendered himself completely to this time. She sat up on him and rocked and he felt a surge of energy. Apparently, he wasn't as tired as he felt. He held her hips and pressed into her. She arched her back and cried out, and he knew the neighbors were hearing all this but didn't even care.

Afterwards he lay there, his arm over hers.

His mind felt empty and peaceful. Last night's events on the expressway faded into a mist. He saw the old man, Ruiz and his wife in it, distant shadows, and he fell asleep.

AND IN WHAT only seemed like five minutes later, he opened his eyes to sun shining in his eyes. He was alone.

The clock said 11:30 a.m.

Holy shit.

Calls to be made. Interviews with the Schuler family.

He sat for a moment at the edge of the bed, rubbing his eyes. Then he pulled on his boxers and went into the kitchen. He checked his phone.

Two voicemails from Mandy at the station.

Mandy had run the SUV's model and make and had three prospects that fit the partial.

After a shower and some leftover Chinese takeout, Flores headed down the expressway again, toward Almaden Valley. At midday, the clouds had cleared and the sun was setting up shop in the sky. As he passed the tree that Schuler had hit the night before, the scene looked empty, all debris removed as if nothing had ever happened.

ROSE SCHULER MULVANEY met him at the door of her neatly landscaped ranch-style home, her eyes red and puffy. She looked to be in her late sixties, but trim and wearing skinny jeans. She had a short, boyish haircut, and her sharp little features made him think of a bird.

She led him through a kitchen that looked as fastidious

and unlived in as a model home. Aluminum appliances polished to a sheen. Labeled drawers. Knives lined up in order of size on a magnetic rack over the oven. Flores liked to keep things tidy, but the feel of this house was too much for even him.

As he sat down at the kitchen table, Flores heard a children's song coming from a TV in the next room, then the delighted belly laugh of a child. It was what this too-perfect house needed. He smiled.

"Sounds like you have a visitor."

"My daughter and her husband are in Puerto Vallarta on a New Year's cruise." Rose took a seat across from him and rested her hands on the table. "I'm watching my granddaughter Chloe."

"I'm sure she keeps you busy." Flores didn't know, just assumed this was the case. He had no experience with young children. Any information he had was secondhand— his older sister, Dawn, was now stepparent to her partner's child and usually in stress mode whenever he called.

Tears filled Rose's eyes and she blinked. "Today, Chloe is a good distraction." Deep lines in her cheeks and brow led him to guess she stored her grief in some labeled drawer in her mind and let out as little as possible.

"I need to ask you some questions about your father, Mrs. Mulvaney. Did you father live alone? Any roommates? Family members?"

"He lived by himself. My son, Randall, lived with him for a few months last year. It was too much house for my father. He didn't throw anything away. There's decades of books, papers, mementos we'll have to clean out." This was a new one for Flores: the woman had received the news of her father's death eight hours ago, and her first concern was to head over and clean out his house.

"Your father worked in aeronautics?"

"For more than seventy years." Rose's voice deepened with pride. "First in Florida, with the fighter pilots who worked in the first astronaut program, then he moved out here to California and worked on high-altitude planes. You've heard of Richard Feynman, the physicist?"

Flores nodded. He'd read about the physicist from Caltech, famous for his entertaining lectures.

"My father was like the Feynman of aeronautics." Rose's expression softened. "He had a way of explaining flight. He made aviation and the sciences interesting and easy to understand—he told his stories, he liked to say. He was a natural teacher. When he retired, it made sense that he began working with high school students."

"He did this at a school?"

"At a tutoring center that helps underprivileged teens on the east side. He worked with students interested in science. Engineering and physics—aerospace, if the kids were interested. He said he wanted to help students who didn't get the same opportunities as other kids in the valley. He had been doing it for about twenty years." Rose Schuler shook her head and seemed to shudder. "It's such a dangerous part of town. I worried about him."

Gang activity was common in East San Jose. Flores wondered if Schuler could have gotten mixed up with kids who had gang connections. Or crossed somebody he shouldn't have. With the drive-by shooting, Flores couldn't rule it out. He'd be talking to Gang Investigations later today.

"Did your father ever mention being threatened by his students?"

Rose looked through the door behind her at Chloe, who was swaying to the song of a singing cartoon shark on TV.

"He didn't. But he wasn't afraid of much. If it happened, he may not have taken it seriously."

Then the big question. Where had Karl Schuler been going on New Year's?

"Do you know why your father would be out driving at that hour? Was he attending a party?"

Rose's mouth twitched, and she looked down into a mug of tea that smelled like cinnamon. She shook her head.

"My father is—*was*—very independent. He made it clear that he lived on his own and we were not to interfere with him. We tried our best to keep an eye on him. He was ninety-two, after all. He often gave us the slip." She clutched her mug tightly, and he noticed her knuckles turned white. "When I called, he'd told me he was planning to stay in last night."

"Unusual to see someone at that age still driving. No problems?"

It had been one of the things he'd thought about this morning on his drive home. Maybe Karl Schuler had cut the wrong person off, triggering an episode of road rage.

"Not that I know about," Rose snapped, her bloodshot eyes turned on him. He wasn't sure if she was irritated at his question or at her own father. "He passed his tests each time. He was determined to keep driving. If it wasn't the students he mentored, it was the senior meals program. I don't know what he'd do if he lost his license."

"What about his cognitive abilities? Any dementia?"

"Not my father." She cut him off in tight, clipped syllables. "I had a few long talks with his doctor. I wanted to be sure. My father's cognitive abilities were just fine."

Flores heard a tapping sound coming from somewhere. The lines around Rose's mouth tightened, and she let out a low sigh.

"Excuse me." She disappeared down the hallway.

Flores used the opportunity to check his phone and messages. There was an Explorer owner registered to a home in North San Jose, fifteen minutes away. After leaving here, he could head up 87, which wouldn't be busy today, then downtown to the station.

Now a ghostly moan echoed from the hallway. The desperate rattling of a doorknob. Rose was pleading.

"Chloe, turn the doorknob."

Another mournful cry. More rattling on the knob. Then faint, disconsolate knocking.

"Hold the doorknob, Chloe. Hold it tight. Then turn it."

Rose came back into the kitchen, her lips pressed together tightly. She opened a drawer, then took out a key. When she came back, she had the two-year-old under her arm. The little girl with wispy white blonde hair looked at Flores solemnly.

"I went pee pee."

The response came out of Flores as if he were commending a rookie after a session of Field Training.

"Nice job."

The little girl smiled at him. She had big blue eyes, pink cheeks and fat hands with stubby fingers. A Cabbage Patch doll.

An unexpected thought ran through his head. He wondered how Oksana felt about having children. They'd never talked about it.

"Chloe, this is Detective Flores," Rose addressed the child in a stern voice. "Tell him how old you are."

Chloe held up two stubby fingers and tilted her head.

At a loss for what else to do, Flores gave her a thumbs up.

"*Hochstuhl*, Chloe." Rose called in what Flores recognized as German.

The toddler lifted her arms. Rose picked her up and settled her into the highchair. She set a plastic container of Cheerios on the tray, which Chloe promptly dumped out.

"She'll be fine for a while." Rose turned back to Flores.

Chloe pulled a wet hand out of her mouth and smacked it down on her cereal-covered tray. She held up a hand bedecked with Cheerios, then smiled and shoved it back in her mouth.

It was becoming clear to Flores that Rose Schuler Mulvaney had as much control over her granddaughter as she'd had over her father.

Karl Schuler had been a man with many connections. Right now, the mentoring Schuler had done in East San Jose interested him most.

"Mrs. Mulvaney, I need the name of the tutoring center in East San Jose."

"East Point Youth Center. It's in south San Jose. Near Monterey Road."

Flores tapped notes on his tablet keyboard. "What other activities was your father involved in? You mentioned a meals for seniors program."

Interesting that Karl Schuler gave so much of his time away, when most men his age would have been trying to enjoy the time they had left. The cynical side of Flores wondered why he was so driven to do it.

"He delivered meals to low-income seniors in the valley. Most of them were younger than he was." Rose threw up a hand in exasperation. "Oh, and a few weeks ago, there was the women's shelter. He'd helped a parent of one of his students get set up at the shelter, and he heard they needed some repairs, so he found volunteers. My father helped everybody."

Schuler, it seemed, was a genuinely good man. As Flores knew, not everyone's father was.

"Your father sounded like a good human being," he said. "I am sorry for your loss, Mrs. Mulvaney."

At his words, Rose Mulvaney broke down completely. She covered her face with her hands and leaned back in her chair, rocking, her body heaving with sobs.

Flores got up and scanned the kitchen. He found a tissue box on the counter near the sink and brought it to Rose. He waited while she calmed down. She pulled out a tissue and wiped her eyes.

"Mrs. Mulvaney, is there anyone else close with your father? Anyone who might have seen him earlier that day?"

Rose nodded and blotted her reddened nose with the tissue. "That would be Duke. Duke Sorenson. He's his closest friend. They knew each other for years. He had a group of guys he met with each week. They got together to tell their stories. I'll get you my brother Christoph's number, too. He's in Florida. He and my father talked every week."

"Did your father have any disagreements with family or neighbors? Can you think of anyone who might have a grudge against him?" He heard the sound of Cheerios skittering across the floor.

Rose shook her head, the creases around her mouth tightening. "That is the hard part. I can't think of anyone."

Rose looked behind her to see the mess on the floor and groaned. She left the room and came back with a broom and a dustpan and bent down to sweep up the Cheerios.

Flores watched Chloe look down at her grandmother and slowly brush more Cheerios off the tray with the back of her hand.

Then the toddler turned to look him straight in the eye. The glint in her eye reminded him of an interrogation he'd had a couple of years ago. An eighteen-year-old who'd killed his mother in cold blood.

Flores had gone soft watching the cherubic toddler. He now firmed up.

He would not bring it up with Oksana.

There was no reason to rush these things.

6

I n his car outside of Rose Mulvaney's house, Flores
checked the address of the registration for the
Explorer in North San Jose. He sent the link to his
phone and reached down for his jacket.

This winter in the Bay Area was cold and wet, not
something he had ever gotten accustomed to. He had
enough friends from other parts of the country who made
fun of him for complaining about temps in the 40s. He'd
come up to NorCal from Orange County to go to college,
and he'd never moved back. His parents in Anaheim
mourned the fact and their phone conversations were filled
with lots of passive aggressive comments.

Truth is, he'd had a string of Northern Californian
girlfriends and the only times he returned to his hometown
was when they wanted to go to a decent beach. Southern
California had it all over NorCal in that area.

He entered the ramp for the 87 north and began the
slow, ambling curve through downtown San Jose, past the
barren white and grey buildings and the purple stucco
Children's Museum, with its giant rubber ducky perched on

top. San Jose wasn't a pretty city. It was San Francisco's left-brained, technology-obsessed brother. Flat and literal, little art, little grace. Buildings that looked like they were created by computer-assisted design programs in the 1970s. But you knew what to expect. No surprises. San Jose was a city you could take at face value.

He took the exit for First Street, heading for the area of condos and apartments that had sprung up amid the wake of high-tech companies on the northeast side of the valley. Land was cheaper here than on the west side, and developers had maximized their profits, stacking boxes upon each other. The tightly packed streets were punctuated by square plots of grass intended to check the box for green space on some planner's map.

The GPS led him to a row of condos that looked like old-fashioned row houses, or more appropriately, row houses as they would look on Main Street USA in Disneyland. Bright pastel tones with white trim. He parked in front of a townhouse painted in light green and white. The garage door, framed in neat, white trim was closed. A squirrel darted across the damp driveway, then shot up the trunk of a tree on the side of the house.

Flores walked up the short path to the gray, paneled front door with tiny square windows at the top. He rang the doorbell. His heart pounded louder as he looked at his surroundings and waited for the home's occupant, who might well be armed and guarding an SUV in the garage.

Light appeared in the door's tiny windows. He held up his badge at the peephole. He heard the click and whir of a digital lock.

A young Asian woman opened the door. From the name on the registration, this wasn't who he'd expected to open the door. In sweatpants and a faded red Stanford t-shirt, it looked as if she was working remotely today. The brown eyes behind her wire-rimmed glasses looked faintly bloodshot as if she'd slept poorly or spent too much time in front of a computer. She looked embarrassed to have been caught in her home-alone clothes.

"Detective Mario Flores, San Jose PD. I'm looking for a Jacob Hollander. Does he live at this address?"

She hesitated, swallowing nervously. "I'm Teresa— Teresa Cho. Jake's my husband. He's on a work trip in Minneapolis and he won't get back till Friday night. Can you come back then?" She smiled politely as she put her hand on the edge of the door to close it, but Flores moved further in on the door mat and her hand dropped.

"Ms. Cho, we're trying to track down a vehicle. A black SUV involved in a shooting on New Year's. The registration shows your husband as the owner of a 2003 Ford Explorer. Is that car at your residence now?"

A sheen of sweat appeared on her forehead. "No, he sold it before Christmas. It took up too much of our garage."

"Ms. Cho, he needs to transfer ownership with the DMV within five days of a sale. Do you remember the date he turned it over to the owner?"

She lifted her shoulders in a shrug. "My grandparents were visiting from South Korea, so I was busy over the holiday. I think he sold it the week before Christmas. Jake's company had a long shutdown, and he gets a little crazy when he's not working. He tries to organize everything and get his life in order. He said he sold it to someone who contacted him. He might have put it on Craig's List, but I'm not sure."

"Would it be possible for you to open your garage door for me, so I can see where the vehicle was parked?" He watched her eyes. No sign of panic. No defensiveness.

He couldn't search the garage without getting a warrant, but if she agreed to open the door, he could at least see where the vehicle had been. If Jake Hollander had been involved in Schuler's murder and the car had come back here in a hurry, there might be some signs in the garage.

She thought for a moment. "I can do that. I'll meet you outside."

He walked around to the garage door and waited. Soon the automatic door opened up with a creak, revealing a small garage packed tightly. A Prius was parked neatly on one side, and shelves on the other side were loaded with Costco-sized packages of toilet paper and paper towels. A small workbench stood near the door into the house—on it, an old Xbox game console and what looked like a computer hard drive and a box of cables.

Teresa Cho came out to meet him from the entrance to the house. The floor was swept clean, and there were faded oil stains on the ground where a vehicle had been. He stood and looked around and saw no shell casings, no skid marks from a sudden entry. Though it could all have been cleaned up since last night.

Flores nodded. "This is a very small garage."

Teresa's phone beeped and she glanced at it before looking up at him.

"When we parked the SUV in here, it was hard to move around. It's not convenient to have only one car, but the Prius is a lot easier to park."

"I'll need your full name and phone number, Ms. Cho." He pulled out his tablet and started a note. "And your husband's cell number."

She gave him Jake Hollander's number. He took out his card and wrote his number on it.

"It's important that you get back to me if you find out

anything that might help us locate the new owner or the car. The victim's family is looking for answers. Call me or email me if you remember anything else."

"Oh, my God. Is that the old scientist who was killed?" The woman was visibly shaken. "Of course. Jake gets busy when he's on site. I'll get him your number, too. If he calls tonight, I'll remind him to call you."

Teresa Cho's garage door slowly closed, as Flores slid back into his car.

He wondered about Jake Hollander and his sudden desire to sell his SUV.

And if Jake Hollander was in OCD mode and trying to get his life in order, why hadn't he taken the time to transfer ownership of his vehicle?

7

A thick layer of fog was drifting down over the hills, filling the air with a damp chill that sunk into your bones. Detectives Dani Grasso and James Ruiz made their way carefully through a muddy front yard as they headed back to their car on the street.

A burglary. A married couple, both software engineers, had a big screen TV, laptops and game consoles stolen. It was a small, 1960s duplex off Foothill Expressway, nothing to look at from the outside, filled with expensive electronics. State of the art, all the accessories and most of them new. The things a two-income couple employed in tech buys when they don't have kids. Ruiz thought of the careful budgeting he and Reyna had to do to afford Jacky's soccer uniforms and school materials.

"A family downstairs in my complex was hit last week," Grasso said. "Three computers and a couple of iPads. While they were out to dinner."

"These guys were skiing in Tahoe." Ruiz said as they got into the car. "Nobody thinks people are watching. Tracking habits and patterns, the days and times. Especially in this part of town."

Ruiz felt his phone vibrate in his pocket. The screen on the dashboard picked up the call and asked if he wanted to answer or ignore it. It was Sergeant Frank Descortes again. The sergeant was rounding up people to watch the Niners game at his new, post-divorce apartment in Milpitas Monday night. Ruiz had done this a couple weeks ago, and the group that gathered had seemed cold and uncomfortable in Frank's bare bones apartment. Vacant stares all around as the group tried to make the best of it, watching a game that wasn't going well for the home team. Frank, who'd drunk a few too many beers, seemed scared that people were going to leave him by himself.

Ruiz tapped a button on his steering wheel to ignore the call.

He gave the department's new Bluetooth-equipped cars a thumbs up. He'd skip the game and touch base with Frank later.

As of last June, Ruiz had worked for Monte Verde Police Department for sixteen years. The small, wealthy community in the south peninsula was very different from the East San Jose neighborhood he'd grown up in, and it had taken him a good year to feel like he belonged there. The custom homes in the hills were owned by young Silicon Valley entrepreneurs, tech company upper management, and older wealthy families who'd moved here before the tech boom.

Ruiz had started on patrol and after five years decided to try out Investigations. In contrast to San Jose, Monte Verde was small—not considered a high crime community. Burglary, domestic cases, noise complaints, neighborhood disputes and drug busts at the local high school. Murders were rare. When they did happen, they usually involved money and family and were as cold blooded as any in his old neighborhood in San Jose.

From the passenger seat, Grasso was watching him with small, black eyes. Her face and tiny nose gave her the look of an alert chihuahua. She wanted to ask him something. He suspected it was something he didn't want to talk about.

"I heard you tell the captain something happened the other night. On New Year's."

Dani Grasso was a year out of the academy, first-generation police, the granddaughter of an Italian-born grocer who had turned his produce stand into a chain of high-end grocery stores in the valley. She had an expensive condo in Cupertino near Apple headquarters, a gift from grandpa. She seemed comfortable right away in upscale Monte Verde. When Ruiz had remarked on how well she was fitting into the community, the captain had laughed and said Grasso had "found her people."

Ruiz drove into the lot behind the station and pulled into a slot near the back door. He turned off the engine.

"Reyna and I saw a shooting on our way back from a party."

Grasso brightened like a student realizing she knew the answer to the teacher's question. "An old man. *Really* old. He used to work at NASA."

Ruiz sat back, his hand on the wheel. Since that night, he'd felt a heavy sense weighing on him that he'd missed something important. That he should have done something to stop this from happening. He'd be damned if he knew what that something was.

"I saw his picture in the *San Jose Mercury News*. Such a tiny guy," Grasso said. "He looked too old to be driving."

"It looked like a gang hit. The kind of thing that

happened in my part of town growing up. The SUV passed us and shot into the old guy's car right after he'd turned onto the expressway."

"He spent his life helping people." Grasso's eyes flashed in anger. "Why the hell would someone kill a guy like that?"

Ruiz tapped his fingers on the steering wheel. "Could have been something he did. Maybe something he didn't even realize he did. Or the killers could have had some liquor in them and gone out with the intention to kill somebody."

He thought of some of the guys he'd met at the New Year's party with Reyna. He'd seen glimpses of it that night. The amped up sense of competition. The tendency to be offended by something you'd normally brush off—like being cut off on an expressway. It didn't take much. He'd seen his own father get violent when he drank. Ruiz had avoided alcohol for years, worried that he was destined to do the same thing.

"The thing that discounts the drinking theory is, this person was a very good shot." Ruiz described the shots, in the left side of Schuler's head, in his chest. "From a moving car."

"But it is possible," Grasso said, almost under her breath, as if she'd started crunching the numbers herself.

Grasso hadn't seen a murder in Monte Verde yet. She was pulling pieces from what she'd learned at the academy, a year of field training and—he knew this about her—a desire to see justice done.

"He was targeted, and they planned it carefully." Grasso was trying to put herself in the killer's place. "He lived nearby, right? Someone called him so he'd leave his house. Then they waited."

"But why was he targeted?" Ruiz rested an arm on the top of the steering wheel. "I've been reading about him. He was a saint. He spent most of his time teaching kids science. In his spare time, he delivered meals to senior citizens."

"There must have been something. Something that made the shooter pick him."

The car grew dark as the sun started its descent behind the coastal hills. The timed lights turned on in the back lot. Ruiz opened his door.

"Sometimes it doesn't make any sense. You want to find the reason behind it—solve the case like a puzzle. But people kill for stupid reasons. The longer you do this, you see that people kill because they're dumb, drunk, high, greedy or just plain evil. Or so twisted by something that's happened to them that they couldn't control themselves."

They walked in through the back entrance, past the break room.

Grasso grabbed her bag from her locker. "You can let SJPD deal with it. You told them what you saw—it's probably more than they'd get from a civilian witness."

He didn't feel like telling Grasso that he hadn't gotten the license plate number, which delayed the search for the SUV. He also didn't want to tell her how much he'd thought about the shooting in the past twenty-four hours. Or that he'd heard the old man's last words. It hadn't been the first time he'd been present when someone died, but that moment with the old man had felt—he could only think of this word—*sacred*. Like Schuler was a man confessing to his priest.

That moment weighed on him. Along with his own failure to do whatever his conscience thought he should have done to stop the shooting.

He had told Flores at the scene that night. But he hadn't told Reyna.

He had decided it might be right to share it with the man's next of kin.

Tomorrow he would call Rose Schuler Mulvaney.

8

Duke sat down at the computer he'd set up on a table in the bedroom.

He turned it on and watched as the screen ran through the Windows bootup sequence. Joanne would have hated that he'd set up the computer in the bedroom. She used to say that was the one place where she had him to herself.

The week after she'd died in her sleep, he'd set up a workplace on the wall opposite the bed, a desk with his computer and his reference books lined up in a bookcase. After Joanne's death and all the work he'd put in to take care of her, he'd gone back to what he knew. The world of specs, of speeds and altitude. It had been more than ten years, but he felt a part of that world again. Even if it was busy work he made for himself.

Today he was here for research of a different kind. He entered "Karl Gerhardt Schuler" in the Google search box and hit return. He received the results he thought he'd get— a brief article in the *San Jose Mercury News* about the shooting, along with a list of Karl's achievements in aeronautics, his inventions and patents. Photos of him receiving an award. Of him on the deck of an aircraft carrier, hand resting on a fuselage. Karl had been as self-effacing as they come, never wanting to talk about his accomplishments, more comfortable with giving credit to his team or to his company. Though from their conversations, Duke had always been impressed by Karl's overall knowledge and decades of experience. The man's memory alone was impressive.

The scariest thing about Joanne's dementia had been the gaps in her memory—they opened up unexpectedly like sinkholes. One day it was the children. Then it was their wedding. Then finally, the day he had to explain to Joanne who he was.

Karl's mind was a precision machine. He could recall a foot race from his childhood in the Harz mountains in Germany as well as a detail of a wing assembly on a plane he'd worked on forty years ago. Duke found this a relief.

Karl's daughter Rose was more involved in Karl's life than the rest of his family. Karl said she sometimes brought meals over and offered to clean. It had been a few years since he'd seen Rose. Duke decided to look her up, to find out what the plans might be for his memorial.

Duke had seen many of his friends die over the years. He held things loosely now. If somebody didn't show up to an outing or get-together, there was a good chance they were ill. The probability of cancer, heart disease or life-changing falls increased with time.

But there was something different about Karl's death. He was ninety-two, and as far as Duke could see, there was nothing wrong with his mind or his body. Or his relationships with family, friends and the people he went out of his way to help.

Duke turned the situation over and over in his head, looking at it from different perspectives, as if it were a scale model of a plane in his hands.

Karl's death did not make sense.

A THRUST of wind rustled through the eucalyptus trees, sending leaves fluttering down. Ruiz pulled the car onto the shoulder, which was muddy from the rains and littered with grey-green leaves and curling strips of bark brought down by the wind.

He parked and stepped out of the truck. The wind felt strong, yet it wasn't raining. He looked around at the site, which was hard to recognize as the scene of the accident. Everything looked different in the light. That night everything had seemed focused, like he'd been in a tunnel —he'd seen the SUV, the old man's white car, and the police cruiser, highlighted on the shoulder in the yellow glow of the streetlights. Daylight transformed and expanded the scene: now he could see the lurching row of trees, the backs of the houses beyond the concrete retaining wall.

The hills in the distance were now bright and green from the rain, a bank of grey clouds piled up over them. Weather reports had been talking about the great storm coming, the atmospheric river that would descend over Northern California in the coming week. From the looks of the clouds today, it was on its way.

He tried to remember which tree Karl Schuler's car had hit. He walked along the shoulder, strewn with eucalyptus leaves, as he eyeballed each tree. The skin on each tree looked smooth, with bark peeled back like brown shipping wrap. He placed his hand flat on one and felt its cool smoothness. Tree after tree seemed the same, little to differentiate them. Maybe the darkness had confused him; it didn't look like anything had happened along this stretch, beyond some quick fast food dining, to judge by the scattered bags and drink cups.

After passing five or six of the large trees, he saw it. The torn-up shoulder should have made it obvious, as well as the skid marks in the lane by the shoulder. Car tracks in the mud, crumbles of car window glass, a curved piece of silver headlight casing. He looked up and saw the side of the tree, a bright gash in its bark.

If the old man had been Latino, there would be a *descanso* here, a cross bearing his name, decorated elaborately with plastic flowers and rocks. A memorial that his soul had departed from his body in this place.

Ruiz walked around the tree, tracing the scars from the damage he'd seen that night. He looked over the skid marks from the SUV in the left lane. He followed the arc the white car had taken from the lane over to the tree.

Ruiz asked himself why he was here. Flores was young, but he seemed capable enough. He wondered if he should give the guy a call. He wouldn't be happy if someone moved in on one of his investigations. But then he'd heard the shots into the old man's car and watched him die. Flores hadn't.

Maybe Grasso had been right—someone had called Karl Schuler out that night. The thought wedged in his head like a splinter. Of course, this was an unusually independent ninety-two-year old. Maybe he'd been going to one of his children's houses. Maybe he'd been out of toothpaste or Depends or something and was making an emergency run to the store.

He thought about touching base with Flores to check in. Flores had interviewed the family by this point. There had to be a way he could finesse this to find out how the case was progressing.

As cars whizzed past on the expressway, he began the walk back to his car, avoiding the puddles and ruts of soft mud. He was looking down when he heard the crunch of car tires on gravel, pulling onto the narrow shoulder about twenty feet ahead of him.

A grey Ford Taurus had parked ahead, not far behind his car. He wondered if it was someone needing help or someone lost, pulling over for a quick check on Google Maps.

The door opened and an elderly man, thin and slightly stooped, stepped out of his car. Ruiz felt suddenly worried for him, on the narrow shoulder so close to traffic. The wind ruffled his stark white hair. He stood up and looked around tentatively. He wore a faded navy-blue windbreaker that looked about fifty years old.

Ruiz approached the car and saw the man's expression. He looked in pain—his face tightened and hard.

He called out to the man. "Need some help?"

The man waved a hand dismissively and shook his head. As he approached the man's car, Ruiz saw his pale, freckled skin and round light-blue eyes magnified behind gold wire rim aviator glasses. "A friend of mine died here on New Year's. I was passing by. I—I guess I needed to see it for myself."

"Karl Schuler." Ruiz nodded. "That's why I'm here. My wife and I saw it happen."

The old man's lips trembled. It looked like the man was trying hard to keep his face immovable as granite. His generation had been taught that.

Not much different than the guys Ruiz had grown up with. *Break and you're weak.*

"Duke Sorenson," the man reached his hand out to Ruiz. The firm grip of his handshake surprised Ruiz. It didn't match the man's appearance.

"Detective James Ruiz."

"Officer, I'd sure appreciate if you could tell me what you saw."

Duke Sorensen faced him in the booth at the donut shop, his pale eyes intense behind his glasses.

The shop smelled like sugar and hot fat. Ruiz's stomach began rumbling.

The morning crowd was long gone in the nearly empty shop and the donuts in the display case looked sparse and worse for wear. The Korean owner was scrubbing the tables around them fiercely, spreading an overpowering scent of lemon surface cleaner.

"Karl and the gang, we met here at Kang's shop. Every Friday morning at nine." Duke looked around the small shop. "Then Joe passed on, and Chuck became a caregiver to his wife until she died. Karl and the rest of us tried to keep things going."

Since his own mother hadn't had the privilege of living past the age of fifty-six and he hadn't seen his father in twenty-five years, Ruiz had only seen the aging process up close when he visited his *abuela* in Salinas. He certainly didn't look forward to it for himself. He'd investigated enough elder abuse cases in Monte Verde to dread that frailty and vulnerability. He fantasized that he'd die in a shootout before he had to face that, though the possibility of that happening was pretty slim in Monte Verde.

"Detective Ruiz." The man's eyes were riveted on him solemnly. "I want you to tell me exactly what the person in the SUV did, what happened to the car, and what you saw when you looked into Karl's car."

Ruiz thought about what he'd say. Duke was a smart guy, and he judged, had a strong streak of pride. He'd be respectful to Karl in telling the story, but he wouldn't soften it either.

"I was in Vietnam, Detective Ruiz," the man said, his magnified eyes still that bleary, angelic blue. "You can tell me the truth."

Ruiz told him about the sequence of events, then the shots into Karl's window. He described Karl's body as he saw it in clinical terms, to explain how severe his injuries had been without painting too vivid of a picture.

"The good news is, he probably didn't suffer." Ruiz hoped his words were accurate. "He couldn't have seen the SUV or the shots coming. There's nothing he could have done to avoid this."

Duke took it in, his eyes as wide and round as an inquisitive baby's. He looked from Ruiz's face down to his coffee. He ran his boney, spotted hands slowly back and forth across the table's Formica surface as if he were treading water.

"Thanks for being straight with me."

Ruiz shook a packet of powdered creamer into his cup. This was not the organic creamer of the MVPD. Clumps floated on the surface till he stirred them in. "Duke, can you think of any reason why Karl would be out that late on New Year's?"

Duke shook his head. "Karl did what he wanted to do. I would say that he might have been out at a party, but he couldn't stay awake past nine." A faint smile crossed Duke's face. "With Karl, the spirit was willing to do almost anything, but the flesh was weak."

The reference took Ruiz back to his church days growing up: Jesus in the Garden of Gesthemane, lecturing his disciples for not being able to stay awake as he wrestled with the prospect of his coming death.

"What could be so important that he would have woken up and gone out?"

"Off the top of my head, I'd say, it had to be an emergency with Rose or his grandkids. They live close by." Duke took a bite of his maple bar. "Or with one of the students he worked with."

Flores must have interviewed the family by now. Maybe he'd found out if someone had called Karl Schuler. If it hadn't been family or a student, maybe Grasso had been right—someone had called the old man out of his house that night with the intent to kill him.

Had Schuler been targeted? He didn't know enough about Karl Schuler to rule out that it wasn't the man himself that the killer in the SUV had been after.

"Duke, when did you first meet Karl?" Ruiz pulled off a piece of the pink-frosted donut on his plate. He hoped Duke was one of those old people who liked to tell stories. It didn't take much to get his *abuela* and her friends launched into the stories they'd stockpiled over the years. He knew them by heart.

"We met years ago," Duke said, continuing the movement

of his hands over the table. "We worked together for years at Lockheed. We'd both been in the valley at different companies and our paths had crossed a few times before that. Karl was a history book of flight—he'd worked in the field for so long. He'd been involved in aviation since after the second world war. We used to joke that he'd probably given the Wright brothers advice on aerodynamics."

"What kind of things was Karl involved in besides aviation? Anything that might have gotten him into trouble?"

Duke let out a laugh, which made Ruiz feel like the man was moving from shock to a place of remembering his friend fondly. "I can tell you. Diddly squat. The guy was a straight arrow. Responsible with his money. Good husband —his wife Aggie died about fifteen years ago and she was the love of his life. He went to church, delivered meals to seniors, and mentored students in science. The rest of the time, he liked to read about anything that flew. That was Karl's life."

Ruiz nodded appreciatively. Then he asked about the thought that his mind had settled on today. That the shooting could have been road rage from an earlier incident: Karl cutting someone off.

"You ever drive with Karl? How was his driving?"

Duke might get defensive. The man had to be in his seventies. From what he'd seen with the elderly residents of Monte Verde who persisted in driving long past their ability to do it, it was the men who fought it most. Not wanting to give up their independence. Which, Ruiz had to admit, he understood.

Duke paused.

"No problems I could see." From the look on his face,

Duke had carefully analyzed all data from his rides with Karl and made the assessment.

"What about his grandkids? Any problems there? Illegal activities?" He wasn't sure if Duke would be aware of these things, but he had to ask.

Duke gave him a sideways look. "Karl said a couple of his grandkids were into smoking *marijuana*." He pronounced the word with the precision of someone who had never come into contact with the substance or anyone who'd smoked it. The man's lips tightened in disapproval.

"Got it. Thanks, Duke." Ruiz smiled. He'd have to talk to the family members if he wanted more information. "Do you know if his family is planning a memorial service?"

"I talked to his daughter Rose this morning," Duke said. "He's being cremated. They're waiting to set a date for the service so the family out of state can be there."

As they left the shop, Ruiz watched Duke make his way back to his car in the strip mall parking lot. Then he sat in his truck eating the last of his pink donut. Reyna wouldn't approve of this afternoon snack. He picked up the chocolate jimmies with his finger and ate them one by one to get rid of the evidence. He balled up the white paper bag and tucked it into his car litter bag.

That night of the shooting still seemed vivid to him. It started up in his mind at random times, when he least expected it.

Something deep and angry in him stirred when the innocent were threatened. It always had.

He felt that same feeling twenty-five years ago, the night the police had come to their apartment, after his father had thrown his mother against the kitchen wall so hard it broke three of her ribs. The police had come before. This was back in the days before the officers could charge someone in a domestic abuse case, regardless of whether the assaulted party agreed or not. At least twice he'd heard his mother's words, denying that her husband had meant to hit her, had meant to shove her—but Ruiz had been there. He'd seen what happened.

Ruiz had studied the officers' faces. They were kind and they gently pressed his mother to describe what had happened. He saw the barely concealed anger in their eyes. anger he now related to, when he saw someone had gotten away with something.

But that night, things were different. As the EMTs did triage on her face and ribs and prepared to take her to Valley General, Lupe Maria Ruiz had turned to the police and said it loud enough that he heard.

Si. Press charges.

After they left, he'd cleaned the blood off the floor and put his little brother Mateo to bed. Then he sat at the kitchen table, waiting to hear from his mother.

He knew what he would do after high school. He'd been thinking about it for a while. That night he said it to himself out loud, and he felt a new strength rising up inside him.

He would join the police force.

10

D uke unlocked the mailbox and pulled out the folded bunch of mail.

Flyers from a local pizza parlor, a utilities bill and a giant 50 percent off coupon from Bed, Bath and Beyond, which he'd never use.

He wondered why he bothered to check the box every day. Did people write letters anymore? He remembered when Joanne was back east at college and wrote him two letters a week. He felt a flutter inside as he remembered her perfectly slanted cursive writing on the envelopes. She'd write about her sorority sisters and what they were planning and funny things her friends had said. He'd been busy in his first job, excited to be working on what he loved, but he felt very alone.

He missed the way her smile opened her up to him, her spunky attitude, and the way her hair turned up at the ends, defying gravity itself. He lived through her descriptions of parties and the hijinks that went on at them. Even in her letters, he heard her laugh. Back in those days, it bubbled out of her so easily. Over the years, that had changed. She'd become tight lipped and withdrawn, communicating mostly about the children, bills or things that needed to be fixed.

The meetup at Donut Haven had raised Duke's hopes. Detective Ruiz wanted to find out what had happened that night; obviously Karl's murder had affected him deeply. Ruiz had reassured him that Flores was trying to track down the SUV.

As he stood in front of mailboxes, the choice wasn't hard for Duke to make: head back to his cold, empty home or keep walking in the sun, now peeking through the grey cloud layer. He tucked the bill in his pocket and deposited the flyers and coupons in the trash can.

It was a mile and a half to Karl's house, longer than he usually walked. Whether for nostalgia or to pay tribute, he headed down the street. He wanted to see his friend's house again.

He made it within a half an hour, taking the side streets, then crossing Almaden Expressway at the light. He remembered the way from driving and turned onto Karl's street. The neat, two-story, white house with black shutters looked no different than it had in the nearly fifty years he'd known Karl. It was midafternoon, and he smelled the powdery floral smell coming from dryer vents as he passed the houses. It filled him with a sense of longing, for a time when he'd lived in a household, not just by himself.

There was a car in front of Karl's. Rose's maroon Honda Accord.

He tapped on the door, and waited, as footsteps approached. Rose usually dressed neatly and fashionably, to accent her figure. Today she wore sweatpants and a t-shirt and was holding a bin full of magazines and newspapers. Without makeup, she looked pale and more her age. It felt odd to see her this way, as if he'd barged into a private space where he didn't belong.

Rose always scared him. He knew from how she'd cared for her father that she must have a kind, loving side. But he always felt he had to be careful or he'd cross her.

"I was out for a walk, and I was thinking about him." He smiled. Rose rarely returned smiles, and he'd come to expect that. "I didn't mean to interrupt anything. I'm sure you've got a lot to take care of right now."

"I'm trying to figure out what to pack up and what to get rid of." Rose set the bin next to the door. It was filled with yellow, dogeared aerospace magazines and aeronautics journals, featuring topics that were big news forty years go. "We've got to clean the place out to sell. The market's on an upswing right now. I want to make sure it's ready when we talk to a realtor."

He wondered if Rose was looking for work to plunge into, to keep her occupied. He could relate to that. The week after Joanne passed away, he'd entered her sewing room to box up her clothes, quilting supplies and craft boxes. It helped to be busy, engaged in a task.

He'd also wanted to get rid of anything that reminded him of the days when she was active and fully herself.

Rose stood in the door for a minute, as if trying to decide whether she'd let him in. "You can come in and help if you like."

Karl's normally cluttered living room was filled with stacks of books and boxes filled with neatly folded clothes. There were stacks of old, framed photos on the end tables. He picked one up—Karl with John Glenn and the 1950s test pilots who became the first astronauts. Another one with Neil Armstrong.

The air was musty, as if Rose's efforts had unwisely

disturbed layers of dust untouched for decades. He noticed a stack of books and pulled up a chair and started going through them. Books about the space program, pilots, and high-speed flight. He picked one about early high-altitude flight and started leafing through the pages.

"Take whatever you want from those piles," Rose looked up from a stack of papers and three-ring binders—notes Karl had made over the years on things that interested him. Duke would love to go through these later and he hoped she wouldn't toss them. "Everything has to go. Might as well go to someone who'll appreciate them."

Duke smiled his thanks and began setting aside a pile for himself. After a few minutes, he realized he had more than he could walk home with.

"Can you go through the books on the shelves by the couch?" Rose waved her hand in the direction of the front window. "I have no idea what he's got over there. There are some boxes by the door. Pull out what you'd like for yourself and for anyone from the donut group, then put the rest in a box."

"Okay if I pick them up another time? I'm walking home."

Rose nodded curtly. "Fine." She finished off another trash bag of notebooks and papers with the resolute jerk of a plastic tie and carried it to the door. "I'll be here tomorrow."

None of her father's warmth. Rose Schuler Mulvaney was a little like her mother. There'd always been something sad about Aggie Schuler, distant and tamped down. Joanne complained that she'd never been able to connect with Aggie. She'd resented that she seemed to end up in the kitchen with her when the families got together. *I'm sure she's a nice person, Duke—but we're nothing alike. I don't even know what to talk to her about.*

Rose went back to the papers, tossing sheafs of paper and binders in the bag. She worked with a steady, rhythmic motion, like a collator on a copy machine.

He'd made his way through the first shelf, when he remembered Detective Ruiz had wanted to know about Karl's memorial.

"Have you set a time for the service, Rose?"

"Probably a Friday afternoon. That works best for the family flying in."

"Christoph will be coming then?" Duke enjoyed talking to Christoph Schuler, who ran an aviation services company in Florida and flew his own plane.

"Of course. And Hermann's grandson and his wife."

Duke looked up at her, startled. Karl hadn't talked about his uncle Hermann much, though they'd come to the U.S. together. They'd worked together for a while in aerospace in Florida, then Karl had moved out to California and married Aggie. Hermann had died in a plane crash in the 1970s. Duke got the feeling that there had been a falling out between Karl and Hermann, but Karl had never talked about it.

Duke finished going through the two top shelves of the massive oak bookshelf. Aviation textbooks, technical journals—most of them outdated and good to throw out. Then biographies of physicists and inventors. There were a few old, cloth-bound books that looked like they were written in German, with elaborate, medieval-looking lettering. He opened one and found his high school German was no help in reading the antiquated script. The yellowed pages smelled good, somewhere between an old library and a forest. He laid one in the box, along with some of the biographies he'd picked out.

Rose returned to her steady churning through the papers and filling bags. After a few minutes, he lost himself in a book about airships stationed at Moffett Naval Air Station in the 1930s. The photographs of the immense ships floating in the giant hangars were mesmerizing. Planes had always been his interest and speed impressed him. But airships had a beauty that was ethereal, almost regal—they moved slowly, not to be rushed. They'd disappeared long before Duke's time, though Karl would have been of an age to see them, as a child.

He looked up at the bay window and saw the colors of dusk outside. Long purple shadows falling across the front yard. How long had he been here?

The room had gone still. Rose's paper shuffling had stopped. She'd settled on the couch, her hand resting on the page of a clothbound notebook. She had her reading glasses on. She was transfixed, her mouth open.

She turned pages slowly. In the few minutes she'd been reading, her face had changed. The harshness of her expression had softened, and Duke swore he saw ruts of tears on her cheeks. He'd never seen Rose cry. He had wondered if she was capable of it.

With light dimming outside and busy streets to cross, he knew he'd have to go. He pulled out a few books, light enough to carry on the walk home, zipped up his jacket and said goodbye to Rose. The soft look on her face went away. She nodded at him, then pressed her lips together. She switched on the end table lamp and returned to the notebook and her perch on the couch.

He would have given anything to know what she was reading.

11

R uiz was alone.

Reyna had gone to bed only an hour after Jacky, since she had spin class at 5 a.m. Ruiz opened the cabinets in the kitchen to look for the potato chips she carefully hid from him. After rifling through the cabinets and drawers, he found the bag in the salad spinner under the stove—a new spot this time. *Nice job, babe.*

He took the clip off the bag and shook some into a bowl, with the exhilaration of having gotten away with something.

He sat down at the computer desk just between the kitchen and the dining room and googled Karl Schuler. All he knew about the man he'd gotten from online news feeds.

The first thing that came up was an article from two years ago in the *San Jose Mercury News* about Schuler's work with students on San Jose's east side.

He remembered East Point Youth Center. It wasn't far from where he'd grown up. If he'd had any interest in science and math in high school, he might have met Schuler there. But math made his head hurt and science seemed all about memorizing things. Criminal Justice had been his interest at that age. That and football, but after his peak playing years in high school, he'd spent most of his community college football games on the bench.

The article listed Schuler's achievements in aerospace and aeronautical technology. He'd worked at Lockheed when he first came to California, in the late 1940s, working with high altitude planes. He'd worked with the U2 spy plane program, then for a couple of aeronautical firms. He held patents for several plane component designs.

Ruiz took a few chips, then wiped his hands carefully on a napkin as he watched a video of Karl Schuler explaining how a plane takes off and stays in the air. The twenty-year-old video was from a presentation at the Smithsonian Air and Space Museum in Washington, DC.

Schuler didn't talk like a scientist. He was a small, white-haired man in a baggy button-down shirt and gold-rimmed glasses, a plastic pen holder in his pocket. It was hard for Ruiz to see this as the dying man in the Camry. He bubbled over with energy, a mischievous look on his face, as he bounced on his heels in front of a white board, a group of students seated in a semicircle in front of him. He explained through a series of drawings, how a plane's engine forced air over the wing. He drew a cartoon wing, with a happy face on it, its eyes closed as the wind passed over it. This caused the plane to lift, cancelling the gravity—an arrow pointing down on the plane with a mean face—that kept it pinned to the ground. This rush of air was able to lift a 200-ton airplane speeding down a runway into the air. Then the pilots tamed that powerful airflow—drawn as a superhero —by using the wing flaps, rudder and back elevator to turn the plane or make the nose go up or down. Schuler imitated the voice of the pilot and even of the plane at one point.

Schuler's goofy presentation made the kids smile. Hearing Schuler's explanation made him wonder why he'd never known this before. He made it sound so simple. It made him want to fly again. He loved the flight to Hawaii he and Reyna had taken last summer—his first flight outside of California. Schuler's excited explanation made flying sound nothing short of a miracle.

Karl Schuler had a Wikipedia entry, though most of it was a list of technical achievements Ruiz didn't know the significance of. Patents for systems on various planes, wing designs he'd worked on. Then his employers, one in Florida, three in Silicon Valley. It gave his birthdate as 1926, Brocken, Germany, which would explain the accent.

His spouse was Agnieszka Kaminski Schuler – born 1923, died 2006. It also mentioned a Dr. Hermann Schuler, his uncle. When he clicked on the man's name, he saw another list of technical achievements he didn't understand. Though he did see that Hermann Schuler's contributions to the United States space program included work on the Mercury and Gemini missions in the 1960s.

Ruiz sat back and finished off his chips, then fluffed up the bag to disguise the fact that half the contents were missing. He placed it back in the salad spinner carefully and noiselessly shut the cabinet.

He thought about the man he'd seen die on New Year's. Karl Schuler had spent most of his life giving to other people. In a valley where young, smart tech types were glorified and senior citizens barely visible, why would anyone track down and kill a ninety-two-year-old man?

He'd meet up with Duke Sorenson to ask more about Karl. He was also curious about Schuler's involvement with East Point Youth Center—could his work there have led to a bad encounter with gang members?

Maybe they'd been making the old man's death too complicated. Maybe Karl Schuler had been unlucky, that's all.

In the wrong place at a very wrong time.

12

Rose called Duke back the next morning, asking if he could come by and do some yard work when he picked up the box of Karl's books and belongings. He agreed.

He had too much time on his hands anyway. Karl had kept his front yard neatly groomed, right down to the edging.

But three days after Karl's death, the lawn needed to be mowed, weeds pulled and the hedge of rose bushes pruned.

It was the least Duke could do. Karl would wince if he saw the yard like this. Taking care of this would honor Karl.

Rose was inside with her daughter, clearing out more of the closets and loading up boxes to take to the Goodwill truck. They stacked the filled boxes on the porch. Duke had volunteered to load them into his Taurus and get rid of them for Rose. He'd go through the boxes first. Sure, it was nosy and he had no business doing it. But he wanted to see if there were any more books he might be interested in. Any papers that might give him a hint of what could have happened to Karl. And if he was really lucky he'd find it—

the book that had brought the cold, no-nonsense Rose to tears.

The weather was biting cold, the skies clear and sharp blue. An airliner, a 747, judging by the nose, cut low across the sky, on its way to San Jose International. It reminded him of brisk days he'd visited Joanne at school in the winter, the kind of day that made her cheeks pink as they walked across campus. She'd been beautiful, dark hair and those blue eyes. Stunning like a movie starlet.

Duke remembered times when he'd put the relationship to the test. Didn't call her back. Let a few of her letters go without writing back. To see if she'd realize her mistake and drift off to someone else. When that didn't stop her, he'd accepted that she would be his, an extravagant gift.

He pulled the lawnmower out of Karl's side shed, pulled the crank and mowed across the yard in neat horizontal rows as Karl always did. He pruned the few winter roses, raking the debris into the pile of lawn clippings, branches and leaves, then push-broomed it all out to the street for yard waste collection.

He looked up when he heard it.

The screech of a car turning too fast, then barreling down the street toward him. Duke stepped back as the car braked abruptly and angled up to the curb a few feet from him.

The young man who got out looked to be in his twenties. His hair was pulled back in a tiny ponytail and he had a full reddish-blonde beard. He wore nice slacks, a sweater vest and a navy-blue sports coat, one Duke himself would have worn with pride in the 1960s, when going to a fancy restaurant.

The young man slammed the car door.

"Is Rose here?"

Duke stood taller and gripped the broomstick in front of him like a weapon.

"Tell me who you are first."

"I'm Randall Mulvaney, old man. Her son."

Duke's heart pounded. He felt an instinctive desire to protect Rose, to warn her. He watched the young man's face as he looked beyond him to the house. *This must be the one who smokes pot.*

Randall headed for the front door and opened it with a carelessness that caused the inner doorknob to bang against the wall. Duke hurried up to the front steps, not knowing what he would do if Rose and her daughter were threatened. He closed his fingers around the cell phone in his pocket, ready to call 911 if he had to.

Duke stood awkwardly in the entry way, waiting. He heard Randall's raised voice from the back bedroom.

"You said you'd give me the seventy-five bucks. I helped the old guy out. What are you doing to me here?"

Duke heard Rose respond in a quiet, measured voice. He heard sound of a zipper, then soft, hurried voices as Rose and her daughter tried to piece together the money between them. Randall raised his voice again.

"I went out of my way and you're both giving me shit now. Fuck you. I deserve more respect than this."

More mumbling between the two women, then Randall came out of the room. He stopped in the hallway and looked down as he slid a thin stack of bills into his wallet. As he headed for the front door, Duke sidestepped into the kitchen to get out of his way. Randall left and slammed the door behind him, with a sound that reverberated from the entry way into the kitchen. Wine glasses in a hanging rack above the counter tinkled against each other, trembling.

Duke looked out the kitchen window and saw the car

wheel into the driveway, then back out, turn and head back down the street. His heart beating, he waited until Randall's car turned onto the main street and disappeared.

"Are you ladies all right?" Duke poked his head into the downstairs bedroom, where Rose and her daughter were sorting pants and shirts into boxes.

Both looked up, surprised. The daughter, a skinny blonde with a sunken face turned to her mother, deferring to her.

"We're fine. Why?" Rose calmly folded the arms of a sweater, then looked up at him, expressionless.

Nothing about Randall Mulvaney's behavior seemed to have bothered the two women. And that's when Duke knew. There was something odd in Karl's family. Something he'd never seen in his times with just Karl.

It made him wonder if there was something about the Schuler family that he'd missed in his years of knowing them.

13

W hen the dental office opened on January 4, Reyna Ruiz was relieved to go back to work. She was happy to get back to a regular routine. Three days after the shooting, she was having trouble sleeping at night.

She'd been shaking when they arrived at her parents' house to pick up Jacky. Her mother in her worn nightgown and robe had asked what was wrong as soon as she'd seen her and Jimmy on the doorstep. They came in, sat on the sagging corduroy couch that her father refused to get rid of and described what they'd seen happen. Reyna slid toward the deep pit in the couch Jimmy made when he sat down and listened to him tell the story. His voice was steady and clear. He spoke slowly and calmly, as if he were reciting the details of a police report. No emotion. Hadn't he felt anything? A man had been killed as they watched.

Wedged in next to him on the couch, she felt irritation, as her father, her grandmother and her mother asked endless questions. Her teeth were chattering, from cold and shock. It was 3:30 a.m. on New Year's. She wanted to go to her own home, curl up in her own bed and cry.

They could have easily shot us instead. My life could have ended an hour ago.

SHE'D WOKEN up at 11 a.m. on new year's morning, her body dull and sluggish, but her mind racing. She asked Jimmy about the old man who'd died. Jimmy had shaken his head, not sharing what he saw when he'd looked into the car. It poured over her: the shaky, weak relief of having just missed death.

Today in room 2, she pulled the shield down over her face and flipped the light on above the dental chair. She went to work on Ben Marsden's teeth.

"Open wide for me now. A little to this side."

She touched the side of the man's chin with her gloved hand and gently shepherded it to the left. A young entrepreneur who had started a company in his 20s, Ben drove a Tesla Model X and wore buttoned-down shirts, the tailored kind that showed off his toned torso. She saw guys with bodies like this at the gym in the mornings, but they bored her. They scanned the line of machines full of women as if it were a restaurant menu. It disgusted Reyna as she did her time on the treadmill. She refused to acknowledge them. She kept her chin lifted and her eyes focused out the window at the parking lot.

It was a small gym in a strip mall, with stained carpeting, the type of business that advertises on flyers stuffed into envelopes with pizza coupons and car insurance ads. It was what they could afford—$15 a month—and she could do spin classes, no extra charge. She went in early, did her time and left.

Her looks were an asset, and she wanted to keep it that way. Not to please Jimmy—he couldn't keep his hands off her. His looks did nothing for her: his flat nose, his barrel chest and belly.

But on one Friday night ten years ago, Jimmy Ruiz had changed everything for her. Pulled her out of a life she could never tell the PTA ladies about.

That afternoon, her boyfriend Mateo Ruiz had been arrested for dealing. She'd found his phone and called his older brother Jimmy after the police left. She and Mateo rented a room in a dirty three-bedroom house in south San Jose, with ten other people she did not know and did not want to live with by herself.

She had nothing but a part-time job at the Dollar Store and a dying, Bondo-covered Corolla.

No matter how desperate she was, she could not call her parents. She'd seen what had happened when her older brother had been arrested the year before. He was no longer allowed in the house. His pictures had been taken down. It was as if he had never existed.

Jimmy had come over, picked her up with her Hefty trash bag of belongings and taken her back to his apartment. He'd slept on the couch and let her have his bedroom. Within a week, he'd found her a small studio off of Alum Rock Avenue, near Japantown. In the summer she started a dental assistant program, with help from Jimmy and her parents.

She'd been so grateful for a new start. When he asked her to marry him after her graduation, what else could she have said?

The wedding in Tahoe and the first year of marriage had gone okay. Then she felt the walls tightening around her, enclosing her with this man who'd fallen into her life and fixed everything. The kindest man she'd ever met, a good man.

A man ten years older than she was. A man her parents adored. A man she wasn't attracted to.

Last October they had gone for a week's vacation in Hawaii, paid for by Jimmy's summer security gig. The hotel on Waikiki made her feel like she was walking through a dream. The way she and Jimmy were treated at the hotel and the restaurants—they were *valued guests*. The warm breeze touching her face, the tropical flowers she started smelling almost as soon as they landed.

That week away, her life matched up with her dreams. Jimmy even looked better to her; in the dim light of the room, with the curtains closed, she saw some of Mateo's features in him—the full curved upper lip, the muscular upper arms. A little pretending didn't hurt anybody. Making love made Jimmy happy and then he fell asleep. She was free.

She could sit on the balcony and read her magazines or go down to the open-air bar, have a drink and watch the torches burn along the beach. Away from Silicon Valley, she moved effortlessly, almost floating. She accepted her drink from the waiter with a slight smile and a graceful, raised hand.

Now she scraped at Ben's front teeth, releasing the fine bits of plaque that had accumulated. It was a satisfying feeling; the same pleasure she got from giving a room a thorough cleaning. She could be as picky as she wanted within the twenty minutes. Just like she was at home, she became protective of her work, wagging her finger at the patients and warning them.

Feel how clean your teeth are now? Don't you dare mess this up.

She wheedled with them to brush and floss. Flirting sometimes worked with the guys. Many of these patients, especially ones working in tech, would leave the chair, then not floss for the next six months. She was tired of picking bits of rotten meat out of their teeth.

Ben was different. He took pride in his appearance. His teeth were perfectly aligned, his gums strong and healthy. His breath smelled faintly of mint.

As she prepared the polishing paste, he smiled up at her. Her first response was to smile back, but she stopped herself. Her cheeks turned warm and she looked away quickly.

After polishing, she pushed the tray aside and slid up her face shield. She tapped the controls to bring the chair up to position.

"Good job, Ben." She kept her tone professional. "Keep up with your flossing routine, and I'll see you in six months."

He watched as she peeled off her latex gloves and revealed her wedding ring. "That's such a long time."

She was ready to smile and hand him his bag of complimentary toothbrush and floss, but the look in his eyes stopped her. She kept her face composed, pushing down the excitement that rose up in her chest.

"There's a great tapas restaurant down the street where I work," he continued. "I was wondering if you'd be up for lunch sometime."

In the look on his face and the deliberateness of his words, she felt a threat. She had come a long way. She and Jimmy now owned a house. Jacky was in a good school. In the back of her mind, there was a plan. She knew this was not part of the plan.

All of this must have shown up on her face. He looked down then shook his head.

"No worries, Reyna. If you change your mind and ever want to meet me for lunch—*just* lunch—give me a call."

He handed her a business card. Bright red shapes, bold black print. Ben Marsden, President and CEO.

She turned to slip the card in her purse. She kept her smile polite.

"Thank you, Ben."

He stood for a moment watching her, then nodded and left for the hallway.

Reyna stood, her stomach fluttering with delicious excitement. Her face felt hot.

She looked down the hall to make sure no one saw her and wondered why she looked so different.

14

J ust when the phone was on its fourth ring and seemed ready to roll over to voice mail, Flores heard a live voice.

"Jake, here."

"Jake, this is Detective Mario Flores of the San Jose Police Department."

"Are you calling about the unpaid parking ticket? 'Cause I paid it online before Christmas." The response was gruff and deep, a note of defensiveness, and heavy breathing as if he'd rushed to find his phone.

"Glad you took care of that, Jake. I'm calling about your 2003 Ford Explorer. I understand you sold it right before Christmas, is that right?"

There was a long pause. "Why are you asking? Did I do something wrong with the paperwork?"

"I'm calling because the car was involved in a fatal shooting on New Year's." The guy had a lot to learn about law enforcement if he thought the police followed up on DMV paperwork issues.

"Oh, shit." More heavy breathing as he seemed to be

adjusting the position of the phone. "I had no idea. Yeah, I sold it. December 23, I think it was. A guy who responded to my ad on Craig's List. It was a hand-me-down from my parents and Teresa hated it. It was time to get rid of it."

"I'll need the name of the person, Jake."

There was fumbling in the background.

"Hold on while I look up the guy's message on my phone."

It took a couple of minutes. Flores took a gulp from his coffee cup and picked at his lunch, a salad bowl from Chipotle gone cold. The lettuce underneath looked wilted and limp. It was what you got when you waited to have lunch at 2:30 p.m. He tapped to refresh his screen, so he could see if he'd heard back from the Gangs Investigations. He noticed he had a text from Jimmy Ruiz. Jake came back before he had a chance to read it.

"You still there? Yeah, the guy's name is Tuan. Tuan Nguyen. He met me at a gas station and paid me cash." *Sure, that's not sketch.* Flores mentally rolled his eyes as he typed the name on his tablet.

"He was a pretty nice guy."

"Did he give you an address?"

Jake breathed heavily into the phone again as he seemed to be trying to look for it.

"I'm still in Minneapolis. I don't have it with me."

"Okay, Jake. Can you describe Tuan for me?"

"Skinny guy. Asian, maybe in his thirties. Kinda short. I'm 6'4" so everyone's short to me. But I'd say 5 foot 8." Flores grunted to himself. *So I'm really short.* "He wears glasses. Crew cut hair. Kind of a nerd vibe."

Not bad, though everything but the height could easily be altered.

"He gave you cash."

"It was kinda weird. But hey, I'm not turning down cash."

"Last time you saw or heard from him was December 23."

"Yeah. Everything must have worked fine with the car, 'cause I didn't hear anything else from him. Then on New Year's Eve I flew out of town."

"Did you send in the change of ownership form to the DMV?"

"Fuck! No, I didn't. I forgot that part. I thought I was taking care of everything too. *Shit*." Jake mumbled and spiraled down into a pit of self- condemnation.

"Jake, I need the info on it as soon as possible."

"I can have Teresa do that, if she can find it on my desk. Shit. Sorry, man." Jake seemed to be going out of his way to beat himself up verbally.

"Have Teresa take a picture and send it to me." If he didn't hear back from Teresa Cho, he'd stop by and follow up with her.

"Got it, man."

Flores ended the call and wrote up his notes. He had a mental picture of Jake Hollander as a big oaf. Brilliant at coding but not so much at practical matters like paperwork and finances. For the sake of the couple's financial future, he hoped Teresa Cho was.

The light outside was dimming as it approached 4 p.m. There was that desolate feeling in the air. The light in NorCal, in his opinion, always seem to slip away too soon.

As he typed up his notes, he wondered if Oksana would be up for a late dinner after her 7 p.m. class. After their New Year's morning, he really wanted to see her again. She backed out on dinner last night, so she owed him one. It was that back and forth that they did. It usually balanced out.

He went back to his computer and saw an email from

James Ruiz. With an amused smile, he clicked on the subject

—**Cerveza Gratis**

I have some info on Schuler if you're interested. Let's touch base. Meet you at Someplace Bar & Grill?

Detective Ruiz was taking Schuler's death very personally. Flores had heard of his performance on a few big cases. Apparently, murder happened even in the quiet, upscale burb of Monte Verde.

Ruiz was a good detective—but he needed to remember this was not his case. It might not be a bad idea to meet up with Ruiz. A free beer was a free beer.

Flores wrote back. *See you at 6. None of that light beer shit, though.*

15

A t 4:15 p.m., Teresa Cho called. She'd searched her husband's desk and found Tuan Nguyen's address.

A half hour later, the setting sun cast shadows through the trees on the green grass of Kelley Park as Flores turned onto Senter Road in East San Jose. He found a parking spot a few yards down from the apartment complex. The patrol officer pulled his cruiser into the space in front of him.

Flores sat for a minute and took a breath, feeling the Kevlar vest tighten over him as he inhaled. He patted his side to make sure his gun was ready. He hoped this would go down smoothly. An easy arrest. An end to a case that had not turned out to be the no-brainer he'd hoped it would be.

He felt a sheen of sweat on his palms as he got out of the car and gave a quick nod to the patrol officer, David Phan. They walked together down the street to the small two-story complex.

Their presence brought immediate attention. Kids on bikes stopped in their tracks, their heads swiveling in their direction. Some dude waved from the window above, intoxicated or a little too manic.

Flores took in the savory smells of fish and something garlicky and fried as they approached the far stairs. They smelled good to him, and he remembered he'd missed lunch today.

The thumping notes of a bass guitar, playing a funk beat, low and slow, drifted down from the second floor. A grandma in a red t-shirt leaned against the rail of the facing apartment walkway and yelled something in a shrill voice, which could have meant, *Keep it down*, for all he knew.

Flores wondered if they were being watched. He monitored their surroundings, looking for cover. He knew Phan a few steps behind him was doing the same thing.

They made their way past a well-kept planter with herbs and a red plastic, foot-powered car for toddlers. There were a lot of children in the complex. Tuan Nguyen's apartment was the middle of the second floor. Flores hoped this would go down easily with no collateral damage.

He knocked on 6B and heard the familiar sound of a cheap, hollow core door, the kind bullets go through like flimsy cardboard. He stepped back and waited.

No sound.

He exchanged glances with Phan. They waited. And listened.

Finally, Flores knocked again, louder.

Quick footsteps, a brush against a wall.

Phan pulled out his gun. Flores had his hand on his. This was where they would use the split-second assessments they had been trained in. It took seconds for something to go wrong. Shoot or be shot. You couldn't take back your response. The results could last a lifetime. For them. For you. For both.

Flores kept his breathing short and shallow. He wanted to hear the smallest sound coming from behind the door.

Phan kept his eyes on the door.

Then the doorknob rattled. Flores's stomach clenched. The door opened.

In an instant, every muscle in Flores's body relaxed. Phan's stance changed, too.

A startled middle-aged woman answered the door, staring in wide-eyed alarm at Phan's gun. She looked between the two of them, then haltingly raised her hands above her head. Smells of dinner billowed out and surrounded them.

"We're looking for Tuan Nguyen, ma'am."

The woman looked puzzled. Flores saw three children pressed up against their mother's back, eyes wide at the sight of the gun. Phan put his away. Flores slipped his into its holster.

"There is nobody by that name here. Just me and my kids. I'm Yvette Tran." Her voice was shaky, but firm. She seemed to be examining them both. Then she nodded, as if she'd made a pragmatic decision—let the police check things out so she could feed her kids dinner. She looked tired.

She lowered her hands and stepped back from the door. "You can come in and take a look around."

Flores took out his badge. Then he and Phan stepped into the apartment living room.

Flores knew. There would be nothing to see here. Toys piled in a laundry basket. Worn, older furniture, covered by colorful blankets. A table with plates set out for dinner.

"How long have you lived at this address, Ms. Tran?"

"We've been here since my husband passed away. Two years in June."

"There hasn't been anyone with the name Tuan Nguyen living here? Any other adult male?"

"As I said, it's just the kids and I."

"Ms. Tran, do you know if there is a Tuan Nguyen in the apartment complex?" Hollander could have written the address down wrong. Flores was relaxed enough now to give Yvette Tran a smile. "He'd be a man in his thirties, skinny. Very short hair. Glasses. About 5 foot 8."

Yvette Tran paused, then shook her head. The kids behind her had lost interest and drifted away. He heard video game sounds.

"Of course, there are a couple of Nguyens in the apartments. It's a common name. We know each other here. I can't think of anyone who looks like that."

Phan and Flores thanked her and made a short, unsuccessful door-to-door survey of the complex, giving the description and name, then they headed back to their cars.

As Phan started up the cruiser, Flores stood on the sidewalk checking his phone messages as the sky dimmed to darkness and kids went inside for dinner. He could go back to Jake Hollander, but he suspected he wouldn't get anything else.

Whoever had murdered Karl Schuler had gone to a lot of trouble to cover their tracks.

16

They were almost done with Karl's house.

Duke understood Rose better now; the work had been hard, but it had felt cathartic to deal with his grief through cleaning, organizing and disposing of things.

At Rose's direction, Duke Sorenson brought the last two moving boxes, labeled KITCHEN, into her tiled entry way and set them down. He'd managed to pack the contents of Karl's cupboards, with the help of Rose's daughter, within the last couple of days.

Everything was clear now, cupboards empty and wiped down, countertops cleared and food thrown out, refrigerator and oven cleaned out.

The house had an antiseptic smell and an echoing coldness that Duke couldn't bear. There was an absence of the life that Karl brought to it: the sound of his warmly accented voice, the smell of coffee always brewing, the German classical music he always had on the radio.

The house reminded him of seeing Joanne's body after

she'd passed in her hospital bed at home, her expression drained of her smile, any trace of her personality. An empty shell.

Rose had decided to rent, since the market was better for rentals right now, with houses in Silicon Valley beyond the reach of nearly anybody who hadn't been working in tech in the valley for at least five years. She told him she didn't want to rush into selling, now that the market was predicted to ease off. She'd wait a few months and see how things looked.

When it came to finances, Rose was a wise woman, as her mother, Agnieszka had been, and Karl had made Rose the executor of his trust.

Maybe Rose wasn't ready to face the fact that her father wasn't ever coming home. She could walk through his house, spend more time with her memories of her father.

Karl would have been much less interested in making money off of the property, Duke thought. He'd have wanted his house to go to someone who needed it. A single mother, a retired couple who'd run out of money. Maybe he'd have wanted to make it a group home for kids in trouble—which of course would have ticked the neighbors off to no end; Duke smiled to himself at the thought.

Rose came in and watched him as he stacked the boxes. She looked at the print on each one. "Bring the top two into the kitchen and I'll start going through them." She gave him a perfunctory nod as he handed her the keys. "Thank you, Duke. For all your help."

Duke turned pink at what was a lavish show of affection, coming from Rose.

"Your father would have done the same for me."

"I have another box that I've gone through that I need to

take to the Salvation Army truck off of Redmond. Would you mind dropping it off for me?"

"Might as well." Duke followed Rose into the living room. "I'm passing right by it."

"This box of books can go." Rose tapped a copy paper box filled with books. "Then I've got a smaller one back in the bedroom. Let me bring it out."

Duke looked down at the box. Curious, he headed for the living room bookcase. He spotted the cloth binding on the journal, the one Rose had been obsessed with the other night when he'd come to help. He pulled on the top of the journal and slid it out easily. He pressed the rest of the books together, so it didn't look as though something was missing. His heart pounding in his throat, he slid the book under a floppy softcover atlas in the giveaway box.

A few seconds later, he heard brisk footsteps coming down the hall. Rose brought out a smaller Amazon shipping box that held books and a few neckties.

He took the box from her and stacked it on the copy paper box. "Let me take these out to my car." He gave her what he hoped was a cordial, nothing-to-see-here smile. "Nothing else for today?"

"There may be more tomorrow, but we're done with the books. Clothes and memorabilia now. We might be able to donate some of it to one of the local air museums. It won't mean anything to anyone else."

They might mean something to me. Duke felt guilty hovering like a vulture over Karl's things, eager to paw through them, while leaving the impression that he was only here to help Rose out.

And now he had *stolen*—something instilled in him not to do since childhood. He saw his mother shaking her head, a look of disappointment behind her spectacles. Guilt came over him as he said goodbye to Rose and lugged the weighty boxes down to his car.

But now he had in his possession the book he'd had his eye on for the past three days.

A ripple of excitement ran through him, crowding out the guilt.

K

arl Schuler's Journal

I started this journal to record what I've seen. I have seen so much, the extremes of human nature: cruelty that put men in their graves and genius that put men out among the stars. And I have seen those two things combined.

Now I am tired.

Two identities live in my head. One real and one pretend. I sometimes confuse them because I am old. Which is the real story? I had to see the words in my own hand, before they blurred again in my mind. So I could face the truth.

I am a coward because I have chosen to write this confession, not say it out loud. I hope my children and friends will consider it fairly. As I near my end, I need to say what I've seen and done. Consider it a warning from someone who remembers. The world is shifting and settling into a pattern. It looks more and more like it did eighty years ago.

If you do not remember your history, it circles back to you, until—if it doesn't kill you—you finally learn your lesson.

Ruiz sat at a high table at Someplace Bar and Grill, trying to pace himself with his bottle of Modelo.

He was not doing quite as well with the almost empty basket of tortilla chips sitting in front of him.

Someplace was one of those 1960s-era bars named as a joke. If the wife asked where you were, you could say, "Oh, I was *Someplace*. Or *Nowhere*. I was at *The Library*." So, as if you were a character in a 1960s sitcom, you technically wouldn't be lying to your wife. Someplace was a tiny bar wedged into an old strip mall, between a vacuum cleaner repair store and a shop for extra wide shoes for women.

The Kelly family had run it for years, and cops, sheriffs and firemen had been stopping in here since before Ruiz was a rookie. Aged indoor/outdoor carpeting, fake wood paneling and patched up vinyl bar stools, but you didn't notice all that if the lights were kept low. The "grill" part of the name didn't really apply; the food consisted of chips and salsa, doughy soft pretzels and almost anything you could heat up in a microwave. It was a place to let down, to relax, a place where you knew you'd be accepted and could have drinks and a conversation in peace.

He'd wanted to get Flores up to date on what he'd heard about Karl from Duke. In return, he was hoping to hear how the young detective was doing with the search for the SUV. It wasn't his business. He was hoping to strike up a camaraderie with Flores and find out what he wanted to know. Have a few beers, share stories and commiserate. He had ten years on Flores and got the feeling the young detective had grown up in an upper middle-class home, one very different from his own. Ruiz hoped they'd find common ground.

About five minutes after six, Flores walked in, scanning the bar and tables. Ruiz watched as a couple of young women at the bar swiveled in their seats to look at him.

"Flores, here." Ruiz waved him over to the table. Flores's eyes brightened and he headed over to the table. Ruiz signaled the waitress, who met them at the table.

"I'll have what he's having." Flores nodded at the waitress, who laughed softly and turned pink as if she'd picked up some clever innuendo in his remark.

"Good choice." Ruiz took a swig and gave Flores a crooked smile. "Don't worry. It's definitely not light beer."

"How's it going at MVPD?"

"Just wrapped up a string of burglaries," Ruiz pushed the bowl of chips toward Flores. "A couple of guys from Redwood City who had been working their way down the peninsula—mostly computers and game consoles. Today someone saw them going through a neighbor's back window and phoned it in. We got there just as they were leaving. I think we had a two-block-long chase."

Flores laughed. He smiled as the waitress set the beer and mug down in front of him.

"So you're from LA." Ruiz launched in. Looking for something to connect with, he headed for sports. "Dodgers fan?"

"You kidding me? Born and raised in Orange County. I'm an Angels fan. I also root for the Ducks." He launched into an explanation why the hockey team's latest lineup was going to make it the best season yet.

Ruiz made sure he looked completely unimpressed and grunted. "You're in Sharks territory now, son. Where'd you go to school?"

"Community college in Anaheim." Flores picked a single chip from the bowl on the table with his thumb and forefinger like a twenty-something woman on a diet. "Transferred up to UC Davis and got my sociology degree."

"What's your dad do? And where did you get the Flores name?"

"You interrogating me, Ruiz?" Flores said it with attitude, pushing back a little. Ruiz laughed. He'd needed to break the ice and the grilling had done it.

"My dad owns a few home furnishing stores. The Flores comes from my dad's parents, who came over from Puerto Rico. Mom's a realtor. They'd like me to move back down south, and they don't like my career choice. I'm happy here."

"Yeah, me too." Ruiz shook his head and leaned on his elbows. "I grew up in San Jose. But it's hard to make a living here if you're not in tech."

Flores pulled out his phone and checked it for a minute, frowning. He mumbled *fuck*, then took a very big gulp of his beer. He moved his thumbs over the phone, texting, then set the phone down.

"Why'd you choose it? Police work." Ruiz was more curious as to why Flores had just sworn at the text message, but he'd finished grilling the guy and it was none of his business.

"When I was sixteen, some friends and I stole a car stereo." The corner of Flores's mouth turned up. "Caught before we left the parking lot. My community service was to join Police Explorers. Some great people spent time with me, something I wasn't getting at home. I wanted to do what they were doing. Maybe help other kids like me."

Flores had gotten off easy with his sentence. But this was an unexpected twist. Ruiz was liking the young detective better. He reminded him of what his little brother Mateo might have been if he'd taken a different path.

"Sounds like a good career move to me."

"I think so."

Flores leaned in over the table.

"We had a lead on the buyer of the SUV. But he gave a false address."

Flores told him about Jake Hollander selling his vehicle before Christmas, and his attempts to track down the man who'd bought it with cash.

"Gangs Investigations says they haven't heard of any activity on that side of town." Flores rubbed his eyes and stifled a yawn. "But I did find out that Schuler got a call at 1:20 a.m. from a payphone near the bus stop at Cherry and Almaden."

"No cameras?"

Flores grimaced and shook his head.

The owner's daughter came by with another round of chips and salsa, placing them, to Ruiz's annoyance, on Flores's side of the table. Flores grabbed a handful.

"On top of my shitty news day, my girlfriend ditched me tonight. This is my dinner."

Ruiz finished off his beer and considered ordering

another. Then he remembered he was on duty tonight for checking Jacky's homework. If it was math, he needed to be stone cold sober.

"I realize it's your case, not mine." Ruiz had to be careful with this. "But how were the interviews with the family?"

"Rose Mulvaney told me her father was very independent. He did a lot of volunteer work, which she thought he needed to cut back on. She couldn't think of anyone who'd want to hurt him. His neighbors said the same thing—he watched their dogs when they went on vacation. Delivered meals to the elderly. Mentored youth in science. By all accounts, a 100-percent good human being."

Ruiz settled back in his seat. The longer he stayed in the profession, the less he trusted the notion of a "100-percent good human being."

"You believe it?"

"In this case." Flores nodded firmly. "I do."

"I wanted to tell you. I ran into one of Karl's old buddies," Ruiz said, taking a small sip of beer and trying to pace himself. "Known him for years. It might be worth talking to Duke. He and a group of Karl's friends meet at a donut shop, not far from Schuler's house. Friday mornings." He took out one of his cards and copied Duke's name and number from his phone.

Flores looked at him, startled and slightly suspicious. "How did you meet him?"

"I went back to the expressway the day after the shooting. I wanted to see where it happened, in daylight. I wanted to see the tree—" Ruiz was surprised to hear emotion in his voice. "That's where I saw Duke, trying to figure out how it happened."

"You really think it would be helpful to talk to these guys?" Flores wasn't trying very hard to mask his skepticism.

Ruiz wondered if Flores saw him as an old guy, too. *Jesus, I don't turn forty till September.*

"He's known Schuler for decades. He and the donut group could be a good source for background on Karl. They've met with him every week for the past twenty-five years."

Ruiz doubted if Flores would contact Duke Sorenson. The young detective didn't need Ruiz's help. But Ruiz wanted badly to see someone behind bars for the murder of the old man. He wanted the young detective to feel that, too.

Flores looked down at Ruiz's card on the table, then picked it up and slid it into his wallet.

Then he gave Ruiz that look again, his big brown eyes shining and that amused smile. Ruiz was sure it worked for women and men alike. Everybody had their bag of tricks when it came to getting through life. But Ruiz didn't want to be condescended to. He would have felt better if Flores told him it wasn't his case and to fuck off and mind his own business. Ruiz would have understood and respected that.

"If I get a chance. Lot going on with this, and I've got quite a caseload. You know how it is, man." Ruiz nodded, and Flores took a last sip of his beer as he thumbed through messages on his phone. A worried look flashed across his face, and he spoke distractedly.

"Thanks for the beer, man. We should do this again."

Ruiz wondered if whatever was blowing up on Flores's phone had to do with the case. Maybe his expectations of getting information from Flores tonight had been unrealistic.

With a nod, Flores got up and headed for the door.

The waitress looked up from pouring a beer from the tap and watched him wistfully as he left.

19

"My office. *Now*."

The sergeant's voice was abrupt on the phone. He'd be passing the verbal beating he'd received down the food chain to him. Flores had read the news this morning. He had a good idea as to what this meeting would be about. That didn't make it any easier.

Flores took a seat in Sergeant Todd Buckley's office and waited while Buckley frowned and tapped on his keyboard.

"It's been four days since Karl Schuler's shooting." Buckley looked up, his face red and his lips under his mustache twitching slightly, further evidence to Flores that the sergeant had just been browbeaten.

"We've got the tech community complaining the case isn't getting the resources it deserves. They don't think we can handle it. They're not the only ones."

"Yeah. I read the editorial in the *Mercury News* today." Flores leaned forward in his seat, his fingers knotted as he looked idly around the room and waited for the full weight of shit to roll down to him.

When he'd joined the department, Flores had some idea

of what he was getting into. Ten years ago, officers had left *en masse*, due to cuts in pensions made to reduce the city's budget. The loss had continued, as officers retired or moved elsewhere, unable to keep up with the high cost of living in the valley. Even now, the department was understaffed. Response times were longer than anyone wanted them to be, and the public confidence in the department had eroded.

"The mayor has a personal interest in this. He gave Schuler an award last year for his work in the community—the mayor considered him a friend. He wants to see an arrest, Mario. An innocent old man, killed in a gang shooting in a safe neighborhood—and we can't solve this? We've worked hard to rebuild the public's trust."

"Gangs Investigations is working with us on this." A fine mist of sweat seeped out onto Flores's neck and arms. With the false address and the phone booth call to Schuler, this was looking bigger than a gang hit, and GI had said as much today. "We're using their contacts to get information on activity that might fit with Schuler's murder."

Buckley looked up at him and frowned. He shook his head and sat back in his chair, which creaked ominously in the long silence.

"Mario, you've moved up quickly here. But I'm not sure you have the experience or maturity for this kind of case."

Anger flared up in him. His case clearance rate was as high, if not higher than anyone's in the department. Flores sat up straight and tried to modulate his voice so it didn't sound disrespectful.

"What specifically in my performance makes you think that?"

Flores was starting to see where this was going. He'd be

taken off the case for political reasons. He'd be sacrificed to reassure the public that the problem was being handled.

"You've got till the 8th. If you haven't put this to bed by then, I'm handing the case over to Jesperson."

Fuck. Jesperson?

Lloyd Jesperson was a fifteen-year veteran who had hung on through the lean years on the force. He'd built up a crust of bitterness and disdain for anyone who hadn't endured that time—especially newcomers like Flores. He'd gone to Buckley twice complaining about Flores's methods.

If Buckley had wanted to piss Flores off, threatening to hand the case over to Jesperson was the best possible way to do it. Flores had worked hard to build his team over the past two years. They worked together well, had a string of successes and genuinely liked each other.

Flores had four days. Four days to find the killers. Four days to salvage his job.

As Flores reached his desk, he saw Jesperson head into Buckley's office, with the speed of someone who'd received the summons he'd been waiting for.

Flores slid quietly into his seat, ready to make phone calls.

And contemplate the fact that he was screwed.

20

The pale man with the aviator glasses—who Flores figured must be Duke Sorenson—nodded at him. "I'm glad you're here, Detective Flores."

Flores sat down in the bright pink chair at the yellow table and looked up to face four men in their seventies. At least.

After the meeting with Buckley, he was open to new angles. Desperation was very motivating that way.

He'd called Duke Sorenson last night, from the number Ruiz had given him. Flores debated calling, wondering if he'd get anything helpful from this group. He decided to find out more about Schuler, to eliminate the possibility that the shooting was related to something happening in the old man's life or family.

Last night at his kitchen table, Flores ate takeout pad thai by himself, instead of the dinner he'd hoped to eat with Oksana. She'd texted that she had a paper due and needed the time to write. Something about the short text bothered him. After today, he badly wanted to see her. The give and take of their times together worked best, Flores thought, when he was able to do as much of the taking as he wanted.

Flores had enjoyed his meetup with Ruiz. The Ruiz he'd seen the night of Schuler's murder was very different than the Ruiz at the bar. While he'd been agitated and angry on New Year's from what he'd just seen, last night he was cordial and relaxed—with a wicked sense of humor.

It both bothered and amused Flores that Ruiz had taken Karl Schuler's murder so personally. Ruiz knew how these things worked; he was a witness. Flores would handle the case his own way. But after Buckley's threat to take away the case, he'd pulled out the card Ruiz gave him and left a message at Duke's number.

From the serious look on his face and his stance at the end of the table, Flores judged that Duke Sorenson had become the de facto leader of the "gang" after Karl Schuler's death.

The man sat with his hands folded, leaning in, a styrofoam coffee cup in front of him. He waited for the other men to stop talking. This was not a social visit. Duke looked like he wanted to conduct a meeting and was prepared to do it.

It took a while for Flores's senses to settle into the place. The smell in the shop was overpowering—a cloying, over-the-top sugary smell that made him queasy. Add to that the bright, circus-color décor. In San Jose, so many businesses were recycled. This might have been an ice cream parlor in its former life.

He looked around to see a motley group of four men. Duke was paler than the rest, with his white hair and papery skin. The other three, an elderly Asian man, a stocky man with salt and pepper hair in an Oakland As cap, and an athletic-looking man with white hair that contrasted nicely with his tan. It looked like the man was younger than the rest—or maybe just well preserved. If there was a way to age well, the man was nailing it.

"Detective Flores, I'd like you to meet everybody," Duke began. "We've been meeting here, with Karl and a few others, for the past twenty-five or so years, give or take a few Fridays. We knew each other's families." He looked down at his hands. "I think I'm saying what we're all thinking. This is something we'd never imagined would happen to our friend." Heads nodded around the table. He gestured to the man to his right.

"This is Arnie Tan. He worked with Karl years ago. He's a research chemist." The man waved sheepishly, caught off guard with his mouth full of donut.

The man in the ball cap nodded, his brown eyes crinkling up. "I'm Aldo Moretti. I worked in aerospace— satellites— before retirement, but Karl also got me involved in the meals for seniors program. And we had an ongoing chess rivalry."

The tanned man looked up and nodded. "Marty Weber here. Karl was my next-door neighbor. We've been friends as long as Linda and I have lived there. Going on twenty years."

Flores took his first sip of coffee from the cup in front of him. It tasted like it had been sitting on a heating element all day. He pushed it out in front of him. He hoped his grimace wasn't too obvious.

"You've all heard the details of Karl's murder by now," Flores started in. "I want you to tell me about Karl Schuler as you knew him. When was the last time you saw him? How did he spend his time leading up to New Year's?"

Flores would interview them separately later, if he

needed to. He'd put feelers out in this meeting to see if these men might have information he could follow up on.

Silence around the table. Marty Weber spoke up.

"Karl was busy during the holidays. I went over to help him put up his lights about three weeks before Christmas. The strings of lights were so ancient, he must have brought them over from the old country. Surprised they worked at all. I helped him hang them along the front of the house. Karl was a healthy guy, but you get a little nervous when you see a ninety-two-year-old on a ladder. Then—he headed out to deliver meals. Before Christmas he'd invited the kids from the mentoring center over for a Christmas party. Some party. It ended at 8 p.m., judging by all the kids I saw leaving." Weber smiled, then his face seemed to crumple. He raised his cup of coffee to his lips as if to hide it.

East Point Youth Center was still closed for the break. Flores had an appointment to meet with Susan Moreland, director of East Point later today.

"He was close to those kids." Arnie Tan smiled faintly, leaning an arm on the table. "He'd do anything for them. Some of them were pretty tough, too. But he'd been doing it so long, he seemed comfortable with them all. They came back to see him later, too. He introduced me to a student he'd mentored years ago – he came over to visit Karl with his wife and kids."

Flores tried to shake the cynicism. Quite possible that Karl Schuler had decided, post retirement, to keep himself busy by volunteering, and he'd found it rewarding. From his interview with Rose, it seemed like a personal mission for Karl Schuler, a decision he'd made much earlier in his life, to do good. Still, there was a hipster devil sitting on Flores's shoulder, in a designer hoodie, fringe of hair dropping down over one eye. *But why did he work so hard at it?*

"Some of the kids have jobs in the valley now. Technicians, engineers." Duke spoke up, his round blue eyes looming behind his glasses. "One of them's at some big tech college back East, Karl told me. Full scholarship."

"Did Karl ever get threats? Either from students at the mentoring center—or anyone else?"

The men exchanged looks in some silent group communication, which Flores tried to read.

"Not from his students," Aldo Moretti started slowly, looking around the group. "They loved Karl. Seemed protective of him. There was a kid who caused some trouble at school. A couple years ago, I think. Brought a knife to school and attacked another kid in the group. It wasn't directed at Karl."

"Remember there was that kid involved in the shootout down on Monterey Road." Marty Weber looked up from his coffee. "From what Karl said, the kid had called him beforehand, pretty scared. The guy had a job, then he screwed up a drug test. He was fired and went home and got his gun. He showed up at his workplace with it. It ended in suicide by cop."

Arnie pressed his lips together and looked down at the table. Aldo shook his head.

Duke looked at Flores, his eyes blinking slowly, as if preparing to speak up. Flores examined his face and tried to imagine what he'd looked like as a young man, his face smooth, his eyes bright and energetic.

"There's something else I think I should let you know about, Detective Flores." Duke paused. There was something in Duke's eyes that looked like fear—or hatred. He couldn't tell which. "Karl has a grandson. Rose's son. Name's Randall. I've been helping Rose. She's trying to get Karl's house ready to sell soon. Yesterday I was doing yardwork in the front, and Randall came by. He yelled at Rose and demanded money from her. Said he'd been helping Karl and deserved to be paid for it. He sounded —threatening."

Flores wrote this down. He needed any lead he could get.

"Karl knew Randall had been in trouble with the law before. In high school. He wanted to spend time with the kid." Arnie Tan smiled sadly. "He said it was kids who didn't know where they belonged who got in trouble. He wanted to let Randall know he was part of the family. He took Randall with him to deliver meals to the elderly. They even built a house together with Habitat for Humanity."

"How did that work out?" Not great, Flores suspected.

Arnie shook his head. "It lasted a couple of months. Karl told Randall he didn't have to do it anymore. Karl said it was more trouble than it was worth."

Flores was curious about Randall's crime. If he'd been a juvenile, he couldn't access the records, but there were ways. He'd ask Rose. Or Randall himself.

"What's the guy's last name?"

"Mulvaney. Randall Mulvaney." There was a look of relief on Duke's face that he'd spoken up about his concerns. "Last I heard, he lived down by San Jose State. He was going to school there, but he dropped out."

Flores's phone buzzed and he checked it quickly. Mandy Dirkson. A lab report had come in.

"Was it a surprise to you that Karl was out driving on New Year's? Was that the kind of thing he'd do?"

More looks around the table. Then Duke spoke slowly and with a conviction in his voice that didn't match his frail appearance.

"Detective, there's only one reason I can think of that

Karl would be out at that time of night." Arnie glanced at Duke and nodded.

Duke's lower lip wobbled, but he looked like he was trying hard to control it as he spoke.

"He'd be out if somebody called and said they needed his help."

FLORES HEADED to the parking lot, relieved to be free from the shop's overpowering smell.

His job brought him in constant contact with death, but he didn't fear it. Not as much as he feared the slow dismantling of life that happened before it. The loss of control. The slowing down. The loss of hair and the loss of looks.

His father was approaching retirement age, ten years behind the donut gang. The last time he'd visited his parents, Anthony Flores looked off kilter, a record spinning too fast on a turntable. There was a new Mercedes in the garage, plans for a beach house—and he suspected, another woman in his life. Which his mother would ignore, never confronting him about it.

Four hundred miles was a good buffer zone between him and his father. Flores wanted to keep it that way.

21

Karl Schuler's Journal
After the students left my house this evening, I walked out the back door and stood on the deck. I breathed in the crisp air that reminded me of my hometown in the Harz mountains.

My town was scarred by the first world war, so many men lost. My father had served in the great war, his left leg amputated after an explosion in his trench. This was the obvious injury, but beyond that there was a dullness in his eyes, a hollow look as if part of him had been opened up and emptied out. My mother told me how he used to be before the war. How he'd played music on the accordion and drawn cartoons that made her laugh. He'd wanted to be a botanist. She loved the man he used to be and cared for the man he became.

When Hitler became chancellor, we had hopes that he would bring new life to our country. At last, someone who could make Germany great, build us up again as a people. We didn't know the horrors to come. If there had been warnings about this man, we closed our ears to them. We only knew we needed life, energy, something to live for. He promised it.

Our country started to rise again. We saw impressive buildings and great airships like the Graf Zeppelin cruising across the sky with that mark—the mark that is now so hated—we watched it proudly, as a symbol of ourselves and our new power.

The summer that Britain entered the war and the attacks started, I turned twelve. My mother made me a cake out of ingredients she'd taken from her bakery job and gave me a new school bag she'd saved for.

My father put in my hands an apple he had picked from the tree in our backyard. I remember feeling nothing but disappointment looking at it. An apple? I could have picked this myself.

I still see the color of it and feel the coolness of it in my hand. The last thing he gave me.

That day my mother was at the bakery. My father as usual stayed at home, lying down in the dark on a cot so his head didn't hurt, sometimes working on the small garden he kept in the backyard. Perfect rows, marching like soldiers, with carrots, turnips and beans strung up on poles. It was hard for him to kneel with his leg. My mother had given him a bench to sit down near the plants. He tended the garden carefully and the food helped us in the hard times in winter. His father had been a successful shopkeeper in town; his brother Hermann had gone to university in Berlin, received his doctorate and worked for the Reich in aeronautics research. My father grew vegetables.

I walked home as usual from school with my friends, talking and racing down the road. Peter Gruber and I were both very competitive and liked to show off, especially for any girls that might be watching. We were set to run a relay race on athletic day at school the next week. That's all we were thinking about— and we'd run the race a dozen times before we were set to actually compete.

I ran up the front steps, full of energy. As soon as I entered the house, it was as if I had run into an invisible brick wall. I felt a prickle on the back of my neck.

Something was different.

Everything was normal in the front hall and kitchen. Bread from the bakery sat out on the counter, ready for dinner. I called for my father. I heard no response.

I heard water dripping in the bathroom sink, so I pushed open the door. My father lay across the floor, a pool of blood around his head, his eyes open. There was blood on the edge of the tub, dark red running from his mouth.

The rest of the day moved in slow motion. It was as if everything from that day and afterwards moved in a slow progression toward my destiny.

I ran to our neighbor, Herr Muller, and told him. Frau Muller kept me in the kitchen, while he went to get my mother.

When she came, she called for me first. I couldn't move from the kitchen table. It would hurt too much to see her face. I felt bad for that afterwards, that I couldn't look at her. She had wanted to see me, to have the reassurance that her only child was okay.

Then I heard loud sobs from the bathroom.

My Uncle Hermann and Aunt Uli and my three cousins came for the funeral. The day after the service in the old church and the burial in the cemetery, my mother and I went back to the still, dark house. My dad had been a soft-spoken man, but the absence of his voice created a silence that was unbearable. Without his care, the garden became a mass of rotten vines and leaves.

For six months my mother drifted between work and home like a ghost. When influenza came through town, she was one of the first to catch it. I found her one morning in her bed, her eyes glazed, her skin hot to the touch. She died at the hospital that night.

Within a week, I was sent to live with Uncle Hermann in Peenemunde, the location of the Peenemunde Army Research

Center, the Heeresversuchsanstalt or HVP, where Hermann worked—the Reich's secret weapons development facility.

HIS EYES STINGING, Duke Sorenson shut the clothbound journal. He'd known Karl for decades, talked with him about any number of things. He was only now hearing the story of his childhood.

He took a deep breath.

That was enough for tonight.

22

Tiffany's car smelled like sweaty workout clothes. Since Reyna was shortest, as usual on these after-work get togethers, she got the back seat. As she slid over on the seat, she tried to avoid stepping on the empty Red Bull cans littering the floor mat.

"When's the last time you cleaned out your car, Tiff?"

"You could have offered to drive, Reyna." Tiffany snapped back from the seat in front of her.

Reyna hadn't offered to drive her Land Rover, because it didn't always start up. Jimmy had been trying to delay replacing the engine. They didn't have the money yet. That's all they needed, a group of women after a couple rounds of drinks, stuck in a parking garage after dark.

Rocio the receptionist slid in next to her. Alicia with her long legs took shotgun. Tiffany pulled out onto the expressway, heading for Santana Row, the upscale luxury mall and night spot in Santa Clara.

Reyna hadn't been out with the girls from work since before Thanksgiving. Energy buzzed through her. She was free tonight. Free from making sure Jacky got his homework done, free from trying to put together an inexpensive dinner Jimmy and Jacky would both eat, free from doing dishes and cleaning up. Jimmy would take care of dinner for him and Jacky. Even if that was something she didn't approve of. She didn't even want to know what fast food Jimmy would pick up. She had no one to think of but herself tonight.

When she got home, she'd pay for the evening out by having to go over the kitchen one more time and picking up whatever Jacky left out in the living room. Socks, books, felt pens and construction paper scraps from school projects. Things left out didn't bother Jimmy; he seemed incapable of seeing them.

Tiffany barreled down Stevens Creek, a woman on a mission. A Hyundai sedan full of young guys looked over at them and waved. Tiff, Alicia and even Rocio laughed.

The car kept pace with them and at the stop light at Stevens Creek, the guy in the front passenger seat rolled down his window and waved to them.

The women in the car, except the quiet, older Rocio, exchanged glances and started laughing. As soon as the light changed, Tiff floored it, leaving the car of guys behind. Reyna felt her stomach muscles go soft, trying to keep from laughing.

They pulled into the parking garage at Santana Row and because it was a weeknight, found a decent spot on the second floor. The night felt sharp and cold. There was energy in the air. Santana Row made Reyna feel rich.

You could walk the streets past shops full of things you'd never be able to afford, sit down in a Tesla and dream of owning one, as you listened to the music of street performers and bands playing. The smells of pasta, gourmet tacos, and French food seeped out of the restaurants. You could walk the streets for free. Reyna had talked Jimmy into bringing her here once. He didn't like it. But she felt wonderful walking under the lights, seeing all the beautiful things. It felt like Hawaii had—beautiful and unreal.

"Mexican or French?" Alicia threw the choice out to them as they walked down the main boulevard.

It felt extravagant to have a choice, but Reyna would have to watch what she spent.

"French," Reyna called out. Champagne, even if she could only get one glass. She still had memories of New Year's replaying in her head, and she needed a break from sadness. She had heard someone say once that it was impossible to drink a glass of champagne and feel unhappy.

"Aren't you fancy," Tiff shot back at her.

They walked into the restaurant and were seated at a table in the bar. Reyna ordered her glass of champagne and looked around the room. It smelled like warm bread and onion soup, both of which she wanted to order. She had a new Visa card in her purse, to be used for emergencies.

Tiff took off her jacket and draped it over the back of the chair. "Night classes start next week, so I'll miss our nights out for the rest of the semester." Her face looked mysterious in the dim light of the restaurant. "Let's make this one count, ladies."

"Jimmy's watching your son?" Rocio smiled politely across the table at Reyna. She was a tiny woman with hair cut short, circles under big, round sad eyes. They had never asked her age; Tiff said she was in her fifties, Alicia guessed thirty-five.

Alicia groaned. "He's not 'watching' the kid if he's the dad. It's called parenting. Let's not act like he's doing something above and beyond here."

"Jimmy makes sure Jacky gets his homework done and

gets to bed." Reyna spoke up. "He won't do dishes or clean, but he's great with Jacky."

When the ladies went out, it often became a slam fest, everyone competing to put down their husbands and boyfriends. Jimmy had his issues, but being a father was not one of them.

The waitress brought their drinks. Rocio's diet coke, Alicia and Tiff's rum and Cokes and then Reyna's champagne, in a crystal glass that flared at the top like a trumpet. Tiny bubbles raced up from the bottom of the glass in lines.

"That's fucking beautiful." Alicia stared over at the champagne, mesmerized. The overhead light shining on it made it look golden. She looked about ready to cry. "Jesus."

Reyna raised the glass and everyone lifted theirs.

"To girls' night out!" They clinked their glasses over the tabletop.

After they'd ordered their food, Tiff began talking about her recent move to an apartment in Gilroy, after her divorce.

"I'm paying $400 less a month. But I'm driving over an hour into the office in the mornings. If I drop Aiden off at early childcare at 6:30, it's not so bad. Maybe fifty minutes. If he gets sick, I'm screwed. I don't have my sister down there to take him. Tag, I'm it. Out a day of work."

"Is it worth it?" They all knew Alicia's husband was a software engineer, and they owned a house in Mountain View. She turned to Tiffany, and said, "Maybe it makes sense to tough it out in the valley. Find a cheaper place."

Tiff took a gulp of rum and coke and glared at Alicia. "Nothing is cheap here. If I had a husband who made money like yours—"

"Can you get more child support from Jeff?" Reyna asked. "It's not like he had to move or anything. Why should you have to move with Aiden, when he's still living up here with his girlfriend?" *He's the one who couldn't keep it in his pants*, she wanted to add, but she wasn't sure she had a right to say it.

Tiff waved her hand dismissively. "We came out here to have a good time, not talk about our problems. Let's have some fun."

The champagne was starting to have an effect on Reyna. She felt like she was floating, suspended a few inches above her seat. The lights outside and the lights inside made everything around her seem to glow.

Tiff leaned in over the table, whispering. "Look at the bar. The guy near the end."

As Alicia turned around in her seat to see, Tiff nudged her with the menu. "Don't all look at once."

Rocio, who had been quietly sipping her diet Coke, even turned to get a look.

"You're all being so obvious." Tiff hissed through her teeth.

"Oh my God. Oh, my God!" Alicia turned back to them, her eyes wide. "I haven't seen a guy like that around here in —forever. He has that SoCal look."

Reyna looked up from her onion soup and saw the man, listening to a woman at the bar. He wore a thin black sweater and she could see the muscles in his arm as he leaned against the edge of the bar. There was something familiar about him.

"What do you think he does for a living?" Tiff asked nobody in particular.

"A guy like that's not in tech, that's for sure," Alicia raised her eyebrows and they all laughed. "It looks like he's with somebody." A blonde woman with exotic features sat on the chair next to him, looking like she wanted to be somewhere else. From the frown on the man's face, he wasn't enjoying the discussion.

They watched him for a while, until their food arrived and they began eating. Reyna finished her soup and bread and took delicate sips of the last half of her champagne. She'd make it last as long as it could.

"Hold on." Tiff looked over their heads to the bar. She kept her voice low, like a commentator on a golf show. "The blonde has left the bar. I repeat. *The blonde has left the bar.*" They all turned to watch the blonde woman, purse slung over her shoulder, make her way hurriedly to the front of the restaurant and out the door.

All four women looked back to the bar. Rocio wiped her lips with her napkin and sat back calmly, waiting to see what would happen next.

Then suddenly, to their horror, the man raised his head from his drink and looked down the bar directly at their table.

Tiff made a gargling sound. Alicia sucked in her breath. Rocio turned around to face the table, seeming to bow her head in prayer.

Reyna looked right back to face the man.

"I know him." She smoothed her hair back. "That's Officer Flores. We met him the night of the shooting. He's investigating the old man's murder."

The man looked back at their table with a crooked smile, then ducked his head down as if he were shy. Reyna smiled back. When she looked at him again, he was talking to the bartender, and she was relieved. He'd moved on.

Alicia began telling a story about scrambling around the office to look for a missing scraper while a patient lay, mouth wide open, in the chair trying to continue a conversation with her. Alicia had told the story before, but it was funny, and they all laughed. Reyna looked over at the bar, and there he was again, looking directly at her. When their eyes met, he had a guilty look on his face, as if he hadn't wanted to be caught looking her way. Then he smiled. He was good looking—something she hadn't noticed that night.

She liked the attention. She enjoyed looking at him. But she was out with the girls, and they all knew Jimmy.

Five minutes later, a waiter came to their table with a glass of champagne on a tray.

He set the flute down in front of her and took her empty glass.

"Compliments from the gentleman at the end of the bar."

Reyna's cheeks felt warm, and a feeling like electricity raced through her body. Everyone at her table was looking back and forth between her and Flores, and nobody was being subtle about it.

"Reyna! *Oh, my God.*" Alicia started giggling so hard, she had to put a hand over her mouth to stop herself. Tiff laughed and whispered something to Rocio, who smiled. All three looked at Reyna to see what she'd do.

Reyna nodded to Flores, raised her glass slightly and smiled her thanks, making sure to keep her response restrained.

"I'm going to find the restroom." Reyna set her napkin down on the table, grabbed her purse and got up. She expected at least one of the ladies to follow her, as usually happened on these nights out, but Tiff had launched into a story about a guy she'd met at the grocery store, and everyone was leaning forward, listening.

She headed down the aisle to the back of the restaurant, where she saw the script on the doors *Les*

Hommes and *Les Femmes*. Ben Marsden had described a business trip to Paris after one of his cleanings. Someday she would visit. Musicians in the streets, beautiful buildings, and everyone dressed so well. After that, when she'd picked up school supplies at the dollar store, she'd found a coin purse with an Eiffel Tower on it. She bought it and kept it in her purse, a reminder. She would go someday.

When she wanted something, she knew how to make it happen.

She scrimped, shopped frugally. One of the dental patients told her where she could invest some money. After five years, they had been able to afford a house of their own. Jimmy made a decent income as a cop. He didn't know how to plan, to save and invest. She, not Jimmy, had put them in a position to buy the house.

She pushed the *Les Femmes* door, opened a stall, pulled the lid down and sat. She needed space to herself. To quiet the noise in her head. She felt at the edge of something, a change coming. She wasn't sure what it was, but at this point, she wanted it. Almost no matter what it was.

She heard a cough and footsteps. Someone else had come into the restroom. Reyna stood up, flushed the toilet and went to the sink. After the woman went into her stall, Reyna looked up at herself in the mirror. Brown eyes, oval face, the thick, black wavy hair that Jimmy loved and asked her not to dye or highlight like her friends did. On that, he had been right. She'd stopped doing that after she moved out of the house in San Jose.

She washed her hands and looked down at the long fingernails with French tips that she guarded so carefully. Refined and understated, not the hot pink polish that she'd worn when Jimmy had first met her. She had learned a lot in ten years. She had always wanted more, but back then she hadn't known what more was.

She went back into the restaurant, as French accordion music played in the background. As she opened the door, he was still at the bar, a drink in one hand, his phone in the other. He had a ragged look about him, and from this angle, his hair looked a little greasy.

Maybe it had been the champagne. She still felt that light feeling, as if she were gliding down a smooth, silver track. It led her to the bar.

"Officer Flores. I thought it was you."

He looked up abruptly, his eyes wide. "Mrs. Ruiz." He broke into the easy, lopsided smile men got when they've had a few drinks.

"That sounds so formal." She laughed. "My name is Reyna. You probably forgot."

"Oh, I did not forget." He put down his phone. Up close, he looked paler than she remembered him. "I was trying to be respectful. Looks like you're out with the ladies tonight. Can I buy you another glass of champagne?"

She looked back at her table. The women were whispering, their heads leaning together, as they watched her and Flores. Alicia said something and they all cracked up.

Reyna had to be careful. Too much champagne and she couldn't trust her judgment. She was on a tightrope right now.

"I'm fine with what I have, Detective Flores."

"You can call me Mario. I'm not on duty." His eyes were fastened on her, trying to take her in. Normally when men did this, it made her nervous. His look made her feel warm, at ease.

"How's the case going, Mario?" She tried out his name

and liked the way it felt to say it. "You've found the guy in the SUV? Jimmy and I have been upset about this since New Year's."

"We thought we'd found him." He took a sip of what looked like bourbon. "Turns out we didn't."

He motioned to the bar chair next to him and smiled, though it looked more sad than happy this time. "Please, have a seat." She stepped up to the seat and brushed her hair back from her face. He rubbed the back of his neck and finally looked away. "I came here to meet my girlfriend. She picked the place." He frowned and a dimple appeared in his cheek. "She broke up with me."

His brown eyes looked red and tired, but he was still good looking. He was the actor a movie studio would hire to play Jimmy in the story of his life—a white version of Latino —someone who looked nothing like him. Fit, handsome, a nice profile. Strong, long fingers. Powerful shoulders.

Next to his drink lay two shredded cocktail napkins and a drink stirrer he'd bent into a triangle.

The champagne, and the good-looking man next to her, made her head light.

"Mario, she made a bad decision." Reyna laid her hand next to his, which she'd meant as a comforting gesture. She'd always been a hugger and a toucher.

He looked down at her hand as if trying to figure out what to do with it. He clapped his other hand over hers for a moment. The warmth of his hand sped up her arm and into her bloodstream. He pulled it back quickly.

He searched her face, then took another napkin and began shredding the edges again as he talked.

"It was someone in her grad program at Santa Clara. A guy named Tim." From her perspective next to him, she looked down at his bowed head. He was one of those men who actually had eyelashes. "She said she made her decision days ago."

The bartender set down a glass of water, which she needed to dilute the alcohol in her system.

"You can do better." She didn't know where that came from, but it flowed out of her like warm honey. She wondered if he had never been dumped before. He looked like he was feeling sorry for himself.

He looked down into his glass, then turned to her, the corner of his mouth turning up. "That's kind of you, Reyna."

The water was clearing the champagne haze from her head. In the corner of her eye, she saw the women at her table. Heads bent together, watching her. But the laughing had stopped.

"I need to get back."

"Of course." He licked his lips and looked down at his drink. He had that look about him, his confidence worn through in spots, so that she could see the holes. Very different than he'd been on New Year's, directing the crime scene on the expressway.

"Thank you for the drink, Mario."

He watched her as she got up to return to her seat. "My pleasure. You know, maybe—" he began, then looked down and shook his head. "I shouldn't drink any more. Enjoy the rest of your night out, Mrs. Ruiz. Say hi to Jimmy for me."

Reyna walked back to the table and sat back down calmly in her seat.

She caught the eyes of Alicia and Tiffany.

They were mouthing *holy shit.*

23

R ose Mulvaney brought out a tray with cups of coffee and a small plate of butter cookies. The cookies looked homemade. Ruiz's eyes lit up. He grabbed his cup and a cookie.

Rose was petite, her hair cropped even shorter than Grasso's. She looked like someone who walked five miles a day. Compact and wiry. Her voice was precise and efficient, as if she tossed out the excess words and only used the ones she needed.

"My wife and I told Detective Flores what we saw that night. I'm doing what I can to help with the case. I am sorry for your loss, Mrs. Mulvaney. I had the opportunity to meet Duke Sorenson, your father's friend, when I came back to look at the scene the next day."

Rose nodded, almost begrudgingly. "Duke's been helping me with my father's house."

Rose's living room was decorated with antiques and a large, ancient-looking cuckoo clock over the fireplace, with a little bird that had popped out and whistled on the hour.

Framed black and white photos were grouped on the surrounding walls. He went over to look at them.

"Is this your father here?" Ruiz asked. He paused at a series of photos and framed awards grouped together. It looked like Rose had made a shrine to her father.

There was a black-and-white photo of a young man with that upward glance and backlighting he'd seen in old photographs. He looked like he was gazing up at his bright future.

Ruiz saw the resemblance between the photo and the old man he'd seen breathe his last breath on New Year's. It was the eyes. They'd been open then and seemed unusually light to him.

Rose stood up. "That's him. Right after he came to the U.S."

Ruiz looked at other photos. A middle-aged Karl Schuler, with a group of astronauts, then another of him giving a speech on a stage, in front of a large crowd. In another photo, a white-haired Karl waved as he sat on the wing of a jet on a runway. It reminded him of the goofy presentation Karl had given to the students at the Smithsonian.

No wonder he spent so much time with kids. Karl Schuler seemed like kind of a kid himself.

At the other end of the wall, Ruiz noticed a young woman with sharp features and dark, haunted eyes. Her hair was pulled up in rolls on the side of her head, the way he'd seen women wear it in old movies. She wore a simple white blouse.

"Is this your mother?"

"Yes, before she married my father."

Getting Rose to give any more details would require some work.

"Did they meet in the U.S.? Or back in Germany?"

After her terse replies, a slight smile emerged on Rose's face. It surprised him, since it seemed out of character for what he'd seen of her so far.

"Both."

"Sorry. Can you tell me what you mean by that?"

Rose looked at the photo. "They met at a military facility in Germany. They became close. There was a bombing at the facility. After that my father moved with his uncle to a town in the mountains. My mother ended up in a camp. Her life was very different after that."

"She was German?"

"Polish." Looking back at the photo, Ruiz could see facial similarities between Rose and the woman in the photo.

"My father didn't think he'd see her again. After he came to the United States, he worked here in the valley. When he was in San Francisco to pick up his passport, he ran into her. She was on lunch break from her job as a secretary at a bank. My father thought he had seen a ghost. He'd never expected to see her again. They were married in two months."

"Such a nice story." Ruiz realized after he said it that it sounded as if he didn't quite believe it.

"They stayed married for fifty-seven years."

He and Reyna had been married for ten years. He loved her, but marriage was a lot of work. Fifty-seven years seemed unimaginable.

"I read there was an uncle—someone who brought your father over to the U.S. with him."

"Hermann. He's over here."

She walked over to photos on the other side of the room. They passed a newer photo, in color, of a young, blond soldier holding a rifle. She gestured to another photo, a balding man with spectacles and the face of a mild mannered, absent-minded professor.

Uncle Herman looked like a friendly old guy.

"Your father came over with your Uncle Herman?"

Rose nodded. A cold look passed over her face.

Rose didn't look like she wanted to say anything else about Uncle Herman.

Ruiz coughed and took a sip of his coffee. "Do you think someone from your father's past could have come back to threaten him? Did he ever mention someone contacting him?"

Rose shook her head and glanced back at the backlit picture of her father.

"I can't imagine that." She snapped. She zeroed in on some crumbs he'd dropped on the coffee table and carefully picked them up with a napkin. "He never mentioned anything. He seemed happy. And very much living in the present."

Ruiz wondered if a Mr. Mulvaney would have a different perspective on Karl Schuler.

"Are you married, Mrs. Mulvaney?"

"My husband and I divorced twenty years ago." Her clipped voice shut down the topic.

"You say your father lived a very routine life. Why would he be out so late driving?"

A look of pain crossed Rose's face. "I don't know."

"Your father mentored at-risk youth, didn't he? Maybe a kid he knew got stuck somewhere on New Year's and called him for help."

Rose swallowed hard. "He did a lot for those kids."

"Sure." He dipped a butter cookie into his coffee. "East Point Youth Center's a great place. What exactly did your father do there?"

"He came and talked to them about science. He helped with homework and took the students on field trips sometimes. Some of the kids ended up being the first in their families to go to college. But there were only a few real success stories. Out of all of the time he spent there, in that dangerous part of town."

It must seem that way to Rose Schuler Mulvaney, living on the southwest side of the city, in upscale Almaden Valley. Many people lived, worked and raised their families on the east side.

"That's where I grew up, Mrs. Mulvaney."

Rose looked at him suddenly, as if reexamining the man standing in her living room, eating her cookies and drinking her coffee.

What kind of person had Karl Schuler really been? Could there be something more sinister hiding beneath the surface? Pedophilia? Or just an obsession with helping. Maybe he had some kind of a white savior complex.

"Any idea why your father was interested in this kind of work?" he asked, throwing it out there to see what happened.

"He couldn't resist people who needed help. Anyone on the fringes. The poor. Troubled students, single mothers." Rose pursed her lips disapprovingly. She walked over to the bookshelf and glanced at the books. She ran her hand over the books on the top shelf, then bent down and ran a finger across their spines as if she were looking for something.

"His father was wounded badly in the first world war," Rose continued, turning to face him. "Friedrich would have had a future in the sciences. His specialty was botany. As smart as Hermann, but he came back with shellshock and an amputated leg. He couldn't go back to university, couldn't work. He had delusions, nightmares. I know it was hard for my father. But he hadn't known anything different. One day when my father was twelve—he found him dead."

Karl Schuler would have had to lock it all away and grow up fast. Suck it up. It had to have affected him. Karl wouldn't have seen a therapist, something that had personally helped Ruiz. People didn't do that back then.

"Did you meet any of the kids he worked with?" Ruiz asked.

Rose shook her head. "That was his business. I tried to get him to give it up. He was too old to be working with those kids. I worried about him."

"East Point would know who your father worked with. Any kids who might have some bad connections."

"If they were a responsible organization they would," Rose eyes darted around the room, as if she were getting impatient with the conversation. She picked up Ruiz's empty coffee cup and put it on the tray. "You'll have to talk to them."

As Rose headed for the cookies on the end table, Ruiz beat her to the tray and took a last butter cookie.

"Part of the reason I'm here is, I wanted to ask you, Mrs. Mulvaney." Ruiz cleared his throat. He had seen this woman's father die. What Schuler had said might mean something to her. "When I got to the car, I heard your father say something before he died. I want to know if it means anything to you."

Rose's eyes got big. Her lips pressed tightly together. He tried to identify the expression on her face. Anticipation, maybe. Fear?

"What did he say?"

Ruiz let the sound from that night play in his head again, as if it were a recording on his phone.

"It was barely a whisper, but it sounded like he said, 'saloon.' Does that mean anything to you?"

Rose let out a grunt. "I can't imagine what that could mean." She continued with the tidying, moving into the kitchen to seal the leftover cookies in a ziplock bag, as if what he'd said had had no effect on her. But the crease deepened on her forehead. The word was rolling through her head as she tried to put meaning to it.

He ate the last bit of cookie.

"Thank you for your time, Mrs. Mulvaney. If you can think of anything about your father that might help the investigation, please give Detective Flores a call."

Rose paused, tray in hand. Her tone softened just a bit, probably as conciliatory as she got. "I'm glad you stopped by, Officer Ruiz."

"I'm sorry for your father's death" Ruiz said, honestly. "I wish I'd known him."

She walked him to the front door, her heels making birdlike clicks on the tile entry way. Then she turned and looked up at him.

"The memorial service is next Friday, at Good Savior Lutheran. 3 p.m. I'm grateful for what you did for my father, and I would like to have you there."

24

W hen Flores's phone rang at 8 a.m., the buzz seemed to originate inside his head, rattling his skull with brute force on its way out. His mouth felt dry and pasty, as if someone had spackled his mouth shut with dental plaque. As he rolled over to his nightstand, he swore he heard his almost thirty-year-old body creak. He fumbled for the phone, which dropped to the floor. He slid his hand under the edge of the bed and felt around till he found it.

"Flores here." The words shot out of his mouth. For all the person on the other end knew, he was awake and perfectly alert.

"Mario, It's Mandy. They've found the SUV. In Gilroy. Near a vineyard off Monterey Road."

Flores sat up in the bed. And immediately regretted it as his head pounded with pain. "Fuck."

Mandy snorted on the other end of the line. "That's a good *fuck* then? Meet you down there in forty minutes. I should tell you—the SUV is burned. Sheriff's deputy says you can smell the accelerant."

"Yeah. Okay. We'll see what we get." He rubbed his eyes and blearily scanned his room for the nearest clothes.

"You know how late you are, right?" Mandy sounded amused. "Buckley's been looking for you."

In ten minutes, Flores had showered, dressed and downed the rest of a leftover burrito and three ibuprofen.

On his way down Highway 85, he thought about last night.

He retraced his steps. The steps of a drunk who'd lost brain cells last night.

He'd met Oksana at the French place, her choice. All seemed fine at first, though she seemed quieter than usual. Fifteen minutes later, while they waited for a table at the bar —she'd broken up with him. He had to ask her to repeat it, since he wasn't sure what was happening.

There's this other student in the program—Tim. There's just something there with us—We have so much in common. Mario, I knew when we were together on New Year's that it would be the last time. I didn't know how to tell you.

His mind replayed the past week. She'd waited for him, on New Year's, hadn't she? They'd made love. They'd been dating exclusively for six months. Things were getting serious. He'd assumed that when she graduated, they'd move in together. Maybe consider marriage down the road. What had changed in a few weeks?

After she left, he'd stayed for a drink at the bar. Okay, three. And then he'd noticed a woman in his peripheral vision. He knew her. Her name escaped him. He watched her with her friends, laughing and talking with her hands. She had an open, sexual way about her that drew his attention. A shiny object he couldn't stop looking at. The way she moved so freely.

She was very different from him. Not college educated.

Grown up on the wrong side of town even. Mired in self-pity after Oksana left, he'd prayed a drunk's prayer that she would come his way. And she did.

Then he realized how he knew her. He'd interviewed her on New Year's. She was James Ruiz's wife. He thought he remembered she worked as a dental hygienist. She was beautiful. But she was no one he'd ever go out with. Or ever cross paths with. So what did he do? He'd bought her a drink and entertained thoughts about what he wanted to do with her. He'd just met up with Ruiz, someone who reminded him of his mentors in Explorers.

The way he remembered it, she had come on to him. An old girlfriend had told him once that all men think women are coming on to them. But in this case, she had. Hadn't she?

The way she'd looked at him. The way she laid her hand down next to his.

Today he needed to focus on the Schuler case. Ruiz had been right. The donut shop meeting had been helpful. He'd talk to Randall Mulvaney and go back for another interview with Rose Mulvaney. Call Karl's son, Christoph Schuler in Florida. He couldn't look past Duke Sorenson's suspicion that Karl Schuler had gone out that night for one reason: somebody told him they needed his help. Someone had called Karl from the public phone at the bus stop —but who?

Facts in this case seemed hard to grasp, clear one moment, faded to nothing the next. But he knew one thing.

The person who'd called Karl Schuler was almost certainly his killer.

25

F lores wound through the bright green hills on Watsonville Road, which ran through farmlands and small vineyards, from the southern suburbs of Gilroy and Morgan Hill down to Highway 152.

It would have taken the killers about forty minutes to get here from the expressway in San Jose.

Not too long after passing a farmhouse with a white picket fence, Flores saw a sheriff's vehicle and two SJPD vehicles pulled off onto the shoulder near a grassy field. He swung the Prius onto the shoulder. He rubbed his face, then got out of his car—willing himself to think clearly. His head throbbed as he stood up on shaky legs. Somewhere, a chicken began squawking, making him want to hold his head and dive back into his car for cover.

In the distance, in the high grass, he found the group's location by the beacon of Mandy's red hair in the sun. He followed the tire ruts of pressed down grass into the field.

The SUV sat, intact near a clump of bushes, a blackened wreck. The plates were still on, but the front two seats, hood, and most of the exterior were charred. He smelled the gasoline as he approached. The passenger and driver side doors were open, and two gloved crime scene analysts were gingerly poking around the dashboard and upholstery.

"Anything that was in the front seat is gone." Mandy took one look at him and pulled a bottle of water from her bag and handed it to him. He accepted it silently, mouthing *thanks*.

He flipped the top and began gulping. She shook her head as they watched

"Whoever set this did a thorough job."

Flores squinted in the sun, as his head started pounding. "Any neighbors who might have seen this at 2:30 in the morning?"

The sheriff's deputy standing on the other side of the SUV spoke up. "Nearest neighbor is by the picket fence, a half a mile up the road. They didn't hear any vehicles, but then they said they went to bed at midnight on New Year's. They didn't see the fire either. This is far enough off the road, so we didn't know about it till this morning. A cycling team riding through the area stopped on the shoulder and happened to spot it."

Flores walked around the SUV, examining the wreck. Could have been due to the damp weather and limited spread of the accelerant, but nothing much was burned but the SUV itself.

"Find anything?" He called to the crime scene pair going through the vehicle.

"It's pretty clean." A woman pulled her face-shielded head out of the SUV. "So far, a receipt, most of it black from the heat. And part of what looks like a boarding pass. We're still checking for any unburnt surface that might hold a print. I wouldn't count on it."

Flores walked around the SUV and followed the tracks

through the brush back to the street. Mandy followed him, shielding her eyes from the sun with her hand. Flores wished he'd remembered to stash his sunglasses in the Prius.

"Whoever drove the SUV here had to have some way to leave," he said, turning around to face Mandy. "Where would that vehicle be stashed, to avoid being spotted?"

They waded through the high grass, following the turn of the road to their right. They had walked about two hundred yards, when Mandy called out.

"There's a dirt road back here. Overgrown, but still a road."

A narrow, muddy path cut through the grass, winding back till it ended at a shabby grey fence. They walked down the path, stepping carefully to avoid clumps of weeds.

Flores crouched down to look at the mud. "It's rained in the past week. But you can still see the traces of it."

As they neared the fence, they saw tracks that looked like a vehicle had driven in, turned and driven out.

"We can still get molds of these," Mandy called, with a sudden burst of optimism, as she made a wide circle around the tracks.

Flores looked down the road back to the street, wishing he could summon her enthusiasm.

"Whatever we can do at this point. We've got three days."

26

R andall Mulvaney opened the door with the sullen face of a kid on a time out. He was a lanky man, maybe twenty-eight years old. He had pale blue eyes, a fussy, neatly trimmed long beard and a mustache that looked like it belonged on a pugilist from the 1890s. He would have fit nicely in one of those old-fashioned, all-body striped bathing suits.

"What do you want, officer?" He stood in the doorway of his apartment in downtown San Jose, leaning against the doorframe as if he hoped that would get the door-to-door salesman to leave.

"Karl Schuler is your grandfather, Mr. Mulvaney. I'm investigating his murder."

"He is. Why do you ask?" Randall challenged, his eyes widening. This was the kind of guy who would fight over technicalities in the answers in a bar trivia contest.

That attitude that would not do him any favors with law enforcement.

"Based on the evidence at the scene and witness accounts, somebody targeted your grandfather," Flores said calmly, settling back into his ready stance, legs apart, leaning toward the door slightly. "I need to ask you a few questions, Mr. Mulvaney."

Randall Mulvaney opened the door and stood back, his hand held out in an overly dramatic manner, gesturing him inside. The room was lit by low light from a purple-shaded lamp. The walls were decorated with fabric wall hangings. Once inside, he realized the room was steeped in the smell of pot, probably not from a recent smoke but ongoing use. Flores could look forward to being teased by his team when he got back to the station. He wouldn't be able to avoid picking up the smell.

Flores took a seat on a velvet overstuffed chair, facing Mulvaney, who sat down on his couch and continued with the sullen looks. Flores looked around at the room, admiring the brightly colored pieces of fabric art.

"Nice wall hangings."

"Shayante makes them," Mulvaney said, as if he should know this person. Of course. *Everyone* knows Shayante.

"Are you a student, Mr. Mulvaney?" Flores tried to establish a rapport. He didn't think it would work, but he'd try.

"I left San Jose State last year. I'm taking a break. I work part time at a thrift shop. Part time at a convalescent home."

"Did you spend much time with your grandfather?"

"Yeah, I lived with him for a few months. I took care of him after he had a hernia operation. I did some work around his house. I trimmed the trees in the backyard, helped him harvest the fruit. My mom and grandma wanted me to spend time with him."

"Did you get along with your grandfather?"

"I was told I should spend time with him. I did what I was told."

What an exemplary grandson. The love and compassion are overwhelming. Flores couldn't tell if he was feeling sick because of Mulvaney's entitlement, the pot smell or his own hangover.

"Randall, where were you on New Year's Eve? Did you go out that night?"

Mulvaney huffed with indignance. "You think *I* killed him?"

"Were you at home or did you go out? Please answer the question, Mr. Mulvaney."

"Shayante and I were at the gallery. There was a party. We were there till about 1, maybe 1:30 a.m."

"People can verify you were there at that time?"

Mulvaney rolled his eyes. "Of course. Ask anyone at the gallery. Fortuna Gallery on First, downtown. Jen Corey is the manager. Call her. She'll tell you."

Flores took a note down on his tablet.

"Did you have any issues or disagreements with your grandfather, Mr. Mulvaney?"

"Did I disagree with his judgmental attitudes? Yes. Did I feel like he loved me just as I am? *No.*" Mulvaney looked as prim and self-righteous as a Puritan, his voice clipped, his posture rigid. "When I was a teenager he was always pushing me to do things. Come volunteer with him. Help him take some kids to the park. It wasn't about whether I wanted to do it or not."

Flores figured Randall was a year or two younger than he was. He tried a "you and me both" strategy.

"When I was a teenager, my mom tried some of the same things. To get me off the video game console."

"Well, it wasn't my thing. He didn't care what I wanted."

Flores remembered what Duke Sorenson had told him about Randall being arrested in high school. Flores's own juvenile run-in with the law had changed his life. He of all people knew that you don't have to stay the person you were in high school. He doubted this was true of Randall Mulvaney.

"When you were in high school, you were arrested. Can you tell me about that, Mr. Mulvaney?"

Randall Mulvaney's prim face came unraveled. He looked panicked. "My records as a juvenile were sealed. Nobody has any business telling you."

"Mr. Mulvaney, why don't you tell me what happened? It's likely to be mentioned by anyone who knew you growing up. Save some time and tell me what happened yourself."

Mulvaney glowered and his leg began to shake. After a long pause, he looked up.

"Fine. I was arrested for stealing a car." Mulvaney crossed his legs and looked down at his lap. "A teacher's at school. I hit another car when I was pulling out of the parking lot. There were some minor injuries."

"Any reason why you did it?"

"I was angry at the teacher. She treated me like shit. Yeah, I was wrong to do it. I was just so mad."

A kid who couldn't control his impulses. Did he know now—eight or nine years later?

"Mr. Mulvaney, can you give me the name of your employer? The convalescent home?"

"Oak View Residential Center."

"And who is your supervisor, Mr. Mulvaney?"

"Barb Danson."

"I appreciate your cooperation."

Flores looked down at the information. He would do all he could to find out about the circumstances of the car theft. He'd talk to the man's employer at the convalescent home.

Then he'd call the gallery to verify Mulvaney's alibi for New Year's.

He stood up and nodded. "Thank you for your time, Mr. Mulvaney."

As soon as he sat down in the Investigations car, he smelled it on his clothes. Wonderful.

The scent would follow him for the rest of the day.

The team was going to love it.

27

I t took Duke till well into the morning to go back to the journal. The entry about Karl's parents had affected him, and he'd had a restless night. He needed to finish it, and then he needed to figure out how to get it back to Rose's bookshelf. This was her father's journal, after all. This in some way was the story of her family, and Duke was beginning to feel guilty for taking it.

He opened the book and picked up where he left off.

KARL SCHULER'S Journal

It was October of 1942. Something exciting was going on at the facility in Peenemunde.

Even as a lowly messenger, I felt it buzzing in the air. Hermann wouldn't tell me. He just walked around with a mysterious smile.

Dignitaries were flying in. A few of the scientists teased me with hints. I had come to the conclusion that there would be a test. I had my suspicions based on sketches I'd seen. Wernher Von Braun had the status of Herr Hitler around the Army special weapons division. It would be a rocket. At that point, I had trouble sleeping at night. I had to know the details.

Hermann and I and his research assistants hiked out to a site in the woods, early on that chilly October morning. We sat on a log and waited, drinking cups of tea that an assistant had brought in a thermos flask. We could see the rocket, the A4 on a mound in a clearing, standing ready in the still morning. Finally, there was a shout, men yelling and talking excitedly. The rumble shook my chest. It seemed to last forever, then the fire spurted out, and the rocket soared upward, far into the atmosphere.

It is hard to describe the feeling we all had. Wonder, awe, fear at this unstoppable power unleashed. This was something human beings created. Human beings who had the knowledge to defeat gravity itself. The Aggregat 4, or A4, was the first manmade object to enter space.

This was the pinnacle of all that was good about our country, that we could do this. At the time of the launch, I did not know the depths to which the human beings of our country were plunging to. I did not know about the costs for this great thing that had just happened. I did not stop to think that this rocket and the ones that would follow would be aimed at other human beings with the intent to kill. If I gave that any thought, I would have brushed it away by saying that these rockets would be heading toward the towns and cities of our enemies—leering, comic book caricatures of human beings.

They deserved it.

THAT FALL SOMETHING else happened to me. For the first time, I fell in love.

As I delivered documents throughout the facility, I got to know the scientists. I got to know the secretaries and clerks, who *were the front line of defense for scientists too busy to respond to mundane matters like the receipt of documents and files.*

She was new that fall. She said her brother had been killed on the front line in Poland. Her mother was left without support, so she quit school to take a job as a typist and earn money. She'd grown up not far from Peenemunde, but across the border.

Agnieszka was Polish.

She was small and thin, with brown eyes. And very shy. For the first two months, we did not talk. We passed each other in the corridor. At first, she kept her eyes down when she passed me. As time went on, she began looking at me with brazen curiosity. I looked back at her and smiled. When I would deliver a file, she would nod, curtly. She was quite serious and that intimidated me. I also took it as a challenge. Somehow, some way, I would get her to talk.

My biggest challenge of all? To get her to laugh.

I wondered if she was trying very hard not to be noticed. She was not German, and she was looked upon as a labor resource, nothing else. She was very good at her job, I knew that. As I got to know her, I would understand her difficult position even more.

One day, I was ready to leave for the day and return to my uncle's home on my bicycle. I saw her walking past the gate, her arms clutched close to herself against the cold. I asked if I could accompany her. She nodded.

I walked my bike next to her in silence as we made our way down the path. I decided to be bold. I asked her name.

"Agnieszka. Agnieszka Kaminski."

Almost in monosyllables, she told me where she lived with her mother. I walked her to the stop for the bus. I asked, like a crazy person, if we could walk together again. Most of our times together were spent after work, walking to the bus. I sometimes lingered at her desk, exchanging a few words, until Frau Kohler gave Agnieszka a severe look, and I knew it was time to leave.

In those months together, one look or a few words meant so much. We rarely touched hands. One evening on our way back, under cover of dusk, I kissed her cheek.

It's something I could never explain to my children and grandchildren—the intensity of that kiss.

It was the happiest day of my life, and it would sustain me for years.

28

Oakview Meadows was a faded wooden one-story off of Blossom Hill in South San Jose.

It didn't look like the kind of place Flores would ever want his parents to live in their declining years. Small sliding windows ran along the side of the building facing the street, and as he pulled closer he saw grubby shades pulled down on each one. In the brochure on assisted living, Oakview looked like the economy option.

The smell hit him as he walked into the lobby. Vegetable soup, disinfectant and urine. He wondered why Randall Mulvaney would have wanted to work here, especially given his feelings for his grandfather.

"May I help you, sir?" The young woman at the desk was a petite blonde with Cindy Lou Hoo eyes and hair piled up in a sort of fountain, in a white scrub top in a Mickey Mouse print. Her name tag read KAYLEY. She smiled as she looked him over.

"Detective Mario Flores, San Jose Police Department." He pulled out his badge and showed her. "I'm looking for Barbara Danson."

"Certainly. Let me give her a buzz." She smiled and picked up the phone. "She was meeting with a patient's family. I think she's done."

Flores nodded his thanks and checked his phone for any updates from his team at the station. His heart sped up a bit when he remembered that Reyna Ruiz had his phone number. Maybe she'd text him. Then he felt a layer of sweat form on his skin as he was filled with terror that she'd do exactly that. He put his phone back in his pocket.

"I'll take you right back, Officer." She led him down the hall, carpeted in a stained olive green, with a few worn spots. They turned the corner and Kayley gestured toward the first door, a small office that smelled like coffee and tuna fish.

"Barb, this is officer Flores."

"Thank you, Kayley." The middle-aged woman in the small office wearing a navy blue blazer smiled as if she'd been expecting him. He hadn't called in advance. The woman struck him as a person who had gotten used to fighting fires in her job, and she'd gotten quick on her feet.

"Barb Danson," she extended her hand and he reached out to shake it. "Now how can I help you, Officer Flores?"

"I'm investigating a possible person of interest in the murder of a man on New Year's. You have an employee named Randall Mulvaney?"

The woman subtly sucked in her breath. "Randall. Yes, he's one of our orderlies. He's worked here for the past year."

"How would you describe him as an employee?" Flores watched the woman, whose face seemed to assume a mask of impassivity. "Is he dependable?"

Barb Danson eased into a smile. "Randall shows up on time and performs the duties he's asked to do. We did have an issue a few months back. He got into an argument with a nurse over the timing of a patient's medication. The shouting disturbed some patients. I sent him home for the day to cool off."

"You didn't notice a pattern of anger with him?" Flores asked. "Did he have any problems with patients?"

Barb shook her head. "I didn't hear of any. I've kept my eye on him to make sure. His attitude doesn't make him any friends here. The well-being of our patients is my utmost concern, but it's hard to keep people in these entry level positions in this valley. We're understaffed as it is. Randall performs his duties adequately. I'm looking at the incident as a one-time thing."

Mulvaney's track record of impulsive anger bothered Flores. What else would he do in anger, especially toward a grandfather he resented?

Flores handed over his card. "We're investigating a shooting. One of Mulvaney's relatives. If you run across any information that might be useful, give me a call."

Barb raised her eyebrows and sighed. "I will, Officer Flores. I just hope it doesn't cost me an employee."

REYNA HAD JUST FINISHED with her 4 p.m. appointment, her last of the day. She cleaned up her station and peeled the gloves off her hands.

She checked her phone and saw that Jimmy had called and left a message. She sped through it, but she caught something about coming home a half hour late. That made things easier. She could pick up Jacky and get him settled in to finish his homework, with no need to rush dinner. She had frozen chicken adobo she could heat up.

She was replacing the polisher, when Tiffany came in

unexpectedly. Reyna knew her face showed her displeasure at this visit and she didn't want to hide it. *Don't slow me down, girl. I want to get out of here.*

Tiffany came into the room and sat down on the chair near the sink.

"Tiff, what's up? Need something?"

Tiffany looked past her, as she watched Rocio tidy up at the front desk, pick up her purse and head for the front door.

"I want to know what you think you were doing when we were out last night," she said, her voice lowered.

"Can you tell me what you're talking about?" Reyna's face felt hot. She pumped soap on her hands, rubbed them together thoroughly and rinsed them off in the sink.

"You know exactly what I'm talking about." Reyna felt her coworker's eyes boring into the side of her face. "The cop. You were flirting with him. We all saw it. What if Jimmy saw what you were doing? Would you be okay with that?"

"We were all out to have a good time last night. You were flirting with those guys in the car on Stevens Creek. What's the difference? I knew the guy, Tiff. It's not a big deal."

Reyna yanked a paper towel out of the dispenser and dried her hands. She wasn't going to let Tiffany pull her off schedule tonight. She was telling her the truth. Flores *was* an acquaintance she'd just happened to reconnect with.

"It wasn't what you think. I was just meeting up with a friend."

Tiffany studied her with an expression somewhere between disgust and pity.

"Don't pull this shit on Jimmy. He deserves better."

With that, Tiffany stood up and pushed past her. Suddenly Reyna felt deflated.

She'd gone home last night with a flutter of excitement.

A surge of something that felt like joy. It had made her everyday life feel so dull, so lifeless in comparison. It flowed through every part of her body like a chemical. It made her feel alive. Her brother Armando had described what heroin felt like to her once. Just like this.

Even looking over at Jimmy that night, asleep on the other side of the bed, couldn't take it away from her. Now that she had this feeling, bubbling up in her, she couldn't imagine living without it.

But she wondered how she would keep it.

29

K arl Schuler's journal

In August of 1943, my life changed completely. It was a beginning. My eyes were being opened. But I was not completely willing to see.

Much had happened since the successful test of the A4 rocket the previous year. Now the new V rockets were in production. With the might of the weapons we were creating, all of us at Peenemunde assumed Germany had the upper hand in the war now.

The night was still, and the moon shone silvery bright outside my window. My cousin Walter had been bothering me to play a game, but I had no patience for him. I went to my room and lay on my bed reading. I began to hear a heavy droning. Soon it got closer and heavier. I knew that sound. Bombers. Bombers that weren't ours.

I looked outside the window and saw them: wings gleaming like silvery insects in the moonlight. Hundreds.

The droning finally stopped. The silence seemed oppressive. After something like that, you tense up and wait for it. The blasts began, thunderous and close.

Later we would find out that two Polish janitors had communicated details of the Peenemunde facility to the Polish Resistance, who had passed them on the British. The RAF had known what to target.

Now all the Polish at Peenemunde were under suspicion for their part in this horrific act.

Even Agnieszka.

The day after the bombing she disappeared.

30

S usan Moreland of East Point had given him names of the students Karl Schuler had been working with. It was nearly 5 p.m. by the time he got to Matthew Le's apartment off Senter Road.

He made his way up the wrought iron and concrete stairs to the second story and knocked on unit 24. A teenaged girl in a hoodie answered the door as she pulled an AirPod from one ear.

"I'm here to talk with Matthew Le."

She looked him over with interest, then yelled *Matt* back into the apartment with the voice of a banshee, before turning back to him as he stood at the door. "Are you the police? Is he in trouble?"

"I'm Detective Flores." He liked to think his choice of suit and tie distinguished him from a patrol officer. The young woman's response made him wonder if the police had been to the apartment before.

Soon a sturdy, muscular young man appeared behind her. He wore a Pokemon t-shirt that looked like it belonged on an eight-year-old.

"Got it, Soph." He nodded at his sister.

The young woman had continued staring at Flores, but when her brother nudged her, she reluctantly put her AirPod back in her ear and walked off.

"Come in and have a seat, officer."

Matt Le was almost Flores's height, but sturdy and muscular. He had a cordial smile on his face, but Flores suspected it was the default face he wore around adults. Or when his mother asked him, *"Drive your sister to school. Clean your room. Why an A- on your final—why not an A?"*

Matt led Flores into the small living room, with a covered sofa and a coffee table piled with textbooks. A black-and-white poster of a martial artist hung prominently over the couch, next to a framed piece of calligraphy. Hung around the room were family photos. Toddlers, children, teenagers, wedding photos, grandparents.

"I'm Detective Mario Flores. I'm here to ask you a few questions about Karl Schuler." Flores took his seat on the couch and turned toward the young man, who stared down at his hands. The polite smile had faded from his face.

"Do you know why I'm here, Matt?" Flores led with this because it was deliberately vague. It left the door open for Matt Le to say anything he might say out of fear or guilt.

Matt turned his eyes on Flores and his lower lip trembled. He spoke slowly. "Yeah, I heard what happened to Mr. Schuler. Another kid from the center told me."

"How long had you known him?"

Matt took some time to clear his throat. When he began talking, his voice sounded hoarse. "I'm a senior this year. I started coming to East Point in my sophomore year. He helped me and a couple other kids with physics. I knew I wanted to go into something related to science. I was doing pretty bad in school back then. My mom said I had to go."

As Matt continued, his voice and face became more animated. The excitement burned through his veneer of teenage toughness.

"Sounds like you didn't mind going to the center."

"The classes were kind of fun. Mr. Schuler talked about how things worked. A group of us built rockets. He did experiments, too. Like he brought in some liquid nitrogen and froze things. He did this thing where he pretended to dip his thumb in the liquid nitrogen. Then he hit it with a hammer and pieces flew around the room. We all screamed. We thought the old guy had shattered his thumb. Then he showed us it was just half a hot dog."

Flores laughed. The students probably loved it. He could see where the old man scared Rose, who was perpetually worrying about him, trying to rein him in, keep him out of trouble.

"Mr. Schuler had you over to his house, didn't he? Some kind of a Christmas party before school let out?"

"The Wednesday group. We all went. We had dinner, then we had a gingerbread house building contest—to see who could make the strongest one. I thought mine was pretty cool. Six stories, with a cantilever roof. But I didn't win."

This would have been a couple of weeks before Schuler's death.

"How was Mr. Schuler when you were over at his house?" Flores asked. "Did he act differently than usual? Did he seem nervous or scared?"

Matt shrugged. "He was in a good mood. Cracking jokes."

"He never talked about anyone who was angry with him —or about being in trouble in any way?" Flores asked. "Any problems the night of the party?"

"Nah. It was maybe ten of us from East Point and Miss Moreland. We all knew each other pretty well. We hung out."

"Did Mr. Schuler talk about anything he'd be doing during the holiday break?"

"He said he had some project he was working on. I thought it was some kind of experiment, because he seemed to do them with us all the time."

Flores wondered what Schuler could have been working on and if it was the project that could have gotten him in trouble. He wondered if Schuler would have confided in Duke Sorenson.

"Can you think of kids at the center who might have a problem with Mr. Schuler? Have a grudge against him?" Matt must have heard the details of the shooting. But if it had been gang-related and Matthew knew any of the people responsible, he wouldn't speak up about it. Peer pressure was a powerful force in normal teenage life. Add gang connections or illegal activity on top of that, and it would be impossible to pry the info out.

Then Flores remembered something the donut gang had talked about.

"Matt—a couple of years ago, there was a student who attacked another student in Mr. Schuler's group." He watched as the kid's face froze. Flores saw a procession of things that looked familiar to him. Panic. The search for a good lie. Then finally, helplessness.

"How did you know it was me?"

The kid's shoulders drew up and he crossed his arms over his chest, as if he wanted to fold himself up into something small.

"Somebody told you."

"Why don't you tell me about it, Matt."

The kid studied him for a minute. He didn't have to tell him, but Flores hoped he would.

"Freshmen year I was hanging out with a bunch of guys I went to middle school with." The arms crossed tighter across his chest and Matt leaned over, looking down as he talked. "We were friends and everything was cool, you know? In high school, they started hanging out with these older guys, who were into some bad shi—stuff. I stopped hanging with them. So they told lies about me to my friends. I got beat up a few times. The one place I felt safe was Mr. Schuler's class. Until one day at the beginning of sophomore year. One of the older kids followed me to the class, just to make fun of me in front of Mr. S and the other students. I couldn't handle it. I had a knife in my jacket—okay, that was dumb, I know. I showed it to the kid, so he'd back off. When he tried to grab it, I stabbed him in the arm."

Matt was still hunched over, his head almost on his knees, as if he was trying to keep from passing out. The state the young man was in told Flores he'd spoken the truth. Certainly, he'd been arrested and possibly spent some time in a facility. The older kid who'd taunted him probably didn't.

"Thanks for telling me." Flores waited for the young man to sit up. When he did, Flores looked him in the eye and remembered why he'd gone into police work. He handed Matt a card. "If you have any more trouble like that, let me know, Matt. Or if there's anything you want to tell me about Mr. Schuler." Matt picked up the card, looked at it and set it on the coffee table.

"Matt, let me ask you something. When you first heard about Mr. Schuler's death." He watched the young man's eyes blinking back tears. "What did you think had happened to him?"

Matt might know more than he was letting on. He might be too afraid to say it now but asking might get him thinking. The young man had trusted him enough to open up about the knife incident.

Matt Le picked at the frayed edge of his Pokemon shirt with a fingernail. "I don't think it was random. That's bullshit. I heard about the shooting—whoever did it knew exactly what they were doing. They wanted him dead."

The teenager brushed tears away with the back of his hand, and he continued, shaking his head.

"Anybody who actually knew Mr. S and did something like this? They would have to be evil."

31

A s the day approached, Ruiz found himself looking
forward to Karl Schuler's memorial service.

It was a chance to see Schuler as his friends
and family saw him. Ruiz was interested in who would
show up.

He was curious to hear what would be said about Karl
Schuler. He knew only what Duke had told him about Karl
and what he'd googled.

Since she'd seen the shooting, too, he asked Reyna if she
wanted to attend. They would drop Jacky off with Reyna's
parents and go to the service at the church Schuler had
attended in South San Jose. Not quite the date night they'd
had on New Year's Eve. He wished it was. It was probably
inappropriate to think about it during a funeral, but the
tight black dress Reyna was wearing made him want to get
her alone.

When he and Reyna arrived, the parking lot was full. He
parked the truck in one of the few spots left on a side street,
and they walked a block to the church.

Rose sat near the front, with a group of what must be

family. The donut gang, including the shop owner Mr. Kang, sat farther back, with another group of white and gray heads. Maybe Schuler's former coworkers.

He scanned the pews for an open spot for him and Reyna. They slid into a pew on the left side, next to a group of teenaged boys with their thumbs twirling over their phones, looking polished but uncomfortable in buttoned-down shirts.

The organ began playing classical music, as people continued entering the church, looking for spots among the pews. Ruiz looked up to see Detective Flores on the side, standing against the wall. Ruiz caught his eye and waved him over. Flores looked over at the Schuler family. He waved his hand to indicate he'd stay put. After a few minutes, he came over and took his place in the pew next to Ruiz.

"Good to see you, Detective Flores." Reyna leaned forward and smiled.

Flores nodded curtly at Reyna, unsmiling, then turned back to Ruiz.

"The mayor and his wife are up front, sitting with Rose." Flores leaned in and whispered to Ruiz. "The tall guy on the other side of her—that's her son, Randall. I interviewed him Wednesday. He's got a record as a juvenile. By his own admission, he stole a teacher's car and wrecked it. He resented his grandfather big time. Apparently, the old man asked him to help build Habitat for Humanity houses with him."

Ruiz grunted. "The nerve of him."

"Looks like Mulvaney was at an art gallery party on New Year's Eve. I need to find out when he left."

Ruiz had no illusions that he was on this case, but he was curious.

"What about Tuan Nguyen? Anything else there?"

Flores frowned and shook his head quickly as he settled back into the pew.

The minister walked up to the podium as the music wrapped up. A quiet hung over the room. A baby behind them shrieked and split the silence. Then a wave of coughs. Ruiz realized as he looked around the room that not only were the pews filled, there were people standing along the walls and along the back. He turned around and saw people lined up in the foyer of the church, waiting to get in.

"We are here today to honor a good man." The minister's voice echoed throughout the church. "He was a man who impacted all of us. And left us better people. We are here to honor Karl Schuler. A man who lived to the age of ninety-two. Yet—I think we all agree—he died too young."

The pastor gave an overview of Schuler's life, from his birth in Germany in the 1920s and his parents' deaths, to his emigration to the United States after the war. The pastor talked about Schuler's love of aviation, his desire to create things that flew, and his fascination with flight. The hardships of his childhood had given him a compassion for others. A desire to help the hurting and to bring help to anyone who needed it. He'd tried to bring the wonders of science to youth who didn't have the opportunities to pursue it.

At that, the teenagers next to Ruiz launched a round of applause, picked up by the rest of the attendees. Ruiz watched the group of boys in uncomfortable formal clothing and a few young women nod. One of the young women wiped away tears as the pastor went on to introduce the next speaker.

Arnie Tan slid out of his pew and walked up to the podium. He pulled a notecard out of his blazer pocket and began telling the story of how Karl Schuler had helped him right after his wife died. How he'd organized outings for the group to get him out of the house and around people.

Then Duke Sorenson got up and made his way up to the front. Today Duke had shed the windbreaker for a black sports coat. He looked frailer than when Ruiz had seen him at the donut shop. Farther away, he saw the whole man: a little unsteady on his feet, pale and drawn in his face. Duke looked to the pastor who stood by and cleared his throat.

"Karl Schuler was my friend for almost fifty years. We first met at Lockheed, working on the U2 program. We found ourselves staying late at the same time, trying to bargain with our wives for just a little more time before we came home. We weren't always successful. We both loved what we did."

"We got to know each other's families. I got to see up close what kind of man Karl Schuler was. A man who loved the science of flight more than anyone I knew. A man who loved his fellow human beings more than anyone I knew. There was not a bad bone in his body. Ask anyone here today and they will tell you the same thing. I was privileged to be his friend. He did not deserve to die the way he did." At this, Duke's voice grew hoarse. He closed his eyes and waited for a few seconds till he regained his composure.

"Karl's death, at the hands of a murderer, did not suit him. If I could imagine an appropriate way for Karl to die, it would have been doing what he dreamed of—flying. Soaring into the sky, past the grief of his lost childhood, past the loss of his wife, Aggie. He would have loved to make his final escape by flying away into the clouds."

"Karl was good at doing something I'm not so good at: forgiving. I can never forgive the people who did this to him on New Year's. But Karl? He would have it in him to do that."

Duke bowed his head, slipped his note card into his pocket as applause swept across the room.

Ruiz leaned into Flores and spoke in a low voice.

"What do you know about Schuler's childhood in Germany?"

Flores shrugged. "Rose Mulvaney said he became an orphan at the age of twelve."

"Would you mind if I did some research on my own?"

Flores's face tightened and Ruiz thought he heard a sigh. "Why?"

Here he was again, butting in. "I'm just curious. It may not make much difference. It may be nothing. But I'd like to find out a few things about his life in Germany."

Flores gave an abrupt nod and looked back to the front. "Touch base with me and let me know what you find out."

Ruiz clapped the younger man on the shoulder.

The next person to come up was a busty older woman in a dark green dress. She moved over to the organ and stood behind a music stand. *Dear God.* Some kind of a song. Ruiz couldn't imagine what song it would be, but he predicted that he'd zone out during it. He looked over at Reyna, who was focused straight ahead, as if she were really excited to hear this one.

The woman opened her mouth and warbly singing spilled out. His worst fear, that it would be some kind of opera, had come true. She was singing in another language, which would probably be German. Ruiz tuned out and started thinking about how he'd find out more about Karl Schuler.

After the singer, Ruiz was pulled out of his haze by a bright voice of a young woman who had stepped up to the podium. She was stocky and tough and wore a maroon dress that wasn't very flattering. He was soon drawn into her story.

"When I met Karl Schuler at East Point Youth Center, I wrote him off. He looked like an old white guy who had too much time on his hands and didn't know or care much about me. I didn't care much about him. But then I heard him talk about planes. About flying them, designing them. I found that I couldn't stop thinking about them. I wanted to find out how I could either fly one or build one myself. He told me I needed to take physics, trigonometry and calculus if I wanted to learn about aviation. I was pessimistic that I could handle those classes. When I decided to try, I found out how much I was capable of. Mr. Schuler was my number one cheerleader."

The young woman wiped tears from her eyes, then smiled. "Three years later, I became the first person in my family to graduate from high school. I went to community college, then transferred to the Georgia Institute of Technology. Last summer I had an internship at Boeing, and in June I'm graduating with a degree in aeronautical engineering."

Ruiz cast a glance sideways and saw Flores's eyes were misty.

The rest of the ceremony continued with funny anecdotes and stories of selflessness and encouragement given. Karl Schuler had been a saint. And not a sanctimonious, self-righteous one. The kind of saint with a sense of humor. It was hard to fault the guy on anything. He was, as he'd heard Captain Coelho say about someone, "a once in a lifetime kind of person."

At the end, as people streamed out, Ruiz and Reyna headed up to the front, with Flores lagging behind them.

Rose stood at the front in a receiving line, as people waited to talk to her. A distinguished man near her age stood next to her. A gawky man with a silly moustache paced a few feet away, looking at his phone. Ruiz guessed this was Randall Mulvaney, Rose's son.

While Flores waited to talk to Rose, Ruiz approached the man next to her. In his expensive navy blue suit, he looked like the CEO of a large company.

"I'm James Ruiz and this is my wife, Reyna. We're the ones who saw the shooting on New Year's."

"I'm Christoph Schuler, Karl's son" He reached out his hand in turn to both of them. "Thank you for all you've done. The family is grateful."

Ruiz wasn't used to the "family" working as one unit. It sounded almost like the mob.

"I'm so sorry for your loss, Mr. Schuler," Reyna said.

"Thank you, Reyna." The man smiled warmly, as everyone always did with her.

"You're from back East?" Ruiz asked Christoph Schuler.

"I flew in for the day from Miami. Rose shouldn't have to handle this herself." He nodded and looked at him and Reyna with interest. "I need to get back tomorrow for a speaking engagement. I'm running for office."

Reyna's eyes lit up. "What are you running for?"

"State senate," Christoph replied. "It's something I've considered for a long time. Now that leadership of my company is in good hands, I'm ready to do it."

"I had a visit with Rose a few days ago." Ruiz leaned in toward Christoph Schuler, as the post-service noise level in the church began to rise. "She was showing me photos of your father and the family. You have an interesting family history."

It was quick, just a small motion. Christoph Schuler flinched and glanced at his sister.

"My father was one of those people who rose above his circumstances. He was definitely a role model for us, and he set a high bar. I hope to bring some of those values to government, as a senator."

Ruiz observed that Schuler was already sounding like one. The older man sighed, adjusted his tie knot, and looked in the direction of his sister, who was still talking to Flores.

"I've had a long, tiring trip to get here," Schuler turned back to Ruiz. "I've got a conference with the governor in about an hour. I'm expecting his endorsement. I'd like to talk to you more, especially about the circumstances of my father's death. Detective Ruiz. Maybe we can meet somewhere tomorrow morning before I fly out. I'm downtown at the Fairmont."

Ruiz wasn't expecting this invitation. He wasn't going to lose the opportunity to hear more about Karl Schuler.

"Why don't I come by your hotel. How about 7:30?"

Flores was still talking to Rose and had missed hearing about his appointment with Christoph Schuler, which was fine by Ruiz.

As Ruiz turned away from Christoph Schuler and prepared to leave, Flores smiled and nodded at him, bypassing Reyna completely. Something seemed weird about that.

Ruiz felt a flash on anger on Reyna's behalf. But he got it. Some people, especially cops, went into hyperfocus mode. Flores was on the job here.

Ruiz put his hand on Reyna's shoulder. "Ready to head out, babe?" She nodded. He gave Flores the "call you later" finger and thumb sign.

As they left, Ruiz saw Reyna in his peripheral vision. She

turned and gave Flores a long, slow look and a smile. He'd seen how the women at Someplace looked at Flores. Maybe that's how all women looked at Flores.

Flores caught her eye, looking wide-eyed as if blinded by a camera flash, then turned away.

32

K arl Schuler's Journal

After the bombing, we left Peenemunde abruptly, moving south to settle in the city of Nordhausen.

One evening Uncle Hermann sat down with me after dinner and finally told me about his work—all of the operations from Peenemunde were now transferred to the Mittelwerk operation, safe from the RAF bombers inside a mountain called Kohnstein.

I wanted so badly to go to his work, to be his messenger, his assistant, as I continued my studies. I remembered the beauty, the glory of the rocket launch at Peenemunde. The new V2 rocket was supposed to be even more advanced.

Since our departure, I had heard no word of Agnieszka. On our last walk, she'd told me something that had haunted my thoughts ever since.

We sat on my coat, spread out on the weeds, near the platform where the V1 had soared up into space. Sea birds flew overhead, crying to each other.

She told me, a little afraid to say it, that she had been married before she came to Peenemunde. To a soldier, a Polish boy. They'd

*been married for about six months before he was sent to the
eastern front to fight for Germany.*

*She found out she was expecting a child. A month later, she
was notified of her husband's death.*

*When the child was born, her mother and sister took her to the
hospital late at night. The labor was difficult because the baby was in
the wrong position. When the baby came, the nurses rushed it away
in a cart, saying it needed oxygen. The next morning, the German
nurse told her that her baby had been born with a serious defect in his
brain. He would never walk or talk. He would always be like a baby.
In the Reich, they told her, we send these children to a special place to
be taken care of. Don't worry, Frau Kaminski. It is for the best.*

*But Agnieszka had heard about other children whose parents
brought them to the special hospitals. They never saw them
again.*

*I pictured Agnieszka's little boy smiling as he lay on the lawn
of some big, clean Kinder center, lovingly cared for by kind young
women.*

*But from the look of pain on Agnieszka's face, she was
imagining a very different picture. And she was right.*

AFTER THE MEMORIAL SERVICE, Flores headed back
downtown.

He flexed his hands to warm them up as he walked
towards First Street to interview Jen Corey at Fortuna
Gallery.

Two more days till Buckley's deadline. Until the case was
turned over to Ass-Kissing Jesperson.

It was late in the day, but he needed something strong.
Espresso.

Downtown San Jose was taking down its annual

Christmas display. Christmas in the Park, a glittery assemblage of decorated trees, Santa's workshop, and animatronic elves, circa 1960. The kiddie rides had been disassembled and loaded onto trucks. The outdoor skating rink was still up, and a few skaters circled the frozen oval, which looked odd juxtaposed against rows of palm trees.

The tall, skinny kid at the counter of the cafe set the espresso shot down on the counter and pushed it toward Flores.

Flores took it and downed it, then set the glass down a little too hard on the counter. He had ten minutes before he'd walk down First Street to the gallery and ask about Randall Mulvaney's alibi.

He needed to pull out of the stupor he felt after the funeral. The overwhelming emotion of a steady stream of people Schuler had helped just drove the point home: he needed to find the man's killer. A reporter had accosted him as he left the church, asking for an update on the investigation. He told the reporter that the team was pursuing a couple of leads and a news conference would be called when there was more information. They'd continued with questions and a small crowd began to gather. Flores quickly ducked into the church.

He should have known Reyna would be there. She sat three feet away from him in the church pew. He smelled the faint scent of peaches on her skin. He felt her presence before he actually looked at her. He stole a glance—she tossed her dark wavy hair and played with her necklace as she sat next to Ruiz, who sat transfixed, his eyes on a young Latina speaking. Reyna's tight black dress fit her curves like a glove and her legs, in sheer silk stockings, crossed revealing those smooth, perfect little calves, like something

Michelangelo had carved out of marble. He made himself look back at the speaker.

He should have pretended not to see the Ruizes. He should have stood on the other side of the church or slipped into a seat when he had a chance. He tried to ignore her. But she was there, and it was nearly impossible to think of anything else.

Maybe the answer was spending more time with Ruiz. If he hung out with the guy, he'd constantly be reminded of how stupid it was to think about his wife.

Ruiz had made it clear that he wanted to do anything he could to help solve the case. The case belonged to Flores and his team. But Ruiz had ten years' more experience than he had. His advice and ideas could help. He made a note to call him and get together again at Someplace.

With the espresso jumpstarting the neurons in his brain, Flores headed out of the cafe.

Then, as Flores turned the corner onto First Street, what he saw made him break out in a sweat.

A blonde woman with a tall man walked close together, backpacks over their shoulders and coffee cups in their hands, laughing. His heart pounded. For the first time since he'd seen Oksana at the French restaurant, he felt pain. The depth of it surprised him. Flores forced himself to turn away and look for the address of the gallery.

He finally spotted it. Fortuna Gallery was a tiny wedge of a storefront next to a stationery shop.

A large, colorful tapestry hung in the window, an abstract blur of colors. He wondered if it was the work of the mysterious Shayante, Randall Mulvaney's girlfriend.

He pulled open the door and walked across the concrete floor till he saw a sign scrawled on a piece of paper and taped to a door: J. Corey, Gallery Manager. He wondered about the rent a gallery like this must pay. It had to be hard for artists to survive financially in the valley.

He tapped on the door. And waited.

The espresso, along with seeing Oksana, made him feel edgy and impatient. He tapped his foot and pulled out his phone. He scrolled through his Facebook notifications. He did a quick search for Reyna Ruiz and pulled up her profile. As soon as he saw her face, he quit Facebook and slipped his phone back into his pocket.

"Detective Flores?" The door opened and a short woman in jeans and a white t-shirt came out. Her hair was short and spiky, but other than that, she could have been a suburban soccer mom. "I was on a phone call. Come on in."

The tiny office looked like a storeroom with a desk. Canvases, bottles of wine, bags of red Solo cups and six packs of soda formed a wall behind the desk.

"Have a seat." She gestured toward a wood and black leather chair that looked like an Eames knockoff. "You wanted to talk about Randall Mulvaney."

Flores took a seat. "He attended your New Year's Eve party. I want to pin down the time he arrived and when he left."

"All I can tell you is what I saw that night. Randall and Shayante came early to help set up. Shayante has a couple of pieces in our show."

"What time was that?"

"They showed up 7-ish." She pushed the spiky bangs off her forehead. "The party didn't go past 1:30. So I have to say, well—they both left earlier than that. They did a lot of work and I think they were beat."

"Were they talking to anyone when they left? Could anyone vouch for the time they left?"

Jen Corey blew out a sigh. "I'm not sure. I can give you a

few names. There's a couple—Ted and Mark Strom." She leaned back in her chair, which let out a squeak. "Shayante's friend, Mira. Mira Davies." She opened her desk drawer and rifled through the contents. She handed him a couple of business cards.

"Thanks, Ms. Corey." He put the cards in his wallet. "Now can you tell me, what is Mr. Mulvaney's relationship to the gallery?"

Jen Corey laughed. "None. Other than he's Shayante's plus one."

"What does that mean, exactly?"

"He comes around with her, because he can't seem to do anything without her. He's been here at lot, helping with her shows, running errands." She smirked. "Personally, I think Shayante's too good for him. But he's free labor, and I'm not going to turn that down."

"Thanks for your help, Ms. Corey." Flores nodded. "Mind if I look around the gallery? I'm curious. Is the work in the window by Shayante?"

Corey stood up, looking amused at his interest. "Yes, it is. Go ahead and take a look. We're not big, so it won't take you long."

He walked back into the entry area and then moved into the main room. There were a couple of sculptures on square pedestals that looked like they were made out of blown glass, with metal strips wrapped around them. On the wall hung fabric art, woven from rough fibers and embedded with something that looked like stones. At first the colors looked mismatched and garish. The more he looked at them, the more the colors seem to complement each other and look like they had been very deliberately and carefully paired together. The placards next to the works read Shayante Miland.

He wasn't sure Randall Mulvaney played a part in his grandfather's murder. But the man hated his grandfather and had a history of impulsive acts. If he'd left before 1:30 a.m., he would have had time to get to south San Jose.

It was time for a conversation with Shayante. He went back into Jen Corey's office and asked for her number. He didn't want to call Randall Mulvaney.

33

Karl Schuler's Journal

At home in the evenings, Hermann would explain the physics behind the rockets. How they worked, why they worked.

I was getting to the point where I could do the calculations. I hadn't gotten over the thrill of seeing the rocket take off in the woods outside Peenemunde. I wanted to see it again. I wanted to see something man had made pierce the sky and enter space.

The work at the old gypsum mine seemed hard to believe. A complete factory had been constructed within the mountain— impenetrable to bombs. Uncle Hermann explained the parts and the different stages of rocket production to me. It was hard to keep workers, he said. But things were progressing well. If I did well in my studies, I would be able to visit the factory at the end of the term.

Uncle needn't have threatened me. My studies, especially science and math, were the highlight of my life. My time with my books in the evening kept my mind busy. Kept me from thinking about Agnieszka. Wondering about her and where she'd gone.

She'd either been transferred, returned to Poland or had been killed. I had to be realistic.

As the term neared an end, my teachers informed me that I was likely to receive an award for excellence in my science and math classes. The fact that I was winning awards didn't excite me. Going to Kohnstein and seeing the work there would be my reward.

That morning of the visit, I woke up early to review every book or newspaper clipping I had that mentioned the rockets.

A driver picked us up and we headed out of town, for the mountains, my favorite place. The hills were lush and green from the rains. A troupe of children with rucksacks hiked along the road, heading for a trail. The clouds hung white and heavy in a clear blue sky. I watched it all pass by me like a movie, a movie of the Germany I loved, my Germany.

Then I saw it: Kohnstein in the distance, a green lion slumbering, its head between its paws. It struck me as an odd image, since the lion didn't seem to be guarding this secret weapon it was hiding. It was sleeping on the job.

We neared the entrance, and the driver pulled us up to the arched entry, hidden in the hillside. Hermann gathered his satchel and waited for me to get out.

As we entered the arch, I smelled an unpleasant odor. Oil and rust and the smell of something like feces and dead rodents. But I was transfixed by the place as it opened itself up to me. Immense caverns, rock ceilings high above me, sides lined with iron racks. Rocket barrels lay on the racks, and a huge crane towered above us. My heart pounded. This was where it all happened. Where the V2 rockets were assembled.

Hermann was excited to show me the place. Today Herr Von Braun was here, and I was to meet him. The man looked like a god from Norse mythology: handsome, with gold hair and a strong jaw. The perfect Aryan. He was the designer of the rocket.

He shook my hand and listened patiently as I excitedly explained what I knew of the V2. He nodded and told me I had a very good understanding of the rocket and that he was quite impressed. I fired off my questions and he took time to consider and answer each one. With my meeting with the architect of the German rocket program, this was officially the best day of my life.

In retrospect, this would be the worst day of my life.

Not long after that, I would fall far. And I would never be the same.

fter the memorial service, Ruiz convinced Reyna she didn't need to cook; they'd order pizza tonight.

Reyna had saved coupons for the local pizza chain. While she reminded him that pizza was a bad nutritional choice, she was happy for a night off. Jacky whooped and ran through the house so much at the idea of this special treat, Ruiz finally sat down and played Minecraft with him on the computer, just to shut him up.

While Jacky continued playing on the computer, Ruiz pulled out his phone and decided to text someone he'd met on a case last year, a history teacher at a private school in the Monte Verde hills. Peregrine Nikolakis wasn't the easiest person to get along with, but as a self-identified history nerd, she might be able to help him. He needed background about Karl Schuler's time in Germany.

Up for some quick research on WWII? I need help on a case.

. . .

HE HEARD his phone buzz an hour later.

Does it involve Nazis? Always up for that. CALL ME.

After giving Perry the details about Karl and Hermann Schuler, Ruiz called in the pizza order.

After dinner, the three of them watched *Toy Story* together. Ruiz had been thinking about the Schuler family since the service and had been longing for some family time.

The three of them huddled on the sofa with a quilt. Jacky recited dialog along with the movie, one he'd watched maybe fifty times since he was a toddler. He and Reyna remembered crazy things Jacky had done when he was young. The boy at first denied having done any of these things, then laughed and acted proud he'd done them.

After Reyna and Jacky went to bed, Ruiz sat down on the couch with a beer, feeling peaceful and grounded after family time.

Around 10 p.m., he got a text from Perry, who apparently didn't have anything better to do on a Friday night.

I struck the mother lode. I'll send something later tonight.

35

T his late in the day, Flores had no problem finding a parking spot on the street near San Jose State. As he turned onto Ninth Street, he spotted Mulvaney's apartment complex and headed for it.

A young woman in a long, colorful dress and a head covering opened the door. She had round brown eyes and her skin was brown, rich and smooth. Wafting out of the door was the same marijuana smell he'd experienced on his last visit.

"Shayante Miland? I was hoping you'd be here. Officer Flores from the San Jose Police Department." He flashed his badge.

She smiled politely. "Randall is working at the thrift store this evening. He'll be back after 8."

"Actually, I wanted to ask you a few questions. May I come in?"

She looked him over then nodded. "Have a seat, please. Can I get you water? A glass of lemonade?" She had the manners of someone who hadn't grown up in California.

Somewhere in the south, maybe. Lemonade was an interesting offer in the relative cold of January. It reminded him of sun and summer and sounded damn good right now.

"I'd love some lemonade, thank you." He took the seat he'd had on his first visit. As Shayante worked in the kitchen, he looked around the room. There was a program from Karl Schuler's memorial service on the coffee table. Flores had seen Mulvaney but didn't remember seeing Shayante there.

She returned with a tray holding his drink, which she set on the coffee table, and took a seat on the sofa.

"I'd like to ask you a few questions about New Year's and the whereabouts of Randall, Ms. Miland."

"This is because of his granddad's death?" She sighed. "Sure, go ahead."

"I'm trying to find out when Randall left the party at Fortuna Gallery. Do you remember when he left?"

"I don't."

He must have looked startled. She explained.

"We came together to help Jen do setup, but I left around 1 a.m. with a friend. Randall got home a little past 2."

Flores made a note on his tablet. "What kind of car does Randall drive?"

"An old white Cadillac. Used to be his grandad's."

Could it be that Randall Mulvaney rode along with someone else or borrowed the SUV that night?

He decided to change tactics. Shayante was much easier to talk to than Randall. He wanted to keep her as a source for information.

"I saw some of your work at the gallery today. Those long fabric and bead pieces. I love the color combinations you use."

Shayante softened, her eyes bright. "Thank you. Those

are a couple of my favorites. I did them for my MFA project last year." She stretched her legs out under the coffee table. She seemed to check him out then took a long drink of lemonade.

"Are you by any chance gay? I get a lot of love from the gay community on my work."

Flores found himself turning red. He laughed. "I'm straight. My mother does sculpture in her spare time. I appreciate good art."

"Ms. Miland. I'd appreciate it if you let me know if you see or hear anything that might be helpful in the case."

"Does this mean Randall is a suspect?" She frowned at him. "I can't see him doing something like this."

"Randall spent a lot of time with his grandfather. We're pursuing all leads."

"Yeah, I get it. Randall can be difficult. He's like a dog I had growing up in Alabama. A poodle and chihuahua mix. He barked at everything. Even things nobody else could hear. We called him Lil Freak. He was annoying as hell." She smiled and looked down. Flores wondered where this was going. "But one night somebody tried to jimmy open our kitchen window. Guess who woke everybody up?"

Flores liked Shayante. He found his thoughts slowing their pace, a relief from the espresso jitters he'd had when he came in.

"You share this apartment with Randall?" Flores wondered if she'd be helpful in pinning down Mulvaney's whereabouts, but he was also curious about their relationship status.

She nodded, looking almost shy. "We met at the gallery. He was very persistent. I finally gave in and we went out. Things moved fast after that."

Flores should know by now that you can't predict what people will see in each other.

As he finished off his lemonade and prepared to leave, he saw Reyna Ruiz in his mind, as she stood next to Ruiz and gave him that long, slow look.

36

Traffic was still light when Ruiz made his way down Highway 880 to downtown.

The just-risen sun burned cold and silvery through the morning haze. It made the rigid, rectangular blocks of San Jose's skyline look glowing and magical—better, he thought, than they usually looked.

He was hoping for fancy hotel coffee, maybe a sweet pastry and some insight from Christoph Schuler into his father and his family.

He found parking at a meter, which, thankfully, took credit cards. Whenever Jacky rode with him in the truck, his spare change disappeared. Ruiz breathed in the cold morning air and headed around the corner and up the steps of the Fairmont.

Christoph Schuler was waiting for him at a table in the restaurant, wearing khaki pants and a pink button-down shirt. Christoph waved him over and Ruiz joined him. The smells of sausage, bacon, pastry and coffee woke up Ruiz's stomach. When the waiter came by, Ruiz asked for coffee and a cherry danish.

"Thanks for joining me, Detective Ruiz." Christoph took a drink of his newly refilled coffee and gave him the same measured smile he'd had at yesterday's service. Under the dimmed lights of the hotel restaurant, Christoph Schuler looked younger. His graying hair looked like it had the benefit of an expensive haircut. He looked like a man who'd spent a good portion of his life in the sun, his skin bronzed. Not the kind of tan Ruiz had gotten from his years in landscaping work as a teen. The even, carefully maintained bronze for those who could afford swimming pools and beachfront property.

"Even after the service yesterday, none of this is real to me." Christoph sat back in his seat and gave him a rueful smile. "I keep expecting we'll be having our weekly phone call this weekend. 11 a.m. on Saturday. My dad never missed it."

The type of relationship Christoph had with his father seemed perfect and scripted, something you'd see on TV. Ruiz was skeptical of it. It was something he had no frame of reference for. Still, he wondered: If Karl Schuler had been such a good father, why had his son moved to the opposite side of the country?

"What was he like when you were growing up, Christoph?" Ruiz took a sip of his coffee, which was strong and full bodied, much better than he would have gotten at work this morning.

Christoph set his fork down and wiped his mouth with his napkin. "He was—*present*. I guess that is what you would call it nowadays. He worked long hours, but when he was with us, he was 100 percent with us. Whether that was him listening to us when we talked about what we were learning in school— or him loading us up in the car to take a trip down to Santa Cruz and going out to the tide pools to look at sea life with us. I can't speak for Rose, but that's what I felt. He wanted to be with us."

"Christoph, you run your own company?"

"I started my own plane maintenance company. I'm in the process of turning it over to my CEO in order to run for the senate." He looked down at his phone. "I've got a phone call with the governor in a few minutes."

"So you followed in your father's footsteps." Ruiz nodded. "And your uncle's, too. I've been reading about Hermann."

Christoph frowned as he sliced into a sausage link. "Uncle Hermann. I suppose, in some way."

"Did you know him well?"

"Of course. I went out to Florida to go to college, and he took me under his wing. At that point, he was a respected scientist in the aerospace community. He passed a lot of opportunities my way."

"He was killed in a plane crash, I read."

"He and a friend took a plane out one day. Flew down to the Keys. There was an engine failure."

"Your father must have been devastated."

Christoph Schuler laid down his fork. "My father didn't get along with Hermann."

Despite the happy photos he saw on social media whenever he logged in, Ruiz knew every family had something. Some families guarded their dysfunctions, took out the dirty things and looked at them with obsessive pride as if they were revered family treasures. He wondered if the Schulers were that way.

Christoph took a sip of his coffee and set the cup down neatly on the saucer.

"Officer Ruiz, there's something I wanted to ask you. I've read the news accounts. But you were there that night." He laid his napkin next to his plate. "I want to know. Tell me how it happened."

Ruiz told him the story, which he'd had plenty of practice telling over the past few days. Christoph asked him about the SUV, and if he'd seen the shooter or driver. He could understand Christoph wanting to know the details. He told the man about his father's last word. He'd told Rose Mulvaney. It was right to tell Christoph, too.

After listening quietly, Christoph shook his head and smiled weakly. "I can't imagine what that means, Officer. But thank you for telling me."

"Now I'd like to ask you something." Ruiz leaned forward, putting an elbow on the table. "Can you think of anyone in the family who might have had a grudge against your father?"

Christoph frowned. When the waiter came by to refill his coffee, Christoph lifted his arm off the table, and Ruiz saw the glint of gold cufflinks on his sleeve. "How could there be? No."

"What about Randall Mulvaney, Rose's son? Your nephew."

"I only know him by reputation. Other family members told me he's rude—even that he's threatened them. I've had very little contact with him."

"Can you think of anyone who might have contacted your father, maybe regarding something from his past?"

Christoph's eyes widened. He sat for a moment, then shook his head. "Not that I can think of. But then, my father lived a very long life."

Ruiz was rationing his cherry danish, taking one bite at a time. Not his usual approach, but this was a cherry danish beyond any cherry danish he'd ever had. But he had to push it aside for what he was going to say.

"Did you know that your Uncle Hermann was listed as a member of the Nazi Party?"

Christoph shifted in his seat. The measured smile on his lips disappeared.

"My father was not a Nazi." Christoph nearly spat out the words.

"I didn't say he was." Ruiz was fascinated by what was going on with Christoph, whose face had slowly turned red. The way it was contorting reminded him of the Nazi whose face melted in the *Raiders of the Lost Ark* movie.

Christoph let out a harsh laugh. "Hermann was a scientist. I can't picture him lifting his head from his research for five minutes in order to have a political discussion. If he was, it was in name only. Maybe he had to sign up in order to continue with his job."

Ruiz knew otherwise, thanks to Perry Nikolakis. The smiling, professor-like man on Rose's photo wall was a loyal member of the Nazi Party. But it wasn't his job to persuade Christoph Schuler of that today.

"Do you know about Operation Paperclip, Christoph?"

"I've heard of it." Christoph eyed him suspiciously then glanced down at his phone.

"In the early 2000s, the U.S. government declassified information from CIA files for a program called Operation Paperclip. After World War II, CIA recruited Nazi scientists and brought them over to the U.S. to work. And scrubbed their records of any involvement in the Nazi Party. Many of them committed war crimes. Experiments on concentration camp prisoners. Working prisoners from labor camps to death in rocket factories. These scientists came over to the U.S. and suddenly—they weren't Nazis anymore."

As he spoke, Ruiz saw fear in Christoph's eyes. "Christoph, your uncle Hermann Schuler and his family, including your father, came over to the United States under the Operation Paperclip program."

Christoph Schuler glared at him, brows lowered.

He raised a finger at Ruiz. "Even if this were true, it has nothing to do with my father's death. Instead of digging up rumors, you should be going after the gang members who shot my father."

His expensive suit and haircut said it. His casual references to the governor said it. Christoph Schuler was used to commanding power. Maybe that's why he was going into politics.

He looked across the table at Ruiz. His lowered voice had the threatening edge of a rusty knife.

"What you're saying is slander. I'd be very careful if I were you, Officer Ruiz."

Christoph Schuler stood up and put on his trench coat. Then he grabbed his carry on and headed out to the parking valet. Karl Schuler had seemed like a good man. His son was an arrogant ass.

Ruiz picked at the remains of his pastry and wondered what father and son possibly had to talk about in their weekly conversations.

37

R uiz poked his head over the cubicle wall at Steff Grasso, who was looking up something on her phone. It looked like she was scrolling through a list of movie times.

"Date night?" Ruiz smirked over the wall at his fellow officer, who hurriedly shut off the phone and swiveled her chair toward Ruiz. He wasn't sure if she had somebody in her life. He wasn't sure if that somebody would be male or female. He was still getting to know Grasso.

"My nephew. I'm taking him out for the night to give my sister a break." Grasso looked at him sheepishly. "He wants to see the new Marvel movie. Not that I have a problem with that. I just can't find a showing that isn't sold out."

"Want to walk up to Garcia's?"

"Of course, I do." Grasso grabbed her jacket and they headed out the back exit.

Clouds hung heavy over the valley today, a buildup to the atmospheric river event that was supposed to happen in the next couple of days. Ruiz felt the dampness creeping down his neck, up his pants legs.

You'd think days of rain would be a good thing. Droughts always seemed to threaten California, no matter how much rain fell in any given year. But these rains could be more than the dry valley could handle.

"Anything new with the Schuler case?" Grasso asked as they crossed in the crosswalk and made their way into Monte Verde's small downtown. The outdoor seating at the cafes they passed was empty, the heaters turned off and covered.

"Reyna and I went to Schuler's memorial service." Ruiz began. "And the next morning I pissed off Karl Schuler's son at breakfast."

"What did you say?"

"I told him his uncle was a Nazi scientist, which is true. And that the family came over from Germany under a CIA program that scrubbed his Nazi past."

"Well now. That's a pretty big family secret." Grasso raised her eyebrows. "Maybe he knows at some level. He just can't admit it."

Ruiz heard his stomach grumbling. "It's not that I want to expose someone as a Nazi for the hell of it. I'm looking for reasons why someone would kill Karl Schuler. If you say Karl Schuler or his uncle had anything to do with Nazis, both of Schuler's kids will deny it."

Ruiz had met with mothers of kids he'd arrested for rape or assault, amid stacks of evidence. *It wasn't him. My son's a good kid.* In the compartmentalized brain of an eighteen-year-old, he saw himself as someone who helped out mom, took care of his siblings. But he had this one annoying habit of assaulting people.

"I met up with him the morning after Karl Schuler's memorial." Ruiz zipped up his jacket as the cold wind hit him and he got smacked in the face by a few fat drops of rain. "Karl Schuler would have been awarded the Nobel Prize after that service."

They stepped up onto the curb and Garcia's loomed into view, with its faded sign and windows so covered with hand-drawn prices and images of tacos and Mexican dishes that you couldn't see out of them sitting inside. The restaurant used to be a breakfast diner until fifteen years ago, when the owner passed on and his wife sold the place. In the upscale suburb of Monte Verde, Garcia's tackiness was allowed because it was the best Mexican food within a ten-mile radius. Ruiz had seen the mayor, the police chief and local tech bigwigs eating here. If you wanted good food, you avoided the dimly lit foodie cafes and trendy spots and came to the Naugahyde booths of Garcia's.

They did what he and Grasso usually did—Ruiz stood in line and put in the order, while Grasso nabbed a booth. Grasso swore they got more beans and rice when Ruiz ordered in Spanish. Ruiz brought two plastic tumblers of iced tea back after ordering.

"Hey, how's Jacky doing?"

"He won't get off the damn computer. He's obsessed with video games."

"Yeah, me too." Grasso grinned. "What's the problem?"

"Reyna's worried that he won't do his homework. She's always worried that he's going to go off the rails."

"Video games aren't going to do that. You guys are good about limiting his screen time. Remember, he's *eight* years old—"

Ruiz shrugged. "She worries. Jacky's got good friends. She wants to keep him with the right kids."

"Video games aren't a gateway to crime." Grasso took a sip of iced tea and looked at Ruiz from over the glass. "You and Reyna doing good?"

The words seemed to come at him from nowhere. Ruiz felt himself recoiling in his seat.

"Any reason you're asking?" Though he'd tried to modulate it, his voice came out sounding nastier than he wanted.

Grasso raised her hands. "Whoa, dude. Just asking. I haven't seen her in a while, that's all."

"She's fine." Ruiz waved his hand. "Busy with work. She's the head of the PTA landscaping committee at Jacky's school."

Grasso was watching him, with what looked like pity in her eyes, though it was probably his imagination. Then he remembered the look Reyna had given Flores at the memorial service.

"I don't know how you guys do it. Keeping up the house, raising a kid, both of you guys working. The valley's a tough place."

Ruiz laughed from deep in his gut and felt better as he released a huge load of tension. "Great coming from you. You wouldn't know, would you?"

Grasso was a good sport. She laughed good-naturedly, her young, smooth face crinkling up, as she played along. "My Mercedes has been giving me nothing but problems lately. And my butler quit to take a job working for Elon Musk. My life is hard right now. Like you care."

Ruiz laughed appreciatively and gave Grasso a fist bump.

He heard his number called and went to pick up the food. He set the container with the carne asada burrito down in front of Grasso.

"Drown your sorrows, my friend."

. . .

REYNA OPENED the fridge in the back room of the dental office, took out her lunch and sat down at the round wooden table. The office had originally been a house, built in the 1950s and remodeled. This room had been a small bedroom in the house. It was now decorated sparely, with a couch, a table and chairs and a small cabinet stacked with popular magazines that had made their way from the waiting room back to the office lounge. *People, Us, Architectural Digest*—and *Golf Digest*, which Reyna had never seen anyone, employee or patient read.

The room had a view of the parking lot, a strip of four spaces at the back of the building that were tricky to maneuver into. Part of the entertainment value for staff eating lunch in the room was watching patients drive down the narrow driveway to the back then try to fit their cars into a spot. It felt mean to laugh at their predicaments, but sometimes it was funny. A stress release.

Luckily it worked out today that her break followed Tiffany's, so Reyna didn't have to worry about running into her. She didn't want to be confronted again.

As she ate her bowl of chicken salad, she leafed through the office's copy of *Architectural Digest*. The featured home today was a celebrity's in Hawaii, a large open home with an outdoor dining area near a pool. Palm trees and orange and yellow tropical flowers surrounded the dining area and a path of smooth stones led down to the pool. Reyna imagined laying out by the pool, then going over to the cool shaded dining area, where her meal would be brought to her. Far away from teeth cleaning, budget meals and cars that didn't start.

She thought about the plan again. She would make it happen. She wasn't sure when. She would have that life. She was still young. Things weren't quite in place yet. Keeping her focus on the plan kept her from being too distracted by Mario Flores. She thought of him often, remembered the touch of his hand, his strong arms and tight, fit body. She imagined what would happen if they did get together. But he was a cop, just like Jimmy. A smart cop, with an education, rich parents and more potential. Still, a cop.

That night of the shooting, she'd been in shock when she'd first met him, so his looks had been the last thing on her mind. The shooting still lived in her thoughts—surreal, horrific. It had all happened so quickly.

She finished the chicken salad and took her clementine out of the bag and used the edge of a fingernail to make a cut, then peeled the spiral off. She looked up to see if anything was going on in the parking lot. An SUV had made its way down the narrow driveway, just as a grey Hyundai had backed out, only a few feet from the window. The SUV revved its engine. It was a standoff. The Hyundai was trapped. The SUV revved insistently.

As she watched, she broke out in a sweat. It felt like it was all going to happen again. She felt the cold as she huddled in the truck with Jimmy, hearing the SUV rev then roar up behind them and swerve around them. She felt petrified. The peeled clementine sections fell from her hand.

She saw it, the SUV swerving around them. The SUV pulled into the lane next to them, cutting so close to them she screamed. Jimmy was looking straight ahead—she saw his profile. He couldn't have seen what she saw. She glanced quickly at the SUV as it passed. She saw a gun—and behind it a face. She had convinced herself that this was a young shooter. But now a face pulled into clear focus in her mind. It wasn't young. It was an old face, with gray hair. Maybe white.

Reyna's hands were shaking now. She slumped back in the chair and swallowed hard, wondering if this was the right thing to do.

She picked up her phone, weighing it in her hand for a minute. The she decided. She had to call him.

Karl Schuler's Journal
  When I used to walk Agnieszka to the bus after work in Peenemunde, I saw the work camp at a distance

  Some of the men from the work camp—Poles and Ukrainians —did maintenance and cleaning at the facility. I had felt good that the Reich was providing work for these men. When I commented on that to Agnieszka, she stared at me.

  "How can someone so smart not know this? These men are slaves. They live in hell."

  One night a few weeks after we had moved down to Nordhausen, I walked into the study, where Hermann sat puffing on his pipe, reading a technical journal.

  "What is on your mind, Karl?" Herman laid aside his reading. "You seem thoughtful tonight."

  I was afraid to ask it. As I realized later, we were being taught not to ask questions.

  "I was curious about something. The camps. I remember seeing the camp next to Peenemunde. There were facility workers living there."

Hermann pulled the pipe away from his lips and frowned.

"What about it? Most of them were criminals. People who had caused trouble. We were kind to employ them. They showed their lack of gratitude by giving the RAF information for the bombing. You saw the results of that." He raised his eyebrows as if the truth of his words were obvious.

"But what did the men do that caused them to be put in the camps?"

Hermann sat back in his chair. "They are the worst elements in our society. Poles, Jews, Ukrainians. They are not like us, Karl. If part of your body is diseased, you take medicine to root it out, so you can be well. These people are an infection that we must keep out of The Reich if we are to achieve the greatness we are destined for. We must isolate them. And in some cases, well— remove them. They will be hindrances to us if we allow them in our midst."

"I had friends in my town who were Jews. I had a friend at Peenemunde who was a Pole." I was surprised at the strength in my voice. "You can't tell me they were bad people."

Hermann let out a long sigh and gave me an amused smile. "Agnieszka Kaminski. Of course."

I'd been foolish to think that our friendship had gone unnoticed. I'd known instinctively it was something we needed to hide. When I walked her to the bus at the end of the day, we were in a crowd of workers, so I never worried. But there were the other times when we slipped away to the woods or down to the sands. Had we been seen?

"After the war, Karl, there will be a world of women waiting for you."

"I don't want them." My face burned in anger. "You know her name. Tell me where she is."

"The Polish workers could not be trusted. You know how important our work is." He was watching me to see how I was

taking this. And I was watching him. He knew more than he was saying.

"Was she sent to a camp?" My throat hurt, clogged with all the words I wanted to say. Hermann had known. He knew where she'd been sent.

Hermann's face had set in place, stony and immovable.

"You must accept what has happened, Karl."

"I can't." I said it matter-of-factly.

Hermann knew what had happened to Agnieszka. Maybe he had arranged it. In any case, I would never trust my uncle again.

Shaking, I stood up and walked upstairs to my room, where I lay awake for the rest of the night, imagining where Agnieszka could be. I pictured her walking along a country road. Looking out of the back of a truck. Riding on a train.

On her way to a country where she could be safe.

REYNA RUIZ WAS STILL at work, at the dentist's office near Rose Garden, a quaint part of San Jose filled with stucco-covered California bungalows. A neat wooden sign outside with gold script said, *Dr. Robert Hansford, DDS.*

Flores drove down the narrow side alley, carefully maneuvering the car into a narrow spot in the back parking lot. It was 5 p.m., and he wondered why Reyna Ruiz was still there, and why she'd wanted to talk to him at work. He'd taken off right after their text exchange.

Had he responded quickly because she always seemed to be lingering in his head, and he'd been all too ready to rush to her? This was business. A possible break in a hard-to-close case. He was getting dangerously close to Buckley's deadline. He had to follow this up.

As he approached the door, a tall blonde woman walked out, a large handbag over her shoulder. Her eyes blinked suddenly when she saw him, as if she recognized him. For all he knew, she was one of the ladies from Reyna's girls' night out a few days ago. He couldn't remember much from that night.

He smiled as he passed her.

The waiting area was furnished with sleek, white leather couches and a glass coffee table with neatly arranged stacks of magazines. He went up to the receptionist at the counter, an older Latina with glasses, her tiny frame drowning in blue scrubs.

"Detective Flores, here to meet with Reyna Ruiz."

The woman gave him one of those professionally polite smiles that receptionists must be given extensive training in.

"Let me take you back to the break room, Detective."

He followed her down the narrow hallway, which thirty years ago had probably led to bedrooms. And there sitting at a table that looked as if it had sat in someone's kitchen was Reyna Ruiz.

"Hello, Mrs. Ruiz." He kept his voice controlled and businesslike. "May I take a seat?"

One look at her face, and his heart pounded wildly and sweat broke out on his upper lip. Despite the commotion inside him, he calmly pulled up a chair and took a seat across the table from her. He set out his recorder between them.

The last time he'd seen her, at Schuler's memorial service, she looked dressed for a night on the town. Today she looked washed out in her pale pink scrubs. In some way, she looked more appealing today, no makeup, her hair loose and unstyled. She had a vulnerability that he wouldn't have thought was part of her personality. At the bar and at the service, she'd had a confident, playful, even aggressive vibe.

The change was intriguing. He needed to know why she was different today.

His conscience spoke to him in his sister's voice.

That's not why you're here.

He clicked to start the recording.

"Mrs. Ruiz, tell me why you called."

"It happened when I was eating my lunch in this room," she began. She nodded to the window toward the small lot behind the office, where he'd parked. "I saw something that made me think of that night on the expressway. An SUV was trying to fight a small car for a spot. The little car wouldn't move, and the SUV wouldn't back out. So the SUV sat there and revved its engine."

She bit her lip and looked back out the window. The incident could have triggered a memory of that night. These things did happen. But he couldn't help being skeptical.

"That night everything happened so quickly. But when I heard the SUV revving, I remembered something. When the black SUV sped up on New Year's— I saw somebody in the passenger side of the car."

Her hands were shaking. She picked up her water bottle and took a drink.

Flores tried to calculate the odds of this being an accurate memory. It had been late. 1:30 a.m. She'd been tired. She'd been drinking. Eyewitness accounts were notoriously faulty. If Ruiz was questioned, could he back this up? Then again, he'd been on the driver's side, probably looking ahead at the road.

He leaned across the table toward Reyna. He kept his tone impersonal, on the verge of harsh. If this was the truth, he wanted to hear all of it. No coy looks, nothing else mixed in.

"Describe to me what came back to you today. Can you picture the person you saw? Can you describe him or her?"

Reyna brushed her manicured fingers through her hair and scrunched up her eyes.

"It was a man. He had a gun. Like a rifle."

"Give me details. What about the man's age? Hair? Facial features?"

"I could tell he was an older man. He had grey hair. The light from the streetlight was shining in on him. A kind of yellow light, but I could still tell his hair was grey."

"Mrs. Ruiz, again—how many drinks did you have at the party that night?"

She turned red as if embarrassed, which also seemed unlike the Reyna Ruiz he'd met at the bar. "*One* drink."

"Your husband didn't talk about what he'd seen with you at any time since then?"

He noticed her lips twitched when he said *husband*.

"No, he did not."

"Do you remember any other details of that night?"

She shook her head. "That's all."

As he jotted notes on his tablet, the thought entered his head. Maybe she'd conveniently conjured up this memory in order to see him. The times he'd seen her, she'd telegraphed her attraction to him.

Dawn's voice again. *It's all about you, isn't it, Ro?*

"Mrs. Ruiz, there is a penalty for making a false statement regarding a criminal investigation. Are you sure you saw what you've told me?"

She tightened her lips into a pout and looked offended. "I *am* sure. I thought it was important that you know."

"Thank you for calling it in." He said it quickly, feeling now he'd accused her unfairly. Jesus, why did he care how she felt? If it was true, this moved the case in a new direction.

He tried a smile, that one he'd used to smooth things over, the one that always worked. Sure enough, she visibly relaxed,

"I want whoever did this to that old man to be caught."

He nodded. "We all do."

Flores would call Ruiz and follow up, asking if he'd remembered anything else from that night. Great if Ruiz could corroborate what his wife had noticed. Ruiz had the eyes of a cop. If he hadn't mentioned it yet, he probably didn't see it. Different people saw different angles of an incident.

"Please keep this to yourself. What you told me today. I don't want other witnesses to be influenced by your statement."

She nodded and stood up.

"Have a good evening, Mrs. Ruiz. I've got to head back downtown before traffic gets bad."

He passed the front desk, now empty, and headed out the door to the back parking lot.

As he started the car and looked behind him to back out, he saw a flash of shiny black hair turn away in the window.

39

The day's light was fading as Ruiz pulled into the parking lot at extended daycare.

It was on school grounds, so Jacky walked to the classrooms after school. Reyna had interviewed the staff, asking questions about whether there was a time and place for doing homework and what STEM opportunities they offered. Satisfied that Jacky would be sufficiently challenged, she signed him up, basically meaning the boy went to school at 7:30 and got out at 5:30—the equivalent of an adult workday.

Ruiz was conflicted about this. He didn't remember having to work so hard as a kid. Yet he also knew the trouble that he and his brother Mateo had gotten into after school on their own, as kids who wore their apartment key on a chain under their shirts.

He went in and signed Jacky out at the front desk. As soon as Jacky saw him, he came running, grabbed his backpack from the cubby and met him at the desk. Jacky was doing his bouncing thing, excited about something. His eyes had that twinkle in them, so much like his mother's, when he was preoccupied.

"Dad! I want to get the new *Forest of Nevermore* game for my DS."

Ruiz snorted. "Yeah, good to see you, too, *mijo*."

"Oh, hi." Jacky did a reset. He quickly moved into schmooze mode. "Tell me, Dad, how was your day?"

"I arrested a car thief. And filled out lots of paperwork afterwards. That's my version of homework."

"Well, that sucks."

Ruiz flashed him a stern look. "Your mom doesn't like when you use that language. You know that."

"It's not like I'm swearing or anything. Everyone says that. Most of the kids say 'shit' all the time, too. I don't."

Ruiz kept a straight face as they headed outside. It had just started to rain. Jacky ran out to the truck, still in bounce mode. He looked like a cartoon character, gangly twig legs and his mother's big, round eyes.

"Your homework done?" Ruiz asked as he clicked to unlock the doors.

"Of *course,* it is." Jacky leaped up into the truck and fumbled for the seat belt. At eight, he'd finally passed the weight limit for sitting in an actual seat without a booster and seemed to take great pride in sitting up in front instead of the truck's small second row seat. "I finish it first, before I play. They tell Mom if I don't."

They pulled out of the parking lot and headed toward Benton, which was crowded already. Ruiz crept into the intersection, then wheeled in to nab a spot. The sky was darkening, and he felt the growing chill through his jacket.

"So, Dad. *The game,*" Jacky started in. "Colin and Raj both just got it. So I need it. I have $25 saved. It costs $49.99."

"Save your allowance. You're gonna get birthday money from your *lola* in March."

Jacky let out a long sigh of annoyance. "Can't we just go to GameStop? It's on the way home. I need the game now. They're already playing it."

Their budget, which Reyna guarded fiercely, was tight. Living in the valley on their two salaries was getting harder every year. How many fellow cops had moved to the Central Valley in the past year? Every dollar was accounted for. They ate a lot of spaghetti. A lot of specials from the Asian market that Reyna knew how to make, that he hadn't grown up with. Some of which scared him a little.

"We don't have the money for it right now. You're gonna have to wait."

"I won't be able to play with my friends." Jacky began to simmer, his lower lip curling under. "Colin says we're poor."

"We're not poor." Ruiz wanted to tell him what poor was like. Going on an empty stomach, waiting for the breakfast his school provided.

He wouldn't launch into the lecture about how much harder his life had been. Or the value of waiting for something you really want. Even though the words sat on his tongue, ready to roll out. He wondered when he'd become an old person.

"Why can't we afford this one thing?"

"There's yard work to do. As long as your mother says we have the money for it, we might be able to give you some extra in addition to your allowance." He was passing this one on to Reyna. She did have a soft spot for the boy. If she felt this game would keep him hanging out with "kids who were a good influence," like Raj and Colin, she might be willing to give him the money.

"Really?" Jacky's mood swung back into the positive. "I

can do it. I can rake the leaves. I can help you fix the fence. I promise. I'll do a good job."

Based on the boy's usual reluctance to help around the house, Ruiz was skeptical.

"Let me talk to your mother. You have to work hard."

"I will, Dad. I'll do anything. For real. Please talk to her."

This could be an opportunity for the kid to learn responsibility—and for him and Reyna to enforce the rules together. Since the beginning of their marriage, they'd been two people from different backgrounds, thrown together and trying to make the best of it. They usually worked it out because they had at least one thing in common. They loved their son.

Ruiz turned onto Kiely and was paused at the light at Kaiser Drive when it happened. Jacky had just reached down to pull something from his backpack.

He heard a pop then a loud crack.

The bullet came through the passenger window at an angle and exited the windshield. At the exact level where Jacky's head had been.

"Jacky, down!" Ruiz held his son's head below the dashboard with one hand as he hit the accelerator and sped ahead.

He pulled the car into the crowded parking lot of a pet hospital, then punched 911 into his phone with shaking fingers.

FIVE MINUTES later as they pulled into their driveway, Jacky was talking fast, jittery from the experience. Ruiz sat back in his seat and took a deep breath and thanked God.

"Where did it come from? Why did somebody shoot at our car? Were they trying to kill us?" After reeling off the questions, Jacky got quiet and looked over at him from the shadows of the car, his face lit in colors from the Christmas lights still up on the eaves.

"Let's go inside. Let me talk to your mother." Ruiz's stomach had knotted up and he'd lost his appetite.

When they got inside, Jacky ran to his mother and wrapped his arms around her. Reyna looked up at Ruiz, her face drained of color, her lips pressed tightly together.

"Tell me what happened, Jimmy."

"Someone shot at us. At Kaiser Drive. One bullet through the windshield." His heart pounded as he remembered it. "Jacky was bending down to get something from his backpack."

"Was it related to Karl Schuler's shooting?" Reyna stroked Jacky's head.

Ruiz shrugged. "That's not an area known for random shootings." But then neither was the expressway by Karl Schuler's house.

Though nobody but Jacky seemed to have an appetite, Reyna brought out dinner. Arroz con Pollo, with a big kale salad that looked as appetizing as a bowl of lawn clippings. When she set down a plate of *lumpia,* Filipino egg rolls, the boy reached across the table for the plate.

"Salad first, Jacky," Reyna snapped. "Then chicken and rice. *Then* lumpia."

Jacky listlessly ate his salad, leaning his head on his hand, as he eyed the lumpia. Ruiz figured the rule applied to him, too, so he piled a heap of the salad on his plate.

He looked over at Reyna. "I want to meet with Mario Flores after dinner."

Reyna looked startled, her cheeks pink. "You're going to talk about the shooting?"

Ruiz nodded. "We could be a target because of what we

saw. The killer saw my truck that night. We have to consider it."

Jacky cleared his throat. "I ate my salad. I ate my chicken and rice. I can have lumpia now?" From the eager look on his face, he seemed to have recovered from tonight's shooting faster than his parents.

Reyna handed him the plate and he took two of the rolls, which looked like small, tightly scrolled diplomas, the kind they gave out at Jacky's kindergarten graduation.

Reyna folded her napkin on her plate and took a drink from her water bottle. She looked over at Jacky, then met Ruiz's eyes, keeping her voice down. There was a catch in her throat. "Jimmy, he could have been—"

"But he wasn't." Ruiz said firmly. "And I want to make sure this won't happen again."

40

Karl Schuler's Journal

Human beings love certainty. Give them a groove to fall into and they will. They will become calm and happy when the thinking's done for them. It's as simple as falling in line next to someone else and marching, one foot after another. As simple as singing the same song with repetitive words. That is what we did in Hitler-Jugend. There is a big comfort in seeing that everyone around you is doing exactly the same thing.

Look, we are all doing it. It must be right.

The more I have worked with teenagers who have felt lost and depressed, I realize that the Nazi plan was brilliant. Keep the youths busy as much of the time as possible, keep them marching and feeling they are part of something bigger, and you will have their souls.

Since I was older, my HJ group was older and the training more intense. It was late in the war, and the supply of soldiers was dwindling, so we were being trained to be the next wave of soldiers for the Reich. The next fodder for the war machine.

I would be destined for a different machine.

. . .

DUKE SORENSON HAD JUST SETTLED in to read the next entry in Karl Schuler's journal. He'd been staying up for the past couple of nights reading it. Karl had written this over the month of December. In his own neat, tidy print, with dates from December 14 through December 30. Karl's printing grew shakier as he'd progressed. Had he known he was going to die?

Anyone who'd reached the age of ninety-two had to sense that death wasn't far off, but Karl's writing had an urgency in it, as if he had to get something out of him because his end might come very soon.

As he read on, he'd read not only Karl's story, but Aggie's. He thought of the many times he judged Agnieszka Schuler for her coldness, how she'd seemed to keep everyone at a distance. Duke had felt cut out, judged by her reserve sometimes. He understood her better now.

He heard the doorbell ring and audibly groaned. He slipped the book under the cushion of the couch and got up.

Kathleen, his oldest child, stood at the door, wrapped in a huge red scarf. Her eyes burned with indignance.

"You *are* here. Dad, I haven't heard from you in three days. I've been worried sick. You're not answering your phone. Or text messages. Do I have to show you how to text again?" She looked past him into the house, as if suspicious of what he might be concealing.

"I haven't forgotten how to use it. I've just been busy."

She bustled past him to get inside, stripped off her gloves and set them down on the foyer cabinet. Then she went into the kitchen as if it were her own and began making coffee in his coffeemaker. He followed her in, though he wished she'd keep her visit short so he could get back to reading.

"When I don't hear from you, I worry about you. I worry you aren't eating. That you aren't taking care of yourself. It's been almost two years since Mom passed, and I worry that you're all by yourself."

"You don't need to worry, hon. I have my friends. I've been helping Karl Schuler's daughter go through fifty years of stuff in his house."

Kathleen was well meaning, but he couldn't help but feel that he was her pet; she had to spend a certain amount of time with him, take him for a walk and make sure his dog dish was full of water and kibbles.

He enjoyed his kids best when he could just have adult conversations with them.

After spooning coffee into the filter and flipping the switch, Kathleen turned to him, her eyes wide.

"Dad, I'm so sorry, I forgot about Karl. How is Rose? How's the family?"

The Schulers and the Sorensons had spent time together as families, starting from the days Duke and Karl worked together. Kathleen and her sisters and brothers had come to think of Rose and Christoph as aunt and uncle, and Karl and Aggie as grandparents.

"I saw everyone at the service yesterday. Rose and Christoph, the grandkids. Rose is trying to work as hard as possible at cleaning out his house. Probably so she doesn't have to think about losing him."

"Sounds about right," Kathleen said briskly. She poured cups of coffee for each of them and brought them into the living room. "I'm not sure how I'd react if I lost you. Mom was hard enough. But Karl—I can't imagine Rose dealing with the fact he was murdered."

Duke didn't need coffee, especially not this late in the afternoon. But it seemed important to Kathleen to make it for him, and he was grateful he had children who wanted to spend time with him. He settled into his seat on the couch and reached for the mug.

"The fellow who saw it happen—James Ruiz. He's a police officer. A real nice guy. He and his wife, they said the SUV waited on the side of the road for Karl to pull out, then sped ahead of them and shot him."

"There's a lot of crazy people out there on New Year's." Kathleen took a sip of coffee, got a sour look on her face, then went to rummage through his fridge for creamer. He got the feeling she wasn't crazy about Costco bulk coffee.

"San Jose is getting more dangerous every year. Could it have been a group of kids? The news said something about gang activity."

Duke shook his head. "I've been thinking about this all week and haven't come up with anything."

Kathleen unwound the scarf from her neck and settled into the armchair as if she were here to stay. "It's hard for me to see why anyone would want to kill a man like Karl."

Through the cushion on the couch, Duke felt the firm shape of the journal under his thigh.

"You can't know everything about someone." He wondered if he should tell Kathleen. He felt the need to take the burden off of himself by sharing what he'd read. "People don't share all of their stories."

Kathleen's eyes narrowed and she leaned forward in her chair. "What an interesting thing to say. Do you know something about Karl you're not telling me?"

He didn't know if he should tell her. What would Karl have wanted? Karl's journal entries could be misunderstood. Maybe they were why he was dead.

"I found something Karl wrote. I believe he wanted it to be found. About his early life in Germany, in Hitler's time."

Her face brightened. She was obviously eager to hear more. "I always wondered if that Uncle Hermann of his was a Nazi."

"Karl saw a lot of things working with Hermann. He wanted to talk about them, but I think he couldn't bring himself to do it. Maybe that's why he waited so long. Maybe he was afraid he'd be thought of as a Nazi, too."

"What if he was a Nazi?"

Duke frowned. "Karl? Would that change your opinion of him now?"

Kathleen looked down into her coffee. "My husband is Jewish. My kids are half Jewish. They're still finding old men who worked as guards at the concentration camps when they were young. There are organizations who hunt them down, and I think that's right. What they did was mass murder. There has to be a consequence for these things. Or it will happen again."

Duke started to feel queasy. It didn't make sense with what he knew about Karl Schuler—a good man as long as he'd known him—that he would have willingly participated in any of the activities of the Third Reich.

"He was young then," Duke said, trying to picture the teenaged version of Karl in the journal. "I can't imagine it—"

Kathleen set her coffee down. She sounded firm, as if the matter was settled. "Karl had a life before he came to the U.S. He's responsible for his actions."

Duke reached for his coffee and noticed his hand was shaking. If it was true that Karl had been a Nazi, like his uncle had been, somebody may have come looking for him. But had that someone known all that Karl had done—all the lives he'd touched for good?

"What about forgiveness." His voice came out sounding raspy, dry. "What good would it do for Karl to be punished for something he might have done seventy-five years ago?"

He wouldn't give up the book now. He couldn't show Kathleen. He'd wait till she left. He had a few more entries to read.

If Karl had changed into someone who could do evil in his youth, couldn't he change into someone who could do good as an adult?

Duke needed to know the whole story of Karl Schuler.

After returning to the station and writing up his notes, Flores put in a call to Crime Scene, to see if they'd managed to find any prints or salvage any of the items found in the burned SUV.

Nobody answered. He left a message.

Time was ticking. He had one more day to find Schuler's killer. Or hand the whole thing over to Jesperson.

Feeling desolate and unusually introverted, he decided to grab some food then drive down the expressway to check the area where Karl Schuler had been killed.

In the dusk, streetlights were turning on. He drove back to Willow Glen. Lincoln Avenue was still lit by white Christmas lights wound around the trees along the street. When he saw the fronts of familiar restaurants, he realized how hungry he was.

It was Thursday evening, an early start to the weekend. Parked cars lined the street bumper to bumper. He found a spot on a residential side street and parked the Prius. Then he headed back to Lincoln Avenue to see what he could find without too much of a wait.

In a hipster fast-food place, he ordered a burger with Korean toppings and garlic fries. No woman in his life right now, so it didn't matter if his breath reeked. He took a table close to the order pickup counter to wait and decided to make a call. The voice picked up after two rings.

"What's up, booger face?"

"Hey, Dawn. Nice to hear your voice, too."

"You never call me. You must want something."

"I wanted to talk to you. Is that so wrong?"

"Hold on—Em is talking to me at the same time. She's making dinner for Sam."

Dawn's partner had a six-year-old who had recently been diagnosed with autism. From what he heard from Dawn, meals were stressful times, a confrontation with Sam's sensory issues.

"Okay, I'm back. Apparently mac and cheese is what's for dinner. Again. Super excited."

Flores laughed. "I'm waiting for my Kobe beef bulgogi burger right now."

"And I *hate* you."

"You want to give me some advice?"

"Is it about a woman?"

Flores let out a fake cough. "Why would you think that?"

"Because it's always a woman."

"In this case, it's a witness to a crime I'm investigating. I can't get her out of my head. She seems to think the same about me." He told her about Reyna Ruiz, editing a few of the facts out to make himself look better.

Dawn let out a groan. "Of *course,* she likes you, pretty boy. Wrap up the case, then start dating her."

"It's not that easy."

"Married?"

He was silent.

"Don't be an ass, Ro."

"She's not like anybody I know. She's a dental hygienist. She's beautiful and—really different than anyone I've been with. I can't stop thinking about her."

"Did you learn nothing growing up with Mom and Dad? That kind of thing messes up families. She probably has a kid."

Dawn's words hit him in the chest.

"And her husband's a cop."

"You didn't need my advice, Ro. You know what to do. Don't do it."

"I guess I wanted—"

"You wanted me to say something to make you feel better about yourself? To say I understand and it's good to let you feel what you're feeling?"

"Yeah." His voice sounded weak and small. Like he was twelve again.

"You're one of those guys who actually thinks about things. You're better than this, Ro."

He saw his burger and fries wrapped and bagged at the pickup counter. He wanted to eat by himself, watch the Warriors game and sulk. He wondered why he'd bothered calling.

"Still love me, Dawn?"

"Love you, Ro. Enjoy your delicious burger." She made exaggerated weeping sounds and then hung up.

HE WALKED down the avenue toward his car, bag in hand, as he thought about Reyna's description of the passenger in the SUV. If her description was correct, this changed things. This hadn't been a group of young gang members.

Uncharacteristically, he didn't give a fuck tonight

whether the garlic fries stunk up his nice, clean car. He opened the bag and picked at them absently with his non-driving hand as he navigated side streets approaching the expressway. He entered the expressway on the side going against traffic.

In a few minutes he'd approached the site of the shooting. There was the yellow streetlight, casting its sickly light on the asphalt. He pulled the Prius off to the shoulder and sat for a moment, orienting himself.

From Ruiz and Reyna's descriptions, he was approximately at the spot where the SUV would have been idling, waiting for Karl Schuler's car. He pictured the SUV revving, then imagined the Camry pausing at the stop sign, about to turn onto the expressway.

At this point, according to Reyna Ruiz, the unknown, grey-haired man was sitting in the front passenger seat.

To his right, there was the cement retaining wall, intended to block the expressway noise from the backyards of the housing development.

He turned off the engine and got out of the car and began walking along the retaining wall. The mud sucked at his shoes, and he regretted he'd worn good shoes to work today. Avoiding the puddles from yesterday's rain, he walked to within about ten yards of the lamp post. Close to the view Reyna Ruiz had that night.

Tall eucalyptus trees, their bark looking slashed and peeled as if vandalized, leaned toward the road. As he walked over the strips of peeled-off bark, he noticed something amid the tree debris. He kicked with his foot until he saw a piece of muddy paper rise to the surface—printer paper folded in half, then in half again. He reached for his wallet, and pulled out a receipt, which he used to carefully pick up the paper.

He followed the retaining wall to the cross street Karl Schuler had entered from, examining the ground along the way. Footprints, a hubcap, and a few beer cans.

After he'd reached the corner of the side street, Flores stood for a while, trying to picture in his mind Karl Schuler's Camry waiting, then turning left onto the expressway. He pictured Ruiz and Reyna approaching the intersection in the Ford F-150, passing the SUV on the shoulder, and hearing it rev, then seeing it race past them and swerve toward the Camry so the person in the passenger seat could shoot.

He'd been suspicious of Reyna's sudden recollection of the event today, but the brain processed traumatic events in a way that wasn't necessarily linear. What she'd seen in the parking lot could have been part of that process.

The shaken, vulnerable Reyna he'd met with today could have been telling the truth. He began to think about what she'd seen—and in what direction it might take the case.

AS HE FOLLOWED the expressway back to Willow Glen, his phone rang. Flores saw his dad's number displayed on his Prius Bluetooth screen.

He wasn't sure why he answered. Maybe it was nostalgia after his talk with Dawn. A hazy longing for family time that hadn't ever been that great, except his and Dawn's childhood together, in which they had pledged to be allies against their parents' dysfunction.

Maybe he was tired and his defenses were down. In any case, Flores hit answer. It was a mistake.

"Mario, Dad here. How're you doing? We've been

following your big case. The scientist who got shot on New Year's. It's been on the news here."

Flores tensed up, steeling himself.

"On the news in LA?"

"They showed a clip of you at the press conference. We recognized you." Flores didn't know if *we* meant he and his mother or he and whatever woman he happened to be with.

"What was the story?"

"It was about how people are losing faith in the police. They showed people protesting that your police department is understaffed."

More reinforcement for his parents' opinion of his chosen profession.

His dad called out to someone in the background, who started laughing.

"But I tell people my son isn't just any policeman. He's got an expensive education, which we paid for. He even got accepted to law school, but he decided to be a policeman instead. Isn't that right, son?"

His laugh sounded like he'd had a few drinks. This conversation was being broadcast for the benefit of somebody with him on the other end of the line.

Flores's finger hovered over the Hangup button. He watched the lights of Willow Glen pull into view, refracted through the drops of rain on his windshield.

"Is mom there?"

Flores heard music and mumbling in the background. Glasses clinking.

"What? No. I'm not home right now."

"Say hi to her for me, when you see her."

He pulled onto Lincoln Avenue and felt a warm feeling, like he was approaching home. A moth heading home to its soft, comforting flame.

Before his dad could say anything else, Flores ended the call.

s Ruiz stepped down from the truck, he saw Flores's Prius, black and shiny, like an eco-friendly Batmobile.

It was parked in one of the angled spots in front of Someplace Bar & Grill.

When Ruiz told him about the shot through his windshield, Flores said he'd meet him in twenty minutes. He'd beaten him here.

The bar was busy tonight. He spotted cops he knew, clustered in groups in battered captain's chairs around a couple of the low tables. A redheaded female officer from SJPD that he knew vaguely sat at the bar with friends.

His eyes scanned the tables. Flores sat at a high table by himself, hunched over his phone, a beer in front of him. His posture and body language told him the guy had had a hard day.

As Ruiz approached the bar, Tara began pouring him a Modelo without him having to ask for it. Ruiz carried it over to the table and took the stool across from Flores. He turned to keep the door in sight. He was still on edge.

"Thanks for coming." Ruiz nodded at Flores. "You got here fast."

"I can't believe this happened to you and Jacky." Flores rubbed his eyes. He frowned at him, concerned. "He's okay?"

"He was bending down to get something out of his backpack when it happened. He was scared but got over it pretty quick. Reyna and I haven't."

Ruiz looked around the table for chips, out of habit, then realized he didn't want any. "I reported the shot. Not that it will do much good."

"Whoever killed Schuler would know your truck." Flores's eyes looked bleary. "Any idea where the shot came from?"

"My guess is from the apartment complex to the right of us on Kiely—the roof or second story, judging by the angle. It's the route we take back from Jacky's school."

"If it's the same person who shot Karl Schuler, you were lucky tonight."

"This can't happen again. You need to solve the damn case, Mario."

It shot out of Ruiz's mouth like trash talk. When it was out, he was surprised by the amount of anger behind it. He had no control over how the case was being conducted, yet his family almost took a big hit tonight.

Flores looked up at him, his eyes wide. He took a gulp of beer and began tearing a line of fringe along the edge of his cocktail napkin.

"I've got a theory I'm working on right now. I need you to tell me one more time, Jimmy. When the SUV passed you on New Year's, could you see anyone in the driver or passenger seat?"

Ruiz pushed the beer away from himself. He tried to calm down and go back to that night one more time, which required some mental discipline, because he was fucking tired of thinking about it. He pictured everything that happened after he first saw the SUV, as if he were going through a scene in a video step by step, pressing pause and examining each frame. As it rolled by in his mind, he told Flores what he saw.

Flores had pulled out his iPad and was making notes. When Ruiz had finished with his account, Flores set the iPad down.

"You didn't see the person on the passenger side?"

Ruiz took a drink of his beer. The distance between the two of them seemed big right now. This was a very different meeting than they'd had last week.

"I was focused on the SUV itself, making sure it didn't hit us."

"You didn't see the passenger or driver?"

Why was he asking again? He'd given a statement that night. "I was focused on the SUV. I couldn't have seen the driver. I saw there was someone in the passenger seat, but by the time I looked, the SUV had sped ahead of us."

A whoop and cheers rippled through the bar. Tara turned up the volume on the TV over the bar, just as the Warriors scored. Suddenly all heads were turned toward the screen.

Ruiz glanced up at the screen briefly. The game was the last thing on his mind tonight. Neither he nor Flores joined in the cheers. Flores had another gulp of beer. He seemed to be downing it at a fast rate tonight.

"I pulled off on the expressway late this afternoon. I walked the shoulder, to where you showed me the SUV was idling."

"Find anything?"

"A printout for an Airbnb rental confirmation in San

Jose—a house in Dry Creek. I drove past it on the way here. The email confirms two bookings—one for December 23-26, then one for New Year's Eve."

Ruiz shrugged. "You have no idea if that has any bearing on the case."

"I called the host before you came in. She's looking up the name. But she remembered it was someone who flew in regularly from Florida."

Ruiz slapped the table and stared at Flores. "Where's your damn phone?"

Flores took out the phone and made the call, under Ruiz's watchful eye.

AT 6 A.M. THE next morning, Flores got responses from the airlines about his request for flight dates for Christoph Schuler.

Christoph Schuler had flown in on American to San Jose International from Miami at 12:54 p.m. on December 23. Then he'd flown back on December 26.

Another flight into San Francisco on December 31 and a return on January 2.

Then on January 6, a flight into San Jose on Delta—via a connection in Salt Lake City. No return flight was listed. He could be in San Jose right now.

While he'd been interviewing the grieving Rose Mulvaney, Christoph Schuler had been in San Jose—at an Airbnb a few miles away. Rose hadn't mentioned him. She had also made a big deal about how her brother and family back east had to make preparations to fly in for the memorial.

The Airbnb printout had been his. And he'd found it right where the SUV had been idling.

Then there was Reyna's testimony—which he was beginning to believe, with the discovery of the Airbnb confirmation. An older, grey-haired man had been in the SUV's passenger seat.

Christoph Schuler was now a suspect in the murder of his own father.

43

Karl Schuler's Journal
After our conversation about Agnieszka and the camps, my interactions with Hermann changed.
Hermann was a teacher and couldn't help himself; so that part of our relationship remained. With a new distance and sternness, he continued to teach me what he knew and what I loved: the science of flight.

One morning he announced that he was taking me with him to Mittelwerk today. Dr. Von Braun had told Hermann that he had been impressed with me.

The brilliant Wernher Von Braun had thought I was smart, and he had mentioned it to my uncle. I craved that validation, from both Hermann and Dr. Von Braun.

But from the moment Hermann and I arrived, the atmosphere at Mittelwerk seemed different. The cavernous facility still bustled with the energy of production, the clank of steel and the drone of machinery. But there was a smell, that strong smell of something rotten, hanging thickly in the air. When I asked Hermann, he said it was the workers. There were *so many workers here—unwashed, unclean Poles, Italians and French. The stench of the workers was the cost of such an operation.*

Today I turned my eyes from the manufacturing of the huge rocket forms to the line leader who oversaw the operation. Quiet voices, supervisors looking at each other, expressions of grim concern. A supervisor took Hermann aside and talked anxiously. A supervisor ran up to the office and went inside, his face lined and pale. Something was not right. Pressure from Der Fuhrer to increase production, perhaps.There was nothing official in the news about the war, other than the push to give more. Nearly everyone whispered it: the allies were winning. But the message to all Germans was the same as I'd received in Hitler-Jugend: more is required. We need more of you. More sacrifice.

Late in the afternoon, the voices and looks changed. A decision had been made. Supervisors looked relieved. The young supervisor who always tried to act as if he was much older than me walked out of the office and approached my uncle. They talked, and my uncle nodded. And in that moment something lifted. Soon my uncle was laughing at something one of the scientists said to him. A group of supervisors gathered together and began talking, nodding and smiling. A couple of the men walked out of the entrance, one of them holding a pack of hard-to-find cigarettes.

When the young supervisor passed by, I asked if he could tell me what happened. I addressed him as Herr and tried to act naive and in awe of him. He looked around quickly.

"The workers. They demanded changes in their conditions. They revolted. We had to take action to stop it. But don't worry. Everything is fine now, mein Junge."

At the end of the day, Hermann had finished his meetings and waved me over. A strange silence hung over the factory. As we prepared to leave, I turned to look out over the operation, and I saw that a crane had been wheeled into place in the center of the cavern. It stood with its top extended, centered in the work area as if it was meant to be seen. Yet no one seemed to be looking at it. I squinted, trying to figure out why it looked so odd.

Hung upon the crane, swinging in the dim light, were the bodies of eight workers, their heads tilted unnaturally, like children's rag dolls hung on a clothesline.

DUKE RUBBED his eyes and closed the journal.

Karl's descriptions of the conditions at the Mittelwerk plant were painful to read, and Duke's endurance was wearing thin. It was time to take a break.

Last year, he'd started a garden on his small back patio. He'd never had much luck growing things. That had always been Joanne's specialty. But after years of caring for her, he was in the habit and felt the need to tend something. He bought a lemon tree and replanted it to a large pot. He bought some pink impatiens because Joanne had loved them. And lots of succulents, because a lady at the senior center had said they were hard to kill.

The skies were darkening as he stepped out of the sliding glass door and poked around the garden. The succulents were doing well, and he topped them off with a little water, careful not to give them too much, in case the predicted rain came. Two small lemons hung on the tree, not a huge crop, but with his level of gardening expertise, he was proud.

He got the call while sweeping leaves out the back gate of the patio. He considered letting it ring—something he was incapable of doing—then set aside the broom and ran into the house.

When the display announced it was Rose, he felt uneasy.

"Good morning, Rose."

"Duke, I seem to be missing something after our cleaning the day before yesterday. It's an old book, nothing special, but it had a lot of sentimental value to me. The binding is old —black cloth."

Duke paused for a bit, to appear to think about it. "I don't remember seeing a book like that."

"I have no idea where it could have gone." Rose said, her voice sounding like a challenge to confess. "I remember putting it in the living room bookshelf. You didn't take it from there, did you?"

"No, I just took the boxes you told me to," Duke lied.

"You said you were interested in his technical journals. Could it have been in the stack of books you took for yourself?"

"Let me check." Duke set the phone down, then walked back and forth across the kitchen loudly, as if he were running off to look for the book. Then he came back to pick up the phone.

"Rose?" He added a little bit of breathlessness to his voice. "I looked through the books I took from Karl's place. I don't see it here."

He heard Rose sigh heavily over the phone.

"I'll check with Salvation Army then. You took the book boxes to the truck on Redmond, right?"

"That's right."

"I'll stop by and ask. If it turns up later, please let me know. Right away."

"Will do, Rose."

Duke hung up, feeling conflicted. Now he'd lied to cover

up stealing. What else would he do? He didn't want to give the book back. He wanted to finish it.

He was the right person to have the book. He knew Karl. He knew him better and would judge him more fairly than anyone else. Maybe more than Karl's children.

Something stronger than his conscience told him. Giving the book back to Rose would be a bad idea.

44

T hat morning, the threatened rains descended on the valley.

Water puddled in street corners and potholes, flooding drains still clotted with leaves from the fall. Weather reports were warning that the atmospheric river was here, a multi-day rainstorm.

At this rate the Guadalupe River would rise to levels that would threaten nearby houses and businesses. After yearly threats of a drought, San Jose would now be overwhelmed with an excess of rain. Low-lying Highway 880, with its potholes and dips, would flood. Flooded areas would either close or cause long backups, as cars slowly made their way through inches of standing water.

Avoiding the freeway, Flores headed for a short cut he'd found, down Southwest Expressway and onto side streets leading into downtown. He passed city workers in orange raincoats using pumps to clear a drain blockage at a corner.

He'd been an outdoor kid used to biking and skateboarding every day. Any day without sun—and there were a lot of them here— made him feel out of sorts. The clouds were thick and grey today, and it felt as though they were oppressing him personally. Dawn would make fun of him if she'd been privy to his thoughts this morning, rolling her eyes at his feeling that the universe was plotting against him. But it sure felt like that. He might have gotten a break today, but the case was moving slowly.

On top of that, Oksana had come by last night to pick up her *Hamilton* CD and a makeup case she'd left under the sink. She was in a big hurry because her precious fucking Tim was downstairs in the car.

He pulled into the station parking lot into the nearest spot he could find close to the entrance. He'd get wet, that was a given. He covered his head with a magazine, grabbed his take-out latte and made a run for it.

When he got to his desk, Mandy passed by with coffee and a stack of paperwork, an odd look on her face. She raised an eyebrow.

"There someone to see you at reception. Says her name is Reyna."

Something like fireworks went off in his stomach, then shot up his digestive tract, so that when he thanked Mandy it sounded like someone had their hands around his throat.

As he walked downstairs, a feeling of inevitability swept over him, like a dark veil. Fate. A ship headed for him, like in some World War II submarine movie he'd watched with his dad years ago. Proceeding at full speed, estimated time of contact five minutes. He felt he was biding his time until the point of contact. He would go down.

He knew he would.

It was as if the past week was preparation for this. All signs had been leading up to this and he could not redirect at this point. Every thought he'd had, every image that had come into his mind over the past seven days, had led him to this. He could not avert course. He could only wait to see what would happen when impact happened.

His feet led him to the front reception, one foot after the other, with a sureness that amazed him. Energy coursed through his legs, as he remembered it did at the opening shot of his first marathon during college. Muscles taut, yet loose and ready.

She sat with her bag slung over her shoulder, her legs crossed as she looked down at her phone, her black hair swept to one side and falling onto her shoulder. Her bare, muscular legs peeking out from her tight skirt were light brown and smooth. When she looked up at him, she smiled in a way that made his heart pound. An irrepressible happiness welled up in him. The darkness of this, his next-to-last day on the case, was lifting.

There was promise glowing, hidden right behind the warm tan skin and soft smile of this woman.

He remembered standing at the top of a hill in his neighborhood, twelve years old, one foot on his skateboard, looking down to the tree-lined street below—that instant before he started the descent. His friends watched, in awe that he was attempting this.

The anticipation, that moment of hanging on the edge, then the release, his stomach dropping with the initial takeoff.

"My car's in the back," he said with a nod. Even then, he said it casually. As if it was an offer and she could still say no. And in his mind, if she did say no, he would be relieved.

She stood up and smiled, her eyes suddenly wide, soft and brown. He felt so connected to her now. He could feel her eyes on his face.

Every time she took a breath, he felt it.

· · ·

"I DIDN'T ASK you what you wanted." He looked straight ahead as he drove the Prius through the rain, taking the side streets again, avoiding the freeway. He headed south, toward Monterey Road.

"What do you think I wanted?"

"To see me."

She let out a laugh. "You're pretty full of yourself."

"You're pretty brazen."

"That means what—you think I'm a slut?"

Worried, he turned to assess her expression and saw that she was laughing.

"I would never use that language, ma'am. Not about you."

He was off script now. He had no idea what was going to happen. It was terrifying, yet there was a freedom in that. As if he was a kid playing in the sun again, no responsibilities to anyone but himself.

They continued down Monterey Road until the scenery changed from suburban to rural. Not far from the field off Watsonville Road and the burned SUV. Fir and eucalyptus trees, grassy fields, turned bright green from the rains. He opened his window and as a splat of rain hit his face, he sucked in the cool, fragrant air.

"Jimmy told me you were upset about the shooting the other night. Sorry that happened. I'm just glad Jacky's okay—"

"I don't want to talk about Jimmy."

He felt the sharpness in her voice, a slap across his face. He went quiet, as they drove past houses with big, rambling yards and fenced off farms with big, slow cows.

"How do you feel about Morgan Hill?"

"I know a good taqueria."

· · ·

FIFTEEN MINUTES LATER, they were eating big, sloppy tacos at a sticky formica counter, served to them on plastic plates by a large chef with a broken nose. Flores couldn't remember tacos tasting this good, strips of barbacoa slathered with fresh guacamole and tomatoes. They finished off two each, then Flores laid a twenty on the counter and they headed back to the car.

After buckling up, he turned to her and moved toward her tentatively, then backed off. They couldn't do this. Not here.

As he started the car again, she rested her hand on his thigh, and he felt like his groin was on fire.

With laser focus he managed to keep the car pointed forward, following Monterey Road until they came to a stretch that used to be the thoroughfare for tourists headed over Highway 152 to the coast. The motels here were fallen from the grace of their heyday in the 1950s. Signs proudly announced air-conditioned rooms and TVs. He imagined the drug deals and the tricks that took place in these rooms.

He pulled into the potholed parking lot of one that looked in better condition than the rest, and looked around cautiously, scoping out the area. Parolees, delinquents, meth users. All the bad guys. What you'd find scurrying around if you lifted a rock and looked underneath.

"Do you feel comfortable waiting here while I go inside?"

Again, he said it clearly, telegraphing that if she wanted to back out of this, she should say so. Though this was something he'd wanted for the past week, he would have been relieved if she said no and told him to drive her back to San Jose. She didn't.

"I'm fine, Mario. I can take care of myself."

He came back with a key within five minutes, and they

followed the whitewashed, wrought-iron-railed stairs to room 202.

The room smelled of mildew, but that faded to the back of his mind as soon as she started unbuckling his belt.

He unbuttoned her silk top, spotting with interest the skull tattoo above her left breast. She took off her bra and there she stood, as good or better than he'd imagined her this past week. He felt that top-of-the-street-on-his-skateboard feeling again.

She led him to the bed, and he bent over her, unable to stop looking at her. She closed her eyes and he put a hand between her legs. She looked up at him with an expression, half mysterious, half mischievous. He lay down over her, pressing insistently till he was inside. Something like the last chorus of a rock song pounded in his head and he was on his skateboard, flying down the road toward the dip, in an arc that he didn't want ever to end, yet he did very much want to end.

He felt himself release in her, but drove in again, going with the momentum, then he pulled out as gently as he could and lowered himself down on his side next to her.

He didn't know exactly how long they lay there, but at some point he became aware of sounds that he must have blocked out in the excitement of being alone with her. He heard pounding on a door a few rooms down. Creaking bedsprings and moans next door. Voices in the parking lot, somebody letting out a cat-like wail. The sounds of an ambulance siren speeding by, going down in pitch as it passed.

The 1980s-era digital clock read 12:45 p.m.

Now that his primary brain was engaged again, he realized he had a meeting at 2. He reached for his pants to find his phone. He'd have messages needing answers by now. He was laying the foundations of a case against Christoph Schuler. He was careful with his documentation, assembling the pieces needed for the future court case. It was one of his favorite aspects of police work. If he was fortunate, the reports he needed would be there by the time he got back.

If not, the day would go bad fast. A meeting with Buckley, a good-bye speech to the team.

"Hon, I gotta get back."

She raised her head sleepily, an amused look on her face. "You called me *hon.*"

Her eyes were half open and her hair swept messily to one side, rippled like ocean waves. That unprotected, uncomposed look he always preferred over styled, blow dried and made up.

"Does the word bother you?"

She held his face and leaned over him to press her lips against his. Her breath smelled like vanilla. Her breasts pressed against him, which began to get him excited again.

He returned the kiss, but turned away from her, which he made up his mind to do, and reached down to find his clothes. Slowly, she got up, wrapped the sheet around her and headed for the bathroom.

AFTER A QUIET RIDE through the rain, driving as fast as he safely could back to San Jose, Flores dropped Reyna off at her car on a side street, not far from the station. A small river was forming next to the curb by her car. After she buckled up, she reached for his hand. He kissed it furtively, then glanced around.

"I need to see you again." He almost hissed it. It came

out of his mouth like an order, and he didn't know where that came from. "Can you get away tonight?"

"I will call you if I can, Mario."

She smiled and closed the door, picking up her phone.

That's when it hit him. A sick feeling in the pit of his stomach.

He was one of the bad guys.

45

K arl Schuler's Journal
The human mind is capable of amazing feats of self-deception.

If you are in a situation that is unconscionable, it is almost too easy for your mind to contort itself to see the situation as normal, in order to cope. You tell yourself lies every day to maintain that normality. Eventually you lose your bearings entirely: what is horrible and evil begins to look right to you.

After my first meeting with Dr. Von Braun, I gradually spent more of my time at Mittelwerk. I knew the place well. I was given more responsibility than I should have had for someone so young. I was the favored one, the one who understood the operations and the science behind the V2 rockets and V1 flying bombs. Even that young supervisor, who had demanded my respect because he was a year older than me, now listened to me. Even took orders from me.

The workers, brought in from the nearby Mittelbau-Dora camp, lived and worked in subhuman conditions in the tunnels. They worked 14 hours at a time, were fed very little and their work was incredibly dangerous. One third of the slave laborers

died in the tunnels. The first workers had been made to dig
tunnels with their bare hands, because of fears that tools would
turn to weapons in a revolt.

At the end of a few months in Mittelwerk, I had made a subtle
shift in my thinking. I had begun to think of the inmates simply
as units of work that could be devoted to making the rockets.
More workers, working more hours, meant more rockets. These
rockets had become my new love. Agnieszka, for all I knew, was
dead, and it hurt too much to think of her.

But I saw the rockets every day. They were stunningly
beautiful to me, an invention that had pushed the limits of flight.
And we Germans had created them.

So when the workers revolted and committed acts of sabotage
because of their inhumane conditions, I was one of those signing
orders for them to be hanged.

I had sunk to the point that I thought that their deaths would
be a warning to others to continue working. Production of the
rockets could not lag.

It was not until after the war, as Hermann, his family and I
waited in Bavaria for the Americans to come to us, that I woke
up. I began having nightmares. I saw the emaciated faces. I saw
the men, disfigured and broken, continuing to dig with skeletal,
clawlike hands in the darkness of the cavern and its tunnels. The
faces haunted me then. They haunt me now.

All I had done in Mittelwerk was evil: I had condemned to
death people labeled as untermenschen. I had put my stamp of
approval on the orders and values of the Reich. Yet the CIA
program that brought us to America erased this record of my and
my uncle's past—so the U.S. could recruit us and claim our
scientific expertise before the Russians did.

This clean slate seemed like a gift at first. My guilt was
blotted out in the eyes of the world, my family, my employers. I
looked good to everyone, a war refugee, like so many of that time.

But there was a stain deep inside me. I knew what I had done. It was there, dark and weighty, ever before me.

I decided I would wipe that stain out myself. From the moment I came to the United States, I would balance what I had done with only good. I would find the poor, the immigrants, the ones who had fallen by the wayside. The ones with little opportunity or hope. I would help students by encouraging them to study math and science, making sure they got the help they needed.

It made me feel good to see these people benefit from my help. They bloomed like flowers around me. The students saw what they were capable of doing when they cared about something. When someone said, Yes, you can do this.

YET NO MATTER HOW *much I did, the darkness was still deep inside me. I could taste it like bile. And it never left me.*

Five years before I retired, a Frenchman came into my office and shut the door. His father had died in Mittelwerk. He'd gone back to Germany, and he'd seen the documents with my name. And the tie to my uncle Hermann, which as time went by, anyone could look up to verify.

The anger flared in me at this employee, but I kept calm. That man in the documents could not be me, I explained easily, reasonably. There had to have been a mix-up with identification. I had no part in this, I told my company's management. The Frenchman lost his job and eventually his marriage and returned to France.

Everyone had believed me.

"NO SCREEN TIME till I see that your homework is done, *mijo.*"

At some point, Jacky had sneaked into the kitchen and sat down at the computer desk. His hand was busily moving the mouse around.

"I'm looking something up. For my *homework*." The boy said it with the righteous indignation of the falsely accused. But when Ruiz stood up, he could see a helmeted warrior on the screen, with a baggage list of weapons and treasures. The kid earned the money for his game. Now he couldn't stay off it.

"Off. *Now.* If you aren't off in five seconds, no computer till the weekend." Ruiz looked at his phone and calmly began the countdown. Jacky scrambled to shut down the game, click exit, and run away from the desk.

"Bedtime in one hour. Bring out your homework when it's finished, so I can check." Ruiz went over to the computer to shut it down. He didn't use it often. He had enough time on the computer at work. Reyna spent her time on Facebook and watching makeup and decorating videos. With the new game, Jacky had been pushing for computer time whenever he could get it.

They both made him feel old. He saw the computer for work, not for entertainment.

After peeking into Jacky's room to make sure he was at his desk working on his social studies, Ruiz went into the kitchen to clean up. Reyna had left them chicken and pasta to heat up. Afterwards he'd tossed everything into the sink to clean up later.

PTA meetings lasted till 9, so he usually waited till the last minute to clean up and load the dishwasher. A bit of rebellion on his part, since he disliked doing it.

He rinsed the plates and silverware. Then scrubbed the Tupperware containers and loaded them into the dishwasher on the top rack, lids on the side, the way Reyna preferred.

Reyna liked things done a certain way. It had taken them a while to work that out, which meant he learned to pick up after himself after ten years of living on his own. And he learned to never leave dishes in the sink. He knew the look on Reyna's face; her nostrils flared, her lips tightened.

But it all worked out to his benefit. The house was always spotless, unlike the apartment he'd grown up in, which smelled like mold and unwashed dishes piled up. Coming home every night, his house was clean and orderly, the perfect place to be after a day of dealing with difficult and broken people. His refuge, thanks to Reyna. When he thought about it, he felt stupid griping about doing cleanup.

After starting the dishwasher, he looked through the cupboards to see if the chips were still in the salad spinner. It was his own personal challenge—like searching for drugs in a perp's house. He pulled out the spinner and took off the lid. Nothing.

The shelves above the fridge? She'd need the step stool to reach them. So it might have seemed to her like a smart place to hide something, since she'd think he wouldn't expect it. He flipped open the cupboard and rummaged through the serving bowls. Nope.

Then he had an idea. Opening the pots and pans cupboard, he found the rice cooker. He flipped the lid, found the chips and slid the clip off the bag. Then he went to the sofa to enjoy his reward with a beer, as he read over files for the burglary case he was starting the next morning. A series of robberies in apartment complexes near 101. With the scarcity of affordable housing in the valley, the less affluent side of town was coming up in the world, with more young professionals moving in. And the thieves were following them. The flimsy doors and substandard locks and security made it easier for them.

There were two complexes in particular that the thieves seemed to target. Because he worked these things out in a very visual way, he took out a notepad and sketched the two complexes, then opened up Google Maps to look at the neighborhood more closely. Between the two, at the back of the resident parking, there was a fence, with an alley on the other side.

He tried to think like the thieves. He was sketching out an escape route, when Jacky came into the room.

"What's up, *mijo*?"

"I'm bored."

"You finish your work?"

Jacky twisted his face. "Not yet. I'm lonely."

Ruiz set down the drawing. He missed Reyna's quiet presence—even if she was usually on the computer or in the kitchen. The small house seemed bigger and emptier tonight. "How about you sit down and we do our homework together?"

"Can I have chips?"

"Do the homework first."

With Ruiz at one end of the couch and Jacky at the other, they worked on their assignments until Jacky rubbed his eyes and laid down his social studies book. He handed Ruiz his homework sheets.

"Good for you. Now where does this go?"

Jacky intoned it as if forced against his will to memorize it.

"In my Social Studies folder, in my binder."

He ran back to his room and came back with his backpack. He quite pointedly took out his binder, held it up, then opened it and slipped the pages inside his folder.

Ruiz reached up to high five him then passed him the chip bag.

"No chip crumbs on the sofa."

"We both know how she gets." Jacky raised his eyebrows, and Ruiz tried not to laugh.

At nine o clock, Jacky brushed his teeth, and Ruiz made sure he got into bed.

Ruiz glanced at the clock. It was almost 9:30. Anxiety began to build in him. A reflex, since childhood. Back then he worried about his father coming home. Whether he'd be drunk. Or whether he'd hear his father yelling at his mother.

He'd been trained to think that way growing up. Being a cop had added to that. Never let down your guard. Where will the threat come from? What's my plan if something goes wrong?

The kernel of anxiety sat in his brain, growing by the minute. He grabbed a handful of chips and quickly finished them off. He plunged his hand in for another.

Disgusted with himself, he turned over the top of the bag, clipped it and returned it to the rice cooker.

She'd been excited about the PTA's renovation project, so maybe the conversation had continued after the meeting. What was it to him? Jacky was in bed, asleep. He had his own work to do.

Which wasn't getting done because he couldn't let go of his anxious thoughts.

10:15.

Ruiz heard the key in the lock, and his body felt the stress leave him. She flipped the deadbolt, then walked into the kitchen, her purse still over her shoulder as if she'd decided not to stay and was going to leave again. She came out to the living room.

"I lost track of time. I should have texted."

Worry had returned and settled down on him like the lead cloak they lay over you when they take x-rays at the dentist office.

Something was different. Her face was flushed. A new seriousness. A distance.

"Don't worry about it." He tried his best to keep a game face on. "I thought maybe the Range Rover wouldn't start. Jacky tried to sneak in some game playing, but he finished his homework and went to bed on time."

He expected her to comment on Jacky's sneaky attempt to play the game, but she looked distracted.

She headed for the closet, and took off and hung up her coat, then headed for the kitchen. He wanted to follow her, to hold her, to touch her, but he had come to know Reyna and her moods over the past ten years. She wouldn't receive it well.

"I need to get to bed." She poked her face around the corner, from the hallway. In sequence, the lights in the kitchen, the hall, then the bedroom went off.

He must have sat on the couch, staring blankly at his notes and sketch, for over an hour. He went over the past few weeks, the past month, yesterday. Had it been sudden? Had it been something gradual and he'd just missed it?

Something had changed.

Tomorrow he would set to work figuring out what it was.

46

D   uke Sorenson woke up as grey light seeped in
     under his bedroom curtain.
          Rain pelted the window, the taps blending
into a steady stream of noise, as if the skies were assaulting
the apartment. It made him want to stay under the covers. If
he went back to sleep, he could forget about what he'd read
last night.

Duke had read nearly to the end of the journal—
stopping after Karl's confession of what he'd done in
Mittelwerk. The book lay splayed on the nightstand next to
him as if he'd abruptly tossed it aside. His mouth felt sour
and dry. He'd fallen asleep without brushing his teeth and
washing his face. His mind fuzzy and disoriented, he tried to
recall last night.

He couldn't stop reading the story of Karl's life in
Germany, and the horrors revealed as Karl visited the
mountain rocket factory. It turned his stomach to think of
the living conditions in the mountain for the workers, and
the horrific deaths of the men hanged. Karl, at the age of 18,

had seen it and approved it. Eventually he had
recommended the hangings.

Yet he'd told the Americans who came through after
the war.

I saw nothing.

Agnieszka had seen other horrors, her child injured
during birth, taken away and euthanized. She'd been in a
camp after leaving Peenemunde. Karl had eventually been
on the same side as those who had put her child to death,
those who'd imprisoned her. Had Aggie known this?

Even more than he had when Kathleen was here, he
wanted to talk to someone. The weight of what he'd read
made his head throb, turned his stomach. He could not
carry this on his own.

Duke thought of the donut gang. They would be
shocked to hear this—angry even, as he had been. But
perhaps they could separate the actions of the eighteen-
year-old in the rocket factory from the Karl they knew.

He got out of bed and looked himself over in the mirror.
He hadn't bothered to brush his teeth and wash his face
when he'd gone to sleep at 1:30 a.m. He'd call the gang, take
a shower and meet them at Donut Haven.

He set the phone tree in action, calling Marty Weber, who
would then call Al Moretti, who would then call Arnie Tan. It
was the system they'd always had. It got them to the donut
shop, assembled. They had met only once before because of
an emergency: Al's wife's death during the night, due to a
stroke. In a place where everyone seemed to be moving away
to retire or live closer to their children, they still had each
other. Because they had shared so much, it wouldn't be right
to keep this information about Karl from them.

"Marty, I have some things to tell you all. About Karl.

Can you meet at Kang's at 10 a.m.?" Best to do this later, when the donut shop was less crowded.

"You okay, Duke?" Marty asked.

Duke wasn't sure he was.

"Call Al. I want us to talk about this."

"See you at 10. Hang in there, Duke."

After hanging up, Duke laid out clean clothes and took a shower. He brushed and flossed his teeth. He considered how he would tell the gang.

Duke went back to his conversation with Kathleen. Karl had done a complete turnaround once he'd come to the U.S. —as if that could cancel out what he'd done in the rocket factory. He'd decided to live his life as an atonement for the sins he'd committed in Germany. He'd devoted his life to reaching out to the poor and disenfranchised in his community. The testimonies to that had been overwhelming at Karl's memorial service. Didn't that count for something?

Dressed and washed up, Duke felt shaky and weak. Sweat made his thin shirt cling to his neck and chest. He walked through the house, feeling unsettled. He still had an hour before he had to be at the donut shop.

He went to the junk drawer in the kitchen, where he ended up stashing any business cards he received. Joanne had hated the junk drawer, with its stash of rubber bands, odd parts, restaurant coupons and old keys. But anything Duke threw in there, he knew exactly where to find it.

Now he rooted around and pulled out James Ruiz's card. Duke felt he could talk to Ruiz. Flores was fine, but a little too young and slick. Duke could see himself talking to Ruiz about this.

He punched Ruiz's number into his phone and waited. It

rang twice, then rolled over to voice mail. Duke realized he wasn't sure what to say.

"Officer Ruiz, this is Duke Sorenson. I've found out some information on Karl Schuler. In his personal journal. I don't know what to think of it. I thought maybe I could talk to you. I'm on my way to Donut Haven—"

The phone beeped, abruptly cutting off the rest of the message. Duke sighed. So much for having someone to unload on. He'd have to wait for the gang today. Nervously, he got up and tidied the living room, as if anyone would come back here to entertain. He gathered up old socks, a pair of slippers, and took his coffee mug into the kitchen. Then he picked up the clothbound journal. He held it in his hands, ran a finger down the spine. What Karl had written was so intimate—and shocking. He wanted to shove it back under the couch cushion and forget he'd read it.

He thought of Rose and how protective she had been of her father. He'd lied to her. Said he hadn't seen the journal.

He wondered if she'd finished it. Reading what her father had written would have destroyed her. Duke wasn't sure he'd want to deal with Rose right now if she'd read it.

He couldn't leave the journal here. He had to take it with him.

He thought for a moment, how he could carry it with him without looking obvious. He went back to his closet and rifled through his jackets. The windbreaker and sweater jacket he wore had pockets too small. He pulled out his ancient tan overcoat, used mostly when he and Joanne traveled back east in winter to visit relatives. As soon as he put it on, he realized he looked ridiculous. Like a cold war spy.

He put it back and pulled out an old navy sports jacket. It was light for winter but had a nice, big pocket inside the front lapel. He slid the journal in, then walked over to the mirror. He looked too fancy for the donut shop. But no rectangular outline was visible, though he felt like he was wearing some kind of armor against his body.

After some nervous pacing around the house, he grabbed his keys off the rack, took one more look at himself in the mirror and headed out to the car.

IN COLLEGE, in a statistics class he'd been bored with, Flores began using percentages to quantify how he felt. He'd started it with a classmate, who'd text him with a series of percentages that summed up his state of mind. Flores had to supply what each percentage stood for:

60% hungover. 30% horny. 6% terrified of finals. 4% still thinking of that last World of Warcraft quest.

As he downed a glass of cold water to get the cotton mouth and stale whiskey taste out of his mouth, he thought of his percentages this morning.

20% hungover (conservative estimate)

40% thinking about Reyna

20% feeling like a bad person (also conservative estimate)

20% thinking about the Schuler case

TODAY WAS HIS LAST DAY. January 8. Today he would lock himself down, figure out if the passenger Reyna had seen was who he thought he was. After last night, he needed something else to think about other than the mess he'd dived into. Finding Karl Schuler's killer would be his escape and maybe his redemption.

Dawn used to make fun of him for this, but whenever he

felt particularly crappy, he took his clothing game up a notch. It would make up for the grey circles under his eyes, the pinkish tinge of the whites of his eyes, the overall bad hair day. This morning he pulled the black suit and a green and blue tie out of the closet and laid it on the bed.

He knew what Dawn would say to him today, if she were to talk to him. So rather than diminish himself further in his sister's eyes by calling her, he played out the conversation in his mind in the shower.

-*You did WHAT last night? You cheating little shit.*

-*She approached me. I gave her chances to say no. We were only going to have lunch. One thing led to another.*

-*Every one of those "things" was a decision you made, Ro. Take responsibility for your actions. You're a police officer who sees people mess up all the time. How do you not see the irony in this?*

-*Reyna doesn't love her husband. She's figuring out what she wants.*

-*And this is the cop that you've been hanging out with. The one you said reminded you of the guys in Explorers. Nice job, Ro.*

He dressed and then looped and pulled down his tie, eyeing himself in the mirror. He needed a front to present to the world today. *Nothing to see here. Except this body.* It would buy him time and space, so he could figure out what the hell he was going to do about the case. And about last night.

Flores looked down at the pin on his lapel. A black swan encircled by a red band that read SJPD HOMICIDE. He'd gotten it after solving his first case. The swan's wings raised up in the circle, as if ready to attack. It looked a little like a symbol from the *The Hunger Games*, but nobody could say it wasn't bad ass, and he was proud to wear it. It would remind him of his duties today.

He had been distracted lately, but today he would bring this case to a close.

Clouds hung over downtown today, pressing down with their grey weight on the station. It was just a matter of time before the onslaught started again. Nice of it to hold off until he got into the station at least.

Flores entered the back door and passed by the coffee station to grab a cup. There was work to do and he hadn't been able to justify stopping for an espresso drink on the way. He planned a visit to Christoph Schuler at the Airbnb. He sniffed the cup and took a sip. At least it contained caffeine. He'd down it quickly.

When he got to the investigations room, Mandy turned around in her chair, frowning.

"We got the report from CSI. Not sure what you can get from this that we don't already have." She did a second take when she set eyes on Flores. "Why are we all dressed up today?"

She handed him the faxed sheets.

"Can't a man dress a little fancy now and then?"

Mandy gave him a look he'd never seen on her before— cold, angry even. But he was too excited about the report to figure out what it meant.

He leafed through the pages. He had that feeling– something he'd almost given up on was going to happen. CSI had analyzed the items found in the burned SUV.

Flores skimmed the report. A closer examination of the size and shape of the burned boarding pass showed it was for American Airlines, but none of the print was readable. It confirmed what they knew about Christoph Schuler's flights.

Also on the list was a partially melted ziplock bag under one of the backseats. The latent fingerprint examiners were still working on some of the prints, but it wasn't likely they'd get an identification, since the high surface heat evaporated the oil and water that made up the prints.

Flores got on the phone to CSI, to Sam McInerny. He had a few hours left on this case, and he was going to use every damn minute.

"When do you think they'll have definite word on the prints?'

"You don't want to bet the whole race on those prints." Sam grunted.

Flores heard taps on a keyboard. "I have an examiner who's taking this as a personal challenge, but I don't think there's enough there. I'll get back to you."

"What about the plastic bag?" Flores didn't want to sound desperate, but his voice sure sounded that way. "Anything on that?"

"No prints. No drugs in it either, if that's what you were looking for."

"Not looking for drugs. Not in this case. Any idea what was in it?"

Sam chuckled. "There wasn't much left of the contents, but there's a strong smell. It brought back childhood memories for me."

"What was it?"

"Cereal, man. Cheerios."

47

Donut Haven looked quiet, the early morning rush passed.

One young guy sat at the window with his laptop open, absently feeding donut holes into his mouth as he stared at his screen. Duke parked his Taurus facing the front door.

He'd gotten here ten minutes early, probably due to anxiety. He felt the tenseness in his hands, achy and stiff, and in his chest, reminding him of the heart attack he'd had years ago, while he was still working. He got out of his car and locked it.

He was ready to walk in and reserve the usual table, when he felt a hand grip his forearm so hard it hurt. Something hard and cold jabbed into his side. On top of his current fears, it seemed about right.

Some punk kid who would steal his credit cards and leave his body in a dumpster. A voice inside him wondered if it would matter. He wondered who, beside his solicitous babysitter Kathleen, would give a damn. He was seventy-eight years old and frittering away with his useless daily routine, hanging on in a valley that was all about the new and improved. He was a faded token from a bygone era.

Fingers dug into his arm, pulling him away.

"Let's go for a drive, Duke."

The man's voice was familiar, someone he'd heard recently—at Karl's memorial, he thought. The gun barrel was poking his back now, driving him forward. Duke nearly stumbled, trying to keep his stiff legs moving. They reached a white car with a rental company sticker.

Rose Schuler unlocked the back passenger door and nudged him to get in.

"Get in and buckle up." She ordered him, then held out her hand. "And Duke—give me your phone."

With a shaking hand, he pulled his phone out of his pocket and handed it over.

Rose passed it to the man—Christoph Schuler. He slipped it into the pocket of his khaki cargo vest and zipped it up.

"Give me the journal," Rose frowned. "I'm sure you have it with you. You were going to show the gang."

Duke considered lying but figured it wouldn't do much good at this point. The two people in the front seat were experts at it and would see right through it. He slid his hand into his hidden lapel pocket and pulled out the black, clothbound journal. He hesitated, trying to analyze the look on Rose's face. He wanted to know if she'd finished it.

"Give it to me *now*, Duke."

What was this about? He was afraid to ask, unable to think about anything now but the fact that Rose and Christoph Schuler were in the front seat and were driving him somewhere—possibly his last destination.

"How much did you read?" He heard Rose's voice, but she refused to turn around and look at him.

Again, he considered lying. But he didn't.

"I finished it." He heard his own voice, weak and thin.

Rose gave Christoph a smug look.

"Why did you think he wouldn't read it?" She laughed harshly. "I knew he would."

Duke thought about the guys—Marty, Al and Alan—and hope bubbled up in him.

"Rose, the gang will be here soon. They'll wonder where I am."

"No, they won't." Rose snapped. "Marty told us about your get together. I saw him in his front yard when I was at my father's this morning. I told him you called it off. You were coming down with something."

Christoph handed Rose the handgun calmly, as if it were a litter bag or a box of tissues. Rose slid it into the pocket of the car door. Christoph buckled up and started the car. They headed toward the street, and turned west, toward the hills.

Rain started beating on the windshield. Christoph turned on the windshield wipers as drops fell faster. It was 10 in the morning, but as the dark clouds clustered, it looked like it was closer to late afternoon, when winter light eases into night.

Duke knew this had to do with Karl's journal. It was possible that someone else killed Karl—they couldn't have done it themselves, could they? Then Rose found the journal while cleaning out her father's home. She'd discovered her father's confession—and the two siblings wanted to stop it from being made public. After all, Christoph was just launching his campaign for senator back in Florida. He had lots of support and a good chance to win.

But soon the unimaginable began to take over his thoughts. What if Rose and Christoph did have something to do with their father's death? Duke feared for himself. He'd always heard it said that killing someone made it easier to kill the next time. He was becoming surer that the barrier had been crossed.

They followed Blossom Hill Road, the long thoroughfare through southwestern San Jose. The wooded green hills appeared before them, covered in a blurred haze of rain and fog. Christoph turned onto Camden, then Hicks Road, which wound back into the hills. At first, all Duke could think of was the waste disposal site nearby.

They passed pink and white Mediterranean-style homes, as they headed up into the hills, where mercury used to be mined in the small Guadalupe mine. The hills in this area were known for their quicksilver mines. Years later runoff from the mines would poison the Guadalupe River and Lake Almaden, just down the expressway from him.

"So we're going to the dump?" Duke let out a weak laugh, trying to dispel the tension in the car.

No response from the front seat. Christoph's hands were clamped on the wheel. Rose looked idly out the window at the scenery, as if she were on a Sunday drive with the family.

As they neared the gates to the waste facility, Christoph wheeled the car around sharply, pulling into the road's hairpin turn and heading higher up the hill. The turn slammed Duke against the door. He clutched onto the handle near the armrest. Duke started to feel nauseous, as he did when he was a passenger on a twisting road.

Christoph Schuler drove angrily, as if chasing down something just beyond the horizon, something Duke couldn't see. He wondered how Christoph and Rose felt about their father right now. Were they angry? Disillusioned? Duke thought about all he'd experienced with the Schuler family over the past eight days. There was something wrong in the family. Something off. For the first time, he wondered if that had started with Karl.

Karl, the glue that held their group together, the man they had all praised at the memorial service, was not who they thought he was.

It would be one thing if Karl had cooperated with the Nazis, truly believing in their cause. He'd come of age during a time when every youth had to be in a Hitler youth program, and where schools were little more than indoctrination centers. But it was Karl's love for technology that had changed him in the V2 factory at Kohnstein, to the point where production of the rockets overshadowed everything else for him. Duke couldn't excuse it, but he could see how it happened.

He had less sympathy for the lies Karl had continued to tell. He'd lied about his part in the rocket factory to the Americans who'd interviewed him after the war. He'd lied when he'd come to America, with the CIA's help, under the secret Operation Paperclip program, so his records were wiped clean of Nazi involvement. Years later Karl had lied when a man suggested Karl was been responsible for the death of his father in Kohnstein.

They continued up the narrow road in the heavy rain, Christoph making erratic jerks to the wheel as he sped up the twisting road. The car hydroplaned once. Duke's stomach lurched.

As they made a wide turn, Duke looked behind them to see the valley below, smaller and smaller through the haze as they climbed. Downtown San Jose was a tiny collection of upended building blocks, surrounded by flatness.

As they neared the top of the mountain, Duke knew where they were.

Mt. Umunhum. He saw the Cube, the eight-story

concrete block that stood at the rim of the valley looking down.

Mt. Umunhum's old Air Force Surveillance station had opened in the 1950s to monitor radio signals along the coast during the Cold War. On alert for signs of eminent attack from the Russians.

If the Russians had gotten to them first after Germany's defeat in 1945, Hermann and Karl Schuler might have ended up in the Soviet aerospace program, working on the Sputnik satellites, the first Vostok manned flight with Yuri Gargarin and the Luna moon missions.

From what Duke had read about Operation Paperclip, it could have gone either way for Hermann and Karl. The Americans just happened to get to them before the Russians.

As the Cold War came to an end in the 1980s, the Cube was shut down. Duke toured the facility years ago and hadn't been up here since Santa Clara County had recently opened hiking trails around the abandoned facility.

The eight-story building stood monolithic, dark and foreboding over the scenic overlook and empty parking lot. Duke shivered as Christoph parked a few hundred feet from the structure. The temperature must have dropped twenty degrees as they'd driven up the mountain.

Christoph took his hands off the wheel and sat for a moment, his head against the seat rest. After a minute, Christoph and Rose unfastened their seatbelts without speaking. Rose pulled the handgun out of the side pocket. She looked at Christoph for confirmation. Christoph nodded.

Nausea roiled Duke's stomach when he saw they were bringing the gun along. What had he done to deserve this? He was Karl's closest friend. He'd helped Rose pack up

Karl's belongings and memorabilia. Now he wondered if Rose had wanted to clean out her father's place quickly in order to find any other incriminating evidence of Karl's past.

Christoph turned around in the seat to face him. There were bags under his eyes. He looked like he hadn't shaved in a couple of days.

"We're going to the lookout."

Christoph shut the door and locked the car, then came around to walk alongside Duke, with Rose on Duke's other side, as if they were going to frog march him. Christoph held the gun loosely as the three of them headed in the direction of the Cube.

The air was piercingly cold, and the icy wind whipped across the flat mountain top. Duke felt it through his summer sports coat. His jaw hurt from clenching against the involuntary chattering.

Duke looked over at Rose, who avoided his eyes and pulled her wool scarf up around her face.

"Rose—Christoph. Can't we talk?" But his words were slapped away by the wind and he couldn't tell if Rose and Christoph heard him. They continued walking, until they came to a deck, above a sharp drop to the hills below.

Duke knew he was here because of what he'd read. They'd known he was going to tell the gang. They planned to shut him up—whether that meant killing him or threatening him into silence.

He realized it was all about containment. If they killed Duke and had possession of the journal, Karl's confession and possibly his murder stayed a secret. Christoph could go back to Florida and become a senator.

Duke wondered what Nick and Nora Charles in the *Thin Man* movies would do in a situation like this. Some clever trick or diversion, maybe. He wished real life was that easy.

The wooden platform looked down on the green, forested hills, gateway to the Santa Cruz Mountains. The deck was partially protected from the wind, so when Christoph turned to him, Duke could hear what he was saying.

"Sit down here."

Christoph set the gun on the bench next to him and took a seat. He zipped his down jacket up around his neck as he looked down on the drop, as if he were checking it out for later reference.

Rose hurried to sit on the bench next to Christoph. That left Duke with a seat nearest the edge, where rain was blowing in through the slats and puddling on the seat. Duke wiped it off with his hand. The icy water made his hand burn. He sat down on the wet bench, his chest now shuddering in the cold.

"You k-killed Karl." He stared across at Christoph as he tried to control his shaking. "I wondered if it could be you. Karl used to talk about how proud he was of you. F-for y-your shooting record with the army."

Christoph stared at Duke with his oddly light blue eyes, which reminded Duke of a wolf's. Rose turned to him with a pleading look. She put her hand on his sleeve.

"Not Duke. Please, Christoph—"

"I planned it carefully, you know." Christoph looked down at his hands, which he flexed. "I didn't want him to feel any pain. I knew where to shoot him so there would be the least suffering possible. I loved my father very much. I wanted to be like him. I wanted to be that good. As a father, I couldn't fault him for anything. Then I read the journal."

Rose began sobbing into her scarf.

"One Saturday last month he called me for our usual talk. He told me he was ready to make a confession about something in his past. I thought, what could my dad—the great human being, Karl Schuler—have done that was bad? Maybe he cheated on his taxes. Maybe he shoplifted candy when he was a kid."

He shook his head and pulled out a tissue to wipe his nose. "I flew out to spend the day with him. He showed me what he'd written. He told me what he'd done in Mittelwerk during the war. I was—not prepared for that."

Rose's crying subsided. "We sat down with him. He told us both. All the details. Then he said he wanted to hand what he'd written over to a journalist, someone who could tell his story."

Christoph cleared his throat. "We told him not to do it."

Rose began crying again. She closed her eyes, then waited to speak. "If my father were to come forward. He would be sent back to Germany for trial. It would kill him. He couldn't have handled that. Then everything he'd done here, his legacy in aeronautics. His brilliant career. It would be gone."

Duke felt dizzy. He hyperventilated as he tried to suck breath in while his teeth chattered. He tried hard to stay focused on what Rose was saying.

"M-maybe that's what he wanted—to be honest for the first time in seventy-five years. W-why didn't you let him have that?"

Rose and Christoph exchanged looks.

"How could he go back to a country he hadn't seen in years? My father brought innovations to the aeronautics industry. He helped make it what it is today. He inspired generations of students. And now he'd be treated like a common criminal—just like a prison camp guard."

Christoph was talking with an openness Duke hadn't seen in him before. But it was also clear that this was more about what the family wanted, than what was best for Karl. What if Karl had been able to step forward and confess what he'd done? He could have died in peace, on his own terms.

"We didn't feel we could handle that as a family. My father was a good man." Christoph continued. "I still believe that. But he disregarded our advice and did things his own way."

Duke had been right with his suspicion about Christoph's motives. He glared at the man.

"If Karl published his journal, your political career would be over."

All Christoph had to do was pick up the handgun next to Rose. He cocked the trigger.

Duke flinched. He shut his mouth.

Christoph kept the gun in his hand and walked back and forth under the wooden shelter.

"We found a car. A big SUV. Rose's mechanic found it on Craig's List. I wanted this to look like a random shooting on New Year's. We would do this as painlessly as we could for him."

"Tuan found somebody who was trying to sell it fast." Rose talked as if she'd just happened to find a bargain while out shopping.

"How did you get Karl to go out that night?"

Rose looked up at Duke from her spot on the bench. She'd aged years in the past week, her eyes red, her skin pale and sagging.

"I called from a pay phone. I told him I was driving back from a friend's with Chloe, my granddaughter." Rose's voice started to lose momentum. She shut her eyes. It looked like the gravity of what she'd done had just hit her. "I said I'd had a few drinks and was afraid to drive."

Duke had swung from the shock he felt about Karl's revelations to the horror he felt at Rose and Christoph's actions.

"You made this look like a gang shooting, didn't you?" While Christoph watched him warily, Duke stood up, forcing himself to move, to keep his body moving as he fought off sleepiness. "You tried to make it look like the killers came from East San Jose, from the students Karl cared so much about. It worked. That's what people suspected first."

The cold started to fill Duke's head with fog. Now he was Nick Charles, looking down a long dinner table of suspects, as he revealed what the killer had done to get away with the crime.

Now it was time for the police to come in. Like Nick Charles, he would retreat, a drink in his hand.

But Duke was afraid that wasn't going to happen.

He was afraid this was his final act.

48

Early that morning, Ruiz felt the bed move as Reyna got up to go to the gym. He heard the water run as she washed her face and brushed her teeth, as she would any other day. He smelled the peach lotion she rubbed on her face and hands.

Out of the corner of his eye, he saw her slip into her workout clothes and unzip her gym bag to pack clothes for the workday. She pulled her hair back with a flick of her fingers and wound a hair tie around it to keep it out of her face.

He felt a sudden ache. These were things she did every day. Signs that everything was normal. For all he knew, nothing would be normal again. How much longer would he hear her quietly going through these motions in the morning?

He hadn't slept. From the time he'd gone to bed until 5 a.m. when she'd gotten up. Alone on his side of the bed with his obsessive thoughts. Branching out in a hundred different possibilities. Had she met someone? What would happen now? Would she leave? He had seen it in her eyes. A wall.

The partition had slid down, indicating that she was no longer accessible to him.

He lay in the bed pretending to be asleep until she walked out, her bag over her shoulder, and shut the door quietly behind her.

There were things he needed to think about today. He'd do what he could to assess the situation and take the action required. He had no proof of anything, just an instinct. But he'd solved cases on instinct.

He pulled himself out of the bed, feeling a heaviness in his body and a deadness in his brain. Sleep wasn't going to happen at this point. He got up and went out to the kitchen. In the fridge Reyna had left a packed thermal lunch bag for Jacky and a brown paper lunch bag for him—with the standard fat-free yogurt, carrots and cardboard-like crackers. When he opened it to look, it struck him that he'd never once thought of this daily lunch as an act of kindness. He'd only seen it as a slam against him, a statement from her that he needed to lose weight.

He poured himself a glass of orange juice and drank it, as he looked at the photos pinned to the fridge door with misshapen clay magnets Jacky had made in school. A photo of Reyna and the other hygienists from work. Jacky as a toddler in overalls, one strap hanging down, his hair sticking up off his head. Then one of him and Reyna, on the ice with a hockey stick in her hand at a Sharks game.

Ruiz carefully washed out his glass and put it in the dish rack. Then he went to wake Jacky up and start the slow process of getting him dressed, fed and ready to take to school.

.   .   .

It wasn't till Ruiz got to the MVPD station, via a drive-thru Starbucks to get a large vanilla latte, that he noticed he had a message on his phone from an unfamiliar number. He clicked to listen to the voice mail and heard Duke Sorenson's earnest voice, sounding cracked and agitated. He'd found out something about Karl Schuler. It was important and he had to tell someone.

"I need to talk to you, Detective. I know I should call Detective Flores, but I feel more comfortable talking to you. Can you please call me? I'm about to head over to meet with the donut gang."

Ruiz checked the time receipt for the message. Duke had left it forty minutes ago. He hit call back. Ruiz had taken a liking to the old guy, but he also needed to tell him that if this was something important to the case, Flores was the one to call.

The phone rang several times. Ruiz pressed end.

Ruiz sat back and scrolled through a report on a burglary he was about to file. Once he sent off the report, he went back to his phone and called Duke again.

No answer.

Somewhere Ruiz had Arnie Tan's card, from his meeting with the donut gang the day after Karl's death. The guy had mentioned he had season tickets to the Giants, and he sometimes gave away what he couldn't use.

He opened his wallet and flipped through the stack of cards. He'd give Arnie a call and see if he could let Duke know he'd called.

Arnie answered after a couple of rings. Ruiz explained that Duke had called and said he was on his way to meet with the gang.

"I haven't heard from Duke. Marty said he saw Rose at

Karl's house this morning. She said Duke was sick and wouldn't be coming."

Ruiz frowned. Duke, with his old school manners, would have called to tell him about this change of plans. He also knew that Duke wasn't a guy to ignore phone calls. If he was home sick, he'd be answering his phone.

"I'll talk to Flores. He can send a patrol or go check on Duke himself."

"Wait a sec." Arnie paused. "Duke's daughter Kathleen is always checking up on her father. Drives him crazy. She's got an app on her phone that tracks him. Whyn't I give her a call. I'll get right back to you."

While he waited for Arnie to get back to him, Ruiz called Flores.

"Hey, Ruiz. What's up?" Flores sounded suspicious.

"Duke Sorenson called me, told me he found out something upsetting about Karl Schuler. He told me he was heading over to the donut shop to meet with the gang. Then Rose Mulvaney told Marty Weber that Duke called it off. But nobody's heard from Duke."

"Duke should have called me." Flores sounded ticked off. "I've been on the case all morning."

"Yeah, I *told* him that." Ruiz raised his eyebrows. He heard a beep that he had another call. "Hold on."

"Detective Ruiz? Arnie again. Kathleen got back to me."

"Did she find Duke?"

"She checked the location app. Could this be accurate? It's pretty strange."

Ruiz listened, then thanked Arnie.

He got back on the line with Flores.

"I've got some time. You want to take a drive? Duke Sorenson's on top of Mt. Umunhum."

· · ·

RUIZ CHECKED in with the captain and told him he needed to take a break to help a friend. He filed the report he needed to get out today. Then he left a message, so Grasso could follow up on one of his cases.

Duke Sorenson belonged on top of Mt. Umunhum just like Karl Schuler belonged on the expressway at 1:30 a.m. on New Year's. The mountain loomed over the west side of the valley, a high point on the Santa Cruz Mountain range. The strange location along with Duke's new information about Karl Schuler were connected. Duke didn't go for a drive up the mountain by himself.

A half hour later, Flores met him at the MVPD front desk, and they headed to his car in the back lot. Flores looked pale and tense. Angsty. Like an emo kid.

"You ok?" Ruiz called across the top of the car at Flores.

"Yeah. Been a crazy couple of days." Flores shook his head and got into the passenger seat. "I just got some news from CSI. The tire treads on Rose Mulvaney's Honda Accord match those we found in Morgan Hill near the burned SUV."

"I didn't expect that." Ruiz knew Christoph Schuler had a part in this. He wasn't sure about Rose Mulvaney. He pulled out of the lot and headed for Highway 85 South, against the commute at this time of the day.

Flores got on his radio and told the dispatcher to tell the Santa Clara County Sheriff's Department to send a car up Mt. Umunhum--and to approach the scene with caution.

Ruiz shot a look at Flores as soon as he completed the call.

"You want to fill me in?"

"Christoph Schuler is a suspect in the murder of his father." Flores leaned back in the seat and rubbed his eyes. "He flew in before Christmas and then on New Year's Eve.

We also got a copy of his army records. He trained as a sniper during his tour of duty."

Ruiz remembered Rose's wall of framed photos. The photo of a blond, blue-eyed soldier with a military rifle in his hands. A young Christoph Schuler. A man trained to kill quickly and accurately. A man who was feeling like a cornered animal right now.

"If he's up there with Duke, we'll need some help."

Flores nodded, his face looking grim.

49

Ruiz impatiently passed cars ambling with midday ease down Highway 85, as he headed for the Camden Avenue exit.

"I want to hear what Duke has to say about Karl Schuler." Ruiz passed a slow-moving car in the fast lane. "The guy was upset."

"No clue as to what it was?" Flores checked his fancy Apple watch.

"I would have told you if I did." Ruiz heard a snap in his own voice.

Ruiz pulled onto the exit ramp and headed down Camden. Years ago, this had been the far southwestern boundary of the valley, older established neighborhoods with good schools. The green, forested hills seemed exotic compared to the bare, often parched brown hills of the east side of the valley.

Flores then took out his phone and began fiddling with it. From a sideways glance it looked like Flores was texting. Then he quickly switched to GPS.

"Thirty minutes up to the top." Flores finally looked up

from his phone. "Hope Duke's still around by the time we get there."

"I hiked there a few months ago with Jacky. We lost reception as we got near the top." Ruiz gave him an amused look as he turned onto Hicks Road and they began the climb up the mountain. Why would someone need a phone *and* an Apple watch?

Flores was edgy and distracted. Ruiz wanted to tease him out of it. He missed the camaraderie he'd had with Flores in the beginning. Now, no banter. Little eye contact. Flores had pulled back in the past week.

As they headed up the mountain, Ruiz thought about last night. Reyna's face when she came in the door more than an hour late from her meeting. He pushed it out of his mind. He needed to focus right now.

The road twisted and grew narrow as they climbed higher. The windshield wipers were losing the battle against the sheets of rain, as they climbed higher into the hills. There was a cool, earthy smell in the air. They'd left flocks of seagulls in their wake as they passed the turnoff for the dump. A few persistent ones flew idle circles now, as if scouring the landscape for a discard or handout. Or a body.

They were nearing the top, when Flores's radio crackled. The dispatcher.

"Sheriff reports three people at the lookout. A hostage situation. One has a gun and is threatening to shoot. Sheriff deputy is trying to negotiate. Check in at the top and proceed with caution."

DUKE FOUGHT off his sleepiness and tried to remain standing, swaying on weak legs as the wind and rain whipped at him. He waved his arms up and down, like those floppy nylon wind-socks, just to keep his circulation going.

He knew he was in the early stages of hypothermia.

Christoph looked like he wasn't sure what the hell Duke was doing. He eyed him suspiciously and kept his hand clenched on the gun, still aimed at Duke.

As he tried to keep moving, Duke became aware of something that he had not been sure of in two years.

He wanted to live.

Since Joanne died, there were times when he'd felt tired. Tired and obsolete. As if he didn't belong in the valley he'd worked in for so many years.

But now he thought of his apartment and the friends he had left, of his children and grandchildren, and of Kathleen, who wanted to run his life.

He wanted to walk away from this and go watch Nick and Nora Charles. Tend to his still-alive plants. Try to play a video game with his grandkids. Listen to his kids complain about their jobs.

He didn't want Christoph Schuler to kill him. He had more time than this.

And he wanted to live it.

About a minute ago, a Sheriff's car had pulled into the circle and parked by the Cube. Duke practically wet himself with relief. They would come and disarm Christoph, talk through this and maybe even realize that Christoph and Rose had killed their father. Since he'd been keeping his focus on Duke, Christoph hadn't seen the sheriff yet.

The sheriff walked about half the way towards them on the overlook. A young and slightly stocky man. From the sudden look of alertness on his face, Duke saw he'd spotted Christoph's gun, at a distance. He had his own pulled out.

"Deputy Jeffrey Chan, Santa Clara County Sheriff. Drop

the gun, sir. Lay it down on the pavement right here. Then we can talk."

Christoph did not move. Rose started crying.

Looking straight at Deputy Chan, Christoph poked the barrel again into Duke's side.

"I'm killing him, if you don't let us get to our car and leave."

"Why don't you tell me what's going on with you, sir? Maybe I can help. Talk to me."

Duke had gone beyond the chattering stage and felt foggy and disoriented. He was afraid he'd lose the ability to stand up soon, and any move would cause Christoph to pull the trigger.

Through the rain, Duke thought he saw a car slowly round the corner into the lot. He desperately hoped it was real. At this angle, he had a better view than Christoph, who was still focused on Deputy Chan. Detective Ruiz was driving, and it looked like Flores was with him.

Duke wasn't sure if this was a good thing or a bad thing for the standoff. More people with guns seemed like more of a chance someone would get shot. Duke turned his eyes back toward Chan, to keep from alerting Christoph to the police presence.

Duke saw Ruiz and Flores park to the side, on an angle where Christoph would have to turn around and take his focus off Chan to see them. They quietly stepped out and crouched down. Both pulled out guns and crept back behind the car.

"Tell me about this person here." Chan asked. "What's his name?"

"Why the hell should I tell you? Let us go, and no one gets hurt."

Christoph spoke contemptuously, as if he knew Chan was trying to distract him with small talk.

In the corner of his eye, Duke saw Ruiz and Flores move along the edge of the parking lot, heading their way. He hoped against hope that they wouldn't startle Christoph.

Once Ruiz and Flores were about fifteen feet away, he saw Flores nod at Chan, who stepped back.

"Christoph, this is Detective Mario Flores, San Jose Homicide. I know about Karl."

Christoph's head snapped to the right, to Flores, and the gun barrel dropped, no longer pointed at Duke.

There was a look of horror on his face. Christoph Schuler was seeing his options disappear. Any chance of walking away from this with the ability to return to Florida and continue his campaign. Any chance of staying out of prison.

Christoph took the gun away from Duke's side. Then as they all watched, he calmly put the gun to the side of his head and stepped to the edge of the lookout, by the drop.

It happened so quickly, it took Flores, Ruiz and Deputy Chan by surprise. They rushed forward, then stopped abruptly. The shot rang out, echoing like a crack of thunder.

Rose screamed and dropped to the ground. Christoph Schuler's body tumbled into the ravine below.

50

County Search and Rescue arrived to recover Christoph Schuler's body.

Ruiz stood to the side for a while, watching Flores in the outlook shelter, tapping away on his tablet and making calls—the start of the long process of wrapping up the case. Over the next few weeks, Flores would be very busy, writing the novel equivalent of reports. But unlike Ruiz, Flores enjoyed that kind of work.

Today the mountain had accepted the sacrifice of Christoph's death, and the cycle of deceit and death that started seventy-five years ago inside another mountain had ended.

At 12:30, Ruiz tapped Flores on the shoulder. Flores's face had the look of a man who'd just come out on the other side of a war, one he wasn't sure he'd won or lost.

"No worries, man. I'll catch a ride back to the station. I'll be here a while."

Ruiz got in his car and got ready to head down the mountain. Once he started the car, he looked at his messages. He noticed a voice mail from an unfamiliar number. He wasn't able to access it till he got farther down the mountain and his Bluetooth reconnected.

He accessed the message through the car's screen and tapped to play it.

"This is James Ruiz from MVPD, right? My name is Mandy Dirkson. We've seen each other at Someplace a few times. I have some information I think you should know. Call me back. I'm out of the office, and I can talk."

Ruiz felt that feeling in his gut, the kind he got when things slid into place and he was heading to the end of a hunt. Suspicions and glimmers of truth now fell in line, dovetailing neatly together. It left a sinking feeling in his stomach, but his head now felt a rush of relief.

He hit the callback button, passed the sheriff personnel with a wave, and continued down the mountain.

THEIR MEETING at Someplace the next night would be short and neither of them would linger. Ruiz took a seat at the table, near the bar, making sure he faced the door. The place was busy, with the game just about to start. In the corner, Joe Descortes sat with a dispatcher and a couple of guys who looked young enough to be in the academy.

Tara had just delivered Ruiz his beer. The smell of the buttered popcorn turned his stomach tonight, so he refused the bowl when she brought it by.

Flores came in looking disoriented. He spotted Ruiz at the table and headed his way, with a kind of a resolute forward lurch, as if his mind knew he needed to be here, but his body was making the trip unwillingly.

When Flores took a seat on the stool, Ruiz saw that his eyes were red. He could have been crying tears of remorse.

He could have been smoking weed. Which one, Ruiz didn't give a shit.

He leveled a look at Flores, took his time and made sure the young man was focused on him.

"I know."

Flores face turned white, but he didn't look away.

"It happened so fast—and I'm sorry, man I just blew it—"

"Shut the fuck up. Listen to me and do what I say."

Flores' face looked drained. His shirt hung loosely on his shoulders. His eyes started to water.

"Okay."

"You will not call Reyna. You will not message her. You will not check her Facebook page. You will have no contact with her. If I find out you have—and I have my ways—you're dead meat." Ruiz had wanted to say the word *my wife*, but it would not come out. He could not make himself say it.

"Jimmy. I'm so—"

"Shut the fuck up. I don't want to hear it."

"I messed up, Jimmy."

At least there was that. Some claim of personal responsibility. Ruiz wanted to know it existed, but a friendship with Flores was not on his list of things to save right now.

"That's it, Flores. Now get the fuck out."

Flores headed out the way he'd come. Just like that.

Ruiz finished his beer. When the cheers and whoops for the Warriors' score rose around him, he couldn't take it anymore. He left his tip at the bar and headed for his car.

DUKE OPENED the book to read the last entry again. He wished he could have copied it. Memorized it.

Karl Schuler's Journal

Fifteen years ago, as my wife lay in the hospital bed with tubes in her body and needles in her arm, I held her hand and confessed. I wanted to tell her before they began the morphine drip so she could be fully aware and know the gravity of what I was saying. I told her what had happened in Mittelwerk. How I had signed the statements, supported the inmate hangings. With the goal of moving the V2 progress forward at all costs. How I had begun to see these men from the camp who had asked for relief as animals, hindrances to be dispensed with, so the V2 project could move faster.

I held her hand and called her by name. I told her I remembered what she was wearing that day at Peenemunde, when I first met her. What it was like walking along the sand with her on those days we'd managed to slip away together.

Then I told her the truth about what I'd done. I looked into her eyes.

I did not soften it. I did not excuse it.

I wished I'd told her sooner. I felt like a coward having waited till this moment.

After I finished, she gripped my hand. A weak smile crossed her face as she said it.

Keine Zahlung erforderlich

No payment required.

51

That night after Reyna made dinner, Ruiz volunteered to do clean up and load the dishwasher. Reyna looked at him as if trying to figure out what the hell was wrong with him, then went to her phone and began scrolling through Facebook.

After he finished, he went into Jacky's room. The boy was lying on his bed, scribbling away at math problems in handwriting that Ruiz doubted any teacher could read.

"You almost done?"

Jacky nodded. He had a worried look on his face. He was a smart boy.

"Maybe five minutes."

"When you finish, you get an hour of time on the computer for gaming. Just one hour. Headphones on."

The look on the boy's face was priceless. His eyes wide, his mouth open.

"Th-this is a school night."

"This is special. Not a reward for anything. I felt like being nice."

The boy was still stunned. Confused. And perhaps suspicious. But he turned back to his homework pages and continued writing furiously.

Once Jacky was installed at the computer desk, headphones on, full focus on the elves and dragons on the computer screen, Ruiz asked Reyna to meet him in the bedroom.

Reyna didn't often look scared. She rarely showed emotion. But tonight her cheeks flushed. Small frown lines appeared on her forehead.

They settled themselves across from each other on the bed. She pulled back a strand of hair from her face and tucked it behind her ear. She brushed her thigh nervously with the long, polished nails of one hand.

Ruiz wanted to wait, to take it slow. If he did, he wondered if she would admit what had happened—just for the relief of having the tense silence end. This was, in many ways, an interrogation. There were effective ways to do this.

"Thank you for cleaning up after dinner," she said quietly.

Ruiz nodded. There was some hope in that. After thinking about it, he changed his tactics a bit.

"You do so much. You have kept this house spotlessly clean—something I never had growing up. You do laundry, you do the shopping—getting all the bargains at the Asian markets. The only reason we have this house is because you put us on a budget to save for it. You have raised Jacky to work hard, to do well in school, to be respectful. To be different than either of our brothers. Thank you for that."

Reyna's face morphed into something he didn't recognize. Her lips twisted slightly. She looked down at her nails.

"I know about you and Flores."

Reyna closed her eyes. As if she'd been waiting for the blow, and it had hit her, but it had come just a few minutes too late, when she hadn't expected it.

"I don't own you. I know there are many things you want in life. If you don't love me, you can leave. But it will be like that Jenga game we play with Jacky. You pull a piece out, and everything around it falls. Jacky, your friends and the people you work with."

There was a long silence. An uncomfortable one for Ruiz. But he waited.

"Jimmy, you are a good father. You helped me get started again." Her voice was quiet and firm. "But I am not attracted to you. I can't remember the last time I was."

The truth sucked the air out of his lungs, but he'd known it. Though it made him mad that Flores had also known it.

The truth of it slowly became real to Ruiz as the words replayed in his head. He was in a whirlpool, being sucked down, fighting hopelessly against the pull downward.

He wanted to ask: But then what happens? Like Karl Schuler, was there any life after the truth was told? Or did everything have to end?

His life would change. He would be Frank, trying to lure anyone he could to hang out with him so he wouldn't have to be alone.

He cleared his throat.

"Thank you for being honest with me."

He looked over to see she'd turned to face him on the bed. She didn't seem to be avoiding him. He'd hoped she'd show something. Crying. Repentance. Gratitude. Concern for him.

She reached out a hand to him. Put it near his on the bed.

"I have to get to bed now. You know I have—

"I know." He said firmly. "Spin class in the morning."

He nodded and held her hand. It felt warm and soft. He held it up and kissed it lightly. As if it mattered.

Then he got up to put his son to bed.

52

F lores downed the last of the bourbon.

Each sip had slid down a little easier, bringing a golden, numbing burn to his senses.

He wasn't tracking the time. He thought he'd come to Someplace Bar and Grill at 5 p.m., after his difficult talk with Buckley—and, if that hadn't been enough, a meeting with Jesperson, as a new member of his team for the double homicide on Silver Creek Road.

The evening crowd was coming in now, talking and laughing. Stories of the workday drifted in the air above them like smoke. Somebody called out the punchline to a joke and a table erupted in laughter. A hockey pre-game show blared on the TV. The Sharks were playing Detroit.

He couldn't believe he'd been here that long. He looked down at his phone and saw it was 6:30 p.m.

He rubbed his face and looked up. Tara was returning from the tables with a tray of dirty glasses. When she saw him, she raised her finely drawn eyebrows, looking like a very concerned Disney princess.

"Are you okay, Mario?"

"Yeah. Fine." He nodded and tried to smile, but he didn't have the mojo today. He had no idea what his face ended up looking like.

"You've been here a while." She set the tray down on the counter, a look of interest in her eyes. "If you want to talk about anything, just let me know."

It would be so easy. The way she looked at him, had always looked at him. They could go to her place when her shift ended. He knew he wanted her more for her kindness than her body. She was probably willing to give him both.

"Could I get some water, Tara?"

She smiled and brought him a glass, and he drank it down.

The buzz must have worn off, because he began thinking again. He saw the events of the past month as if they were happening to someone else.

How do you become what you've always hated?

He laid the question out there, in his thoughts, but got no answer. Even his sister Dawn's imaginary voice was refusing to talk to him.

He always swore he would never be like Anthony Flores. He was smarter and more self-aware. Things would turn out differently for him. Now he knew that wasn't true. There was a seed planted in him long ago that had grown into something twisted. He had to know where it came from.

He would book a flight into Orange County for the weekend.

Mario Flores picked up his phone and called his father.

THE SMALL PLANE took off early Saturday morning from San Jose's Hillman Airport, racing along the runway, then leaving the ground behind with a sudden thrust upward.

Ruiz pictured the air rushing over the cartoon wings Karl Schuler had drawn in his Smithsonian demonstration. The atmospheric river had finally lifted. On this clear cold day, he looked down at the valley, its business parks and freeways shrinking as the Cessna climbed higher.

Christoph Schuler's son was at the controls, just a few feet ahead of them, yet off in his own world, encased in headphones and exchanging words with the control tower as they headed over the valley to the Pacific Coast. Ruiz was glad that Zach, a flight instructor back in Florida, had volunteered to do this.

Ruiz was Duke Sorenson's guest today. Duke sat in the seat in front of him, wearing his classic blue windbreaker. He gazed out the window, baring his teeth like a dog with his head out of the window of a car. Ruiz had only known Duke during his time of grief. He liked seeing a smile on the man's face.

Before the flight, Duke and Randall Mulvaney had assembled Karl's and Agnieszka's ashes on four sheets laid out on a long table set up near the plane. They solemnly folded the sides of each sheet over the ashes, then rolled them up into bundles, sleeping-bag style. Duke cut a slit at the end of the cloth on each one, then the two of them slipped rubber bands over the bundles to hold them together.

The plan was to slip off the bands and grip the slit at the end. They would open up the plane's side window and let each bundle unfurl, emptying the ashes into the air.

"If you release the ashes too close to the plane, they'll fly back in your face. Believe me, you don't want that," Duke said sternly, as he explained the process to a frightened-looking Randall.

It had been two hard weeks. Rose had been arrested as

an accomplice in her father's murder. Then the family held
a short service at a funeral home for Christoph.

The mood was lighter today. Randall, Shayante Miland,
Duke and Ruiz had met early that morning at the airfield.
Shayante had brought coffee and donuts.

"When are we supposed to do this again?" Randall asked
loudly as he leaned back in his seat, his long legs spread out
in the aisle. Shayante, oblivious to him, had her 35mm
camera out and was absorbed in documenting the flight in
photos.

Duke sighed under his breath as he turned back from
the window. "By law, we can't release the ashes till we're
three miles offshore. Don't worry. When we get to the right
place, Zach will let us know."

The plan was to scatter both Karl and Agnieszka
Schuler's ashes out over the Pacific, releasing them so they
blended as they fell into the ocean. Ruiz was the only one
there who hadn't known Karl or Aggie. He felt like an
outsider, someone who'd come to know Karl only through
the people who'd loved him and wrestled with his sins.

The short meeting at Someplace was the last time he'd
seen Flores, who had not been invited to join the flight. For
a while when Flores had pulled away, Ruiz had missed their
camaraderie. They had managed to work together up on the
mountain. He felt no hatred for Flores. He had been clear in
his words to the young detective. He did not doubt Flores
would abide by them.

His thoughts about Reyna were different. Something
had been torn from him, and the wound still ached. She had
sat at the computer in the kitchen this morning, drinking
her coffee. She said goodbye as he left, looking up only
briefly. Did she care that little for him? Maybe she was
ashamed to have been caught.

After a long flight over the green, misty Santa Cruz mountains, Zach announced they were approaching the ocean. A layer of fog hung over the grey-blue water undulating below.

"If you want to say something, now's the time to do it." Duke addressed them unceremoniously, then returned to his perch at the window, taking in the view.

They looked around at each other.

Shayante started first, resting the camera on her lap and turning toward Randall thoughtfully.

"No payment required. That's what Aggie Schuler said to Karl when he told her what he'd done. That all would be forgiven. The past is with us. It doesn't go away. But now it is washed and renewed. Let the good parts of it remain."

Ruiz finally understood Karl Schuler's last word. After hearing about Karl's confession to Aggie, he knew Karl had said *Zahlung*—German for payment. Maybe he'd felt his children had demanded a payment.

"My grandfather was a Nazi." Randall began, with the seriousness of someone reciting poetry. "The two of us didn't get along. He pissed me off on a regular basis. But he wanted what he thought was best for me, and I'm sorry he's dead."

Duke looked around to see if anyone else was going to speak up. Then he began in a shaky voice.

"Karl was my friend. Nothing he did before I knew him changes that. I hope he's free now. No more guilt."

Duke opened the window. Ruiz noticed Zach Schuler up front, continuing to look straight ahead. Whether he couldn't participate because of his duties as pilot, or whether he was still dealing with disappointment and shock about his father and grandfather, Ruiz didn't know.

As Randall watched Duke holding one of the bundles,

his face changed. The mocking look faded. His voice turned soft, the kind of voice people use when talking to small pets.

"Karl Schuler and Agnieszka Kaminski Schuler, we release you now. Go in peace."

Duke released each bundle of Karl's ashes. Randall Mulvaney and Shayante each took a bundle of Aggie's ashes and let them unfurl out the window. With each bundle, clouds of ashes flew back behind the plane in a puff, swirling together.

Ruiz had moved to the other side of the plane to watch the release. As he watched, the tenseness in him started to loosen. His head felt empty, swept clean. It had been three weeks since he'd sat down with Reyna for the talk.

Every day was something new and uncertain.

He could not see where this story would end.

But he knew now.

He would open his hands and let it all go.

❧

If you enjoyed this book, please post
a review on Amazon, Goodreads or the review site of your choice.

ACKNOWLEDGMENTS

To my husband, Pete, for his love and support. To the writers groups: The Highway group—Leira Lewis, Rie Neal, Rosanna Griffin and Becky Cuadra George. And the Palo Alto group—Pam Milliken and Patrick Andersen, copy editor extraordinaire, for encouragement and commiseration in good times and bad. Thanks to the Sisters in Crime Coastal Cruisers chapter and to Alec Peche, for showing me the ropes of publishing and telling me to just do it.

Also, thanks to Moffett Field Historical Society Museum; to Esther Jude for the German help; to my fellow teacher Pam Stewart for her knowledge of Santa Clara; and for answers to my police questions, Vicinio Mata, and Adam Richardson at Writers Detective Bureau.

I also owe a debt to Annie Jacobsen's great book, *Operation Paperclip: The Secret Intelligence Program that Brought Nazi Scientists to America* (Little, Brown and Company)

Special thanks to Debbie Cunningham, for her support

and the best snacks ever during NaNoWriMo. And to Chris Anderson, for her mystery expertise and the socially distanced porch get-togethers.

ABOUT THE AUTHOR

Victoria Kazarian lives and writes in San Jose, California. A former Silicon Valley marketing professional, she now teaches high school English. Her short story, "Good Neighbors," appears this year in the sixth Sisters in Crime Guppy Anthology, *The Fish that Got Away*. You can contact her and sign up for her newsletter at victoriakazarian.com